The Tanglewood Flower Shop

LILAC MILLS

The Tanglewood Flower Shop

CANELO

First published in the United Kingdom in 2019 by Canelo

This edition published in the United Kingdom in 2020 by

Canelo Digital Publishing Limited
Third Floor, 20 Mortimer Street
London W1T 3JW
United Kingdom

A CIP catalogue record for this book is available from the British Library.

Print ISBN 978 1 78863 766 4
Ebook ISBN 978 1 78863 740 4

Look for more great books at www.canelo.co

Printed and bound in Great Britain by Clays Ltd, Elcograf S.p.A.

2

Chapter 1

Leanne opened the door and breathed deeply, the alluring scent of a variety of blooms wafting across her face as the air in her shop was disturbed. Beneath the heady perfume of the flowers lay a deeper, richer smell of green things, and earth from the pots and hanging baskets dotted around. She loved those smells, lived for them in fact.

Being in the florist's shop was like being inside a jewellery box lined with different shades of green: leaf-green satin, forest-green velvet and sage-green damask. The jewels were the flowers themselves – brilliant shades of fiery orange like sparkling amber, reds as bright as the finest rubies, blues ranging from sapphire to lapis lazuli, the purple and violet of tanzanite and amethyst, with the whites of pearls and the yellow of gold.

Add hot pink and some paler blooms into the mix, and the whole shop was a riot of colour that ebbed and flowed with the seasons and was at its best at the flower farm or the wholesaler.

Actually, having to get up to go and purchase the flowers at ridiculous o'clock was the only part of her job that Leanne disliked, although after years of living on her parents' farm, she would have thought she should be used to getting up before the birds by now. Not that she did it every day, but a couple of times a week was more than enough for her, thank you very much! She mainly sourced her flowers and plants from a nearby flower farm, and sometimes from the garden on the farm where she still lived. For out-of-season or special flowers, she used the wholesaler, which she hated doing but had no choice, though she insisted on visiting it herself to choose her own stock rather than ordering online.

She stepped inside Field Day Flowers, closed the door behind her and headed for the kettle. A cup of coffee was needed before she unloaded the van and tackled today's orders, she decided grimly. The back of the van was full to bursting with roses. Red ones. One of the most lucrative days of the year was looming, but Leanne viewed it more as an endurance test. She hated Valentine's Day, and it wasn't because she lacked a love interest – although it was fair to say there was no romance on her horizon – but because she felt she had little scope for creativity. There was only so much that could be done with a dozen red roses.

She spent the morning making up the bouquets for tomorrow and storing them in the temperature-controlled room out the back. She knew she was lucky to have it; when the butcher's shop that had been here since her mum was a child started selling wild boar and venison three years ago and business really took off for them, they needed somewhere larger. Their move to new premises around the corner gave Leanne an opportunity to jump in with an offer for this one. The room where the meat had once been stored made a perfect place to keep her flowers, and even the meat hooks came in handy for the hanging baskets.

In fact, the former butcher's shop made an excellent florist's. It was just the right size, and she loved the way the shop front angled in a bit so she could put some of her lovely displays outside without blocking the pavement or risk them getting too wet. She made a point of doing a new one every week.

In honour of Valentine's Day, she had borrowed (though her dad would have something different to say about it if he knew) an ancient bicycle from the depths of one of the farm sheds, spray-painted it red and filled the little basket on the front with a heart-shaped box of chocolates and a bottle of wine – both empty, of course. She'd added sprays of artfully arranged roses and gypsophila, and the cutest teddy bear she could find. Then she'd draped greenery and red ribbon all around and placed a bay tree alongside the bike, which she'd trimmed into a heart shape and dotted with roses. Finally she'd filled the inside of the window with a Cupid's bow and arrow made from red, white and gold flowers arranged over a hidden frame. Sometimes she recognised how much of an advantage it had been to grow up on a farm with four brothers – she was a dab hand with chicken wire, a soldering iron and a pair of pliers!

Ken, her part-time driver, popped in at ten o'clock to collect the day's deliveries, and she made a mental note to put aside a small bunch of roses for him to give to his wife. Bless him, he had retired several years ago, but his inadequate pension meant he'd been forced to take on any work he could, and Leanne had been more than happy to ask him if he'd like to drive her van for a couple of hours every day.

It would be more than a couple of hours tomorrow, she estimated, looking at the order book. But for once, the sight of so many orders didn't fill her with joy.

Her window did, though. She loved making unusual displays, the stranger the better, and she knew that her attempts to brighten up her shop were viewed favourably by the rest of the village.

In fact, the whole village was a chocolate-box affair, with its gurgling river, pretty humpbacked stone bridge, old pubs and equally old shops. Some of the smaller side roads were still cobbled, and the residents had fought long and bitterly to keep them that way. The shops reflected the prettiness of the village too, from the baker selling traditional and unusual loaves, hand-baked on the premises, to the quirky craft shops and the tea shop near the river at the end of the high street.

Talking of the tea shop, Leanne looked up when the door opened to see its owner, Stevie, darting inside.

'Roses,' Stevie panted. 'Fifteen, please,' she added, placing her hands on the counter and taking big gulps of air.

'Who's chasing you?' Leanne asked drily.

'No one, but there's been such a rush on this morning, I haven't had a minute to myself. With Cassandra being pregnant, I couldn't ask her to waddle up here – it might take her all day! She's huge already and she's got ages to go yet. I keep telling her to take it easy; she needs to give up work, but I think she and Aiden want to install a couple of beehives and set up the pasteurisation thing for the goat's milk, so she intends to hang on until the last minute.'

'Let's hope she doesn't have it in the middle of your tea shop,' Leanne joked.

'Stop it,' Stevie groaned. 'I don't want to tempt fate.'

Stevie might be rushed off her feet, but she was glowing, Leanne thought. Being in love clearly suited her. As did the fresh air of the stables — if you could call the interesting smells around any stable fresh. She had moved in with showjumper Nick shortly after last summer's ball at The Manor, and was loving every minute of it. Living with Nick, that was, not the stables side of it, although she had confided to Leanne that she was learning to ride, albeit cautiously and with a great deal of clinging onto the horse's mane and shrieking.

Leanne mentally shook her head. Until Stevie had arrived in Tanglewood, she had been a city girl through and through; now look at her — living in The Furlongs, surrounded by fields and horses. She could never have thought her life would change so radically when she first set foot in her tea shop all those months ago.

Leanne was ready for a change herself, but…

'Roses?' Stevie reminded her.

'Yes, sorry, I'll sort you some out now. Will buds be OK? If you put them in their vases as soon as you get back, they should be open by tomorrow, but I warn you, they'll be past their best come Monday.' That was the problem with hothouse roses: they didn't last long, only a few days at the most, before they started to look overblown.

'That's OK, I'll be sick of them myself by Sunday evening. I'll change them on Monday.' Stevie rooted around in her voluminous handbag, coming up with a paper bag. 'I thought you might fancy an eclair,' she said, handing the sweet treat over.

'Yum.' Leanne peered inside, her mouth watering at the sight of the chocolatey, creamy goodness within. 'Have you got time to join me for a coffee?'

'Sorry, no. I've got to get back. It's Betty's day off and I've left Cassandra on her own.'

Leanne watched her go wistfully. That was the main drawback of being a one-man band – the lack of company during the day. When she got home, there tended to be too much of it, but that was another story. Aside from Ken and those customers who lingered for a chat, she was very much on her own. Sometimes she thought it must be really nice to have a companion to work alongside. OK, not a *companion*, because she'd be the employer and they'd be the employee, but someone else in the shop who she could bounce ideas off, or even just have a moan to. Preferably someone who understood the floristry business.

Or – and here was an idea – perhaps she could take on an apprentice? She wouldn't be able to pay them much, but at least it would be a job of sorts. She could train them up, and maybe eventually leave them in charge while she went off and...

And *what*? What did she need time off *for*? What was she actually going to do with it? Go shopping? Unlikely. Maybe she could join a class, like yoga, or spin, or have a facial... No, being realistic, she knew she'd never do any of those things. She had enough exercise with the shop and being on her feet all day, and she wasn't all that bothered about facials. Besides, she knew in her heart that she wouldn't completely relax if she wasn't here to supervise. And it wasn't as though she had a husband or children to occupy her free time. She felt vaguely envious when she thought of her friends Stevie and Tia, both of whom were head over heels in love and planning their respective weddings. Leanne was going to be a bridesmaid at Stevie's, which was the closest she'd get to a wedding of her own any time soon.

'Hiya, love,' a familiar voice called as the postman pushed open the door with his shoulder and placed a handful of letters on the counter.

Leanne smiled and waved as he left, then turned her attention to the post. Flyer, catalogue, spammy pension plan thing – they all went in the bin. The council tax payment request she put to one side, as she did with a beautiful note from a very happy customer (wedding flowers – big job), and she hung on to the floristry magazine. It was usually full of great tips and new designs, and she couldn't resist a quick flick through its glossy pages.

An article caught her eye.

Budding Stars!

Could you be the floristry star of the future? Have you got it in you to create breathtaking designs? Can you wow! *our judges? Do you have what it takes to go all the way?*

If you're frantic about flowers and bonkers about blooms, then this is the show for you.

She scanned further down the page to the small print.

Network UK is seeking florists for a brand-new series, Budding Stars, *which will be aired in the summer. The programme will be in a competition format, filmed over ten weeks, with one entrant being eliminated each week.*

7

The winner will get to design the floral display for the main gate to the Chelsea Flower Show.

To enter, you must be eighteen or over. The competition is open to both amateurs and those who work in the floristry business but who have not previously won an award for floristry and do not hold any qualification in the subject.

Wow! The Chelsea Flower Show was the epitome of everything floral and gardening. To exhibit there was a prize indeed. Feeling a flutter of excitement in her chest, Leanne turned the computer on in the back office, clicked on the website mentioned in the article and had a good look. To apply, all she needed to do was fill in a form.

Admittedly, it was quite a detailed form, and it took her all afternoon, in between serving customers and putting the finishing touches to the orders for tomorrow. After she'd completed it, she read through the reams of information about disclosure clauses (eh?), availability for filming, and so on; then with her heart in her mouth, she pressed send.

She knew there was only a teeny-weeny chance she'd get through the first round of selections, and she made a promise to herself not to get too excited.

But she couldn't help feeling a thrill all the same. This opportunity might be just what she'd been looking for.

Chapter 2

'Rex! Rex!' yelled a voice from behind him, and Rex turned to see a springy Dobermann bounding towards him along the path, all floppy ears and waggy tail, with its tongue lolling out. It bounced to a stop, scattering small stones.

'Sorry, really sorry. Not everyone likes dogs.' The Dobermann's owner hurried up, panting as hard as his pet.

Actually, Rex did like dogs. Well-behaved dogs and well-trained dogs, which this one clearly wasn't. It also didn't help his mood that he'd just discovered he had the same name as a daft Dobermann.

'He's only a puppy, nine months old. He'll settle down soon,' the man said.

Yeah, like in a couple of years maybe, Rex thought, as the dog went into puppy pose, his front legs resting on the ground and his waggling backside up in the air, before leaping to his feet and darting off when his owner made a lunge for him.

'Not got a dog yourself?' the stranger asked, looking around as if he thought Rex might have hidden a mutt in the heather.

'No,' Rex said, his soft Scottish burr drawing out the vowel. His beloved bitch Star had recently passed away, at around the same time as his long-term girlfriend had upped and left. They said things happened in threes, so when the third of his misfortunes arrived barely a week later, he was sort of expecting it. He'd loved that job, too...

Never mind, he'd probably grow to love this one; he was halfway there already. It was just a pity it was so far away from home.

The man stuck out his right hand, intruding into his thoughts. 'I'm Arthur, and this is Rex.' He nodded at the dog, which had reappeared at the man's side.

'Rex,' Rex said, taking the man's hand and giving it a firm shake.

'Yeah, Rex,' Arthur agreed. 'It's a grand name for a dog.'

'No, I mean *my* name is Rex.'

'Oh? *Oh!* Ha, ha. Well I never. Rex, meet Rex.'

Rex the man leaned down to pat Rex the dog, who had calmed down enough to sidle up to this interesting new human for a sniff. He felt a familiar pull on his heartstrings. Star's passing had left a huge hole in his life – possibly even more so than his girlfriend's leaving – but he wasn't yet ready to give his love to another dog. It was too soon; his emotions were too raw. Besides, no dog could ever replace Star. She had been one of a kind. He'd had her since she was eight weeks old, and she'd gone everywhere with him. He'd chosen his profession based on the fact that he could take her to work. He'd even taken her to university with him (she'd had to stay at his digs on the days he had lectures), and she used to like nothing better than accompanying him on his field days. She loved it all – woodland, heathland, the high mountains, the wetlands; as long as she was with him, she was happy.

He was lost without her, as if an essential part of him was missing.

'Lovely up here, innit?' Arthur said. 'I've been walking these hills since I was a lad, rain or shine. Always had dogs, see, and they need walking every day.' He stared out over the valley below, and Rex did the same.

This Welsh mountain range wasn't as impressive as those of Rex's Scottish homeland, but it did have a certain charm, although he was under no illusion that small mountains meant safer mountains. In fact, the smaller ones tended to attract more casual visitors, as he'd found out. On a dry Sunday, the main track up Pen y Fan, the highest peak in South Wales, was akin to a supermarket on Christmas Eve. Last Sunday, which had happened to be dry, sunny and Easter, had apparently attracted a record number of visitors. Some of them had been dressed for it, in hiking boots, fleeces and waterproofs, but others had worn T-shirts and soft pumps, clearly unaware that even on a good day, conditions underfoot could be muddy, rugged and slippery. The weather at the top could turn in an instant from warm and bright to sharp biting winds and lowering cloud.

Mountains certainly weren't to be taken lightly, and that was where Rex came in; part of his job was to educate and advise. Thinking of this very thing, he checked Arthur out, relieved to see that he had a sturdy pair of well-worn boots on his feet and several layers of clothing showing through his partly unzipped waterproof jacket.

They went their separate ways, Arthur up and Rex down. He'd come out early, as he had done every day of the two weeks since he'd relocated to Tanglewood, trying to familiarise himself with the land. He intended to know every inch of his patch by the end of the month, however exhausted he felt – walking for twenty or thirty miles a day took it out of you, but it was the best way to get to know a place.

Right now, though, he was ready for lunch. Breakfast had been a ham-filled bun and a flask of coffee, eaten perched on a spectacular slab of rock that jutted out of the top of one of the smaller peaks. It was about the same length and width as a diving board; in fact, that was exactly what the locals called it! Rex had sat on the edge of it, his legs dangling over the side, perched several hundred feet above an almost sheer drop. If he fell now, he'd thought, it would take more than a plaster and a bit of Germolene to put him back together again.

As he strode back to the village, heather and tufts of grass gave way to enclosed fields surrounded by hedgerows. It was almost lambing season, and the fields were full of pregnant ewes munching contentedly on the new growth. The bit of sun last weekend (Easter weekend and it hadn't rained – a miracle!) had encouraged fresh green shoots to spring up, and the leaves on the trees were starting to unfurl.

He stopped to touch a dangling catkin, smiling at the unmistakable sign of spring. A few wild primroses were scattered at the foot of the dry stone wall, and he was careful not to tread on them. As he walked on, he made a mental note to check the funding situation for this particular path. It was obviously well used and was starting to degrade in places. He wanted to repair any damage now, and not wait until the job became a major one.

A gentle bend in the path brought the now familiar view of Tanglewood into sight. He'd not explored this particular route before, but he had checked on the map before he'd set out this morning and knew it looped around to bring him back to the village from the north-west. Besides, he'd know Tanglewood anywhere, with the ribbon of river running alongside it, the small stone bridge that he could just make out if he squinted, and the crossroads formed by the intersection of the two main streets. The village was nestled at the bottom of a U-shaped valley with the steep slopes of the mountains rising either side, and surrounded by lush farmland.

He had to admit, it was very picturesque, reminding him of a miniature Switzerland, but with rows of stone cottages instead of chalets. Tracing the little streets with his eye, he counted the houses until he came to the one he lived in. From here, it was nothing more than a speck, but he was convinced he could see the ivy growing around the door. He was renting it for now, although if this move worked out and he decided to stay, he might see if he could purchase it once the money came through from the sale of the house in Scotland that he still part-owned with his ex.

Even in his own mind, Rex hesitated to use Jules's name. If he thought of her at all that is, because he was actively trying not to. It wasn't that he was heartbroken (he was heart*sore*, but his heart wasn't shattered – there was a difference), it was just that her departure had been so unexpected. There they'd been, bumbling along – quite happily, he'd thought. Then she'd dropped the bombshell that their relationship wasn't going anywhere and she was moving out.

Looking back, he knew he should have realised. The pair of them had become more like a couple of lodgers than romantic lovers. Maybe it was to be expected when you were with someone for any length of time – perhaps you did lose the spark. How sad if that were true, he mused. During the weeks between the split and moving to Wales, he had found plenty of time to reflect, and had been forced to admit that he was equally to blame. Maybe he should have made more of an effort, wooed her more, made her feel special.

He had also realised something else, which had come as a bit of a surprise to him: that perhaps it was because he hadn't loved her enough that he hadn't made the effort in the first place. After the first flush of passion had worn off, they hadn't had a great deal in common. They'd simply drifted along like two pieces of flotsam on the same tide. Even moving in together had been a matter of finances; their decision to buy had been based on wanting some kind of return on their investment. They'd chosen their house with their heads and not with their hearts. Looking back, that should have told him everything he needed to know.

He grunted, kicking a loose stone down the path. At least the house had increased in value, so they'd both got something out of their failed relationship.

After climbing over the last stile, he picked up the pace. He was starving, and a bowl of delicious soup with a couple of slices of home-baked granary bread was calling to him. He'd taken to popping into Peggy's Tea Shoppe every now and then when he couldn't be bothered to cook. Actually, it was becoming a daily habit, and if he didn't manage to get the same table by the window, he had a tendency to feel a little disgruntled.

'She's made some spinach and cheese patties,' Betty, the old lady who helped in the tea shop, hissed at him as he slid into his usual seat. 'They're not as good as my vegetable pasties, but they'll do.'

'Do you have any of your pasties?'

'No – why do you think I told you about *her* patties? They come on a bed of rocket with home-made onion chutney,' she added.

'I'll have those then,' he replied with a smile, 'and a bowl of whatever soup is on the hob.'

'Tomato and roasted pepper,' Betty said over her shoulder. 'I take it you want a pot of tea?'

'Please.' His order given, he leaned back and studied the noticeboard. He enjoyed looking at what events and activities were on, what was for sale. Stevie, who owned the place, was very strict about what she allowed to be posted on it. Today there were the familiar adverts for a plumber and a handyman, which had been there a while. There were also a couple of new ads for a dance class and an open day at the little primary school, alongside a notice for a twelve-mile walk into the Beacons for charity. Rex knew all about that particular event, because although he hadn't organised it, it was taking place in his area, and he intended to be on hand just in case.

The items for sale included a pram, a garden shed (buyer to dismantle and remove), a chest of drawers and—

'Here you go. Mind that bowl, it's hot.' The younger waitress, who was pregnant and who Rex thought might be called Cressida or Cassandra (he wasn't sure which and he didn't like to ask), placed his meal on the table. 'Can I get you anything else?'

'No thanks, this is perfect.'

15

It was, too, and he set to it with gusto. When he was finally replete – which took a piece of cake and another pot of tea – he leaned back, patting his stomach. If he kept this up, he'd have to double his daily mileage just to keep his weight even. The food here was simply too good.

As he waited for his meal to go down, he found his gaze returning to the noticeboard. Something had caught his interest earlier, but his food had appeared and distracted him before he could read it properly. He scanned the adverts. Ah, that was it. He wasn't really ready, but there wasn't anything wrong with just going to have a quick look. It wouldn't do any harm, and it would let him stick his toe in the water, so to speak. He didn't *have* to buy one, did he?

He fished around in his backpack for a pen and some paper before carefully writing the number down. In case there was the remotest possibility he might forget what it was for, he added *puppy* underneath and underlined the word three times.

Chapter 3

Leanne had been rushed off her feet all day, yet despite that, she was bored.

Maybe *bored* wasn't the right word, but for the life of her she couldn't find a more suitable one. It wasn't as if she hadn't been creative today; she had. She'd spent a good couple of hours stripping the window of its Easter arrangement and designing a bright, pretty spring display – something she always enjoyed doing. But something was missing. She felt restless and out of sorts. Maybe she was coming down with a bug or a virus, and she prayed that wasn't the case – she couldn't afford to be ill. The last time she'd been unwell, she'd had to close the shop for a couple of days.

She was curled up in her favourite armchair at home, with her laptop on her knees, reflecting that if you ran your own business then your work was never truly done. She paid a couple of invoices, moved a few spam emails to the trash and read a sales pitch or two, saving one of them for later. Then she spotted something that almost made her heart jump out of her chest – an email from *Budding Stars*.

Calm down, Lea, she told herself, it's probably a standard rejection, a 'thanks but no thanks'. She recalled how giddy she'd become when she'd received an earlier email from them, until she'd realised it was merely an acknowledgement of her entry. But she was unable to stop her hands from shaking as she clicked on the message.

She read it once, then read it again. She looked up and stared into space for a minute, worrying at her bottom lip with her teeth. She read it for a third time, just to be certain.

She was through to the next round of the selection process! They were inviting her to their studios in London for an interview and a demonstration of her abilities.

She felt sick. She felt excited. And she felt incredibly nervous. What if she made a total prat of herself? What if they didn't like her, or she looked like a hideous witch on screen? She'd heard that the camera hated some people and loved others – what if she was one of the hated ones?

She could always back out now, walk away with no harm done; no one would ever know.

Yeah, right. There was no way she was going to pass up an opportunity like this, no matter how terrified she was at the thought of taking part in the competition.

Then it finally hit her – she was actually through to the next round! *Squeee!*

She had to tell someone. Her mum was out at a planning meeting to raise funds for the church roof, but her dad was around. She vaguely remembered him muttering something about a man and a dog, and she guessed he must be with Bess and her pups, so she decided to go and find him. The puppies were eight weeks old and absolutely adorable. Plus, it was a good excuse for her to play with them, because there was no way she was going to get any more work done this evening – she was far too excited for that.

Bess, like the other farm dogs, lived in one of the old stables next to the house which Leanne made her way over to now. She couldn't ever remember there being any horses in them. The dogs usually bunked down together, but Bess had been moved to a pen of her own when the birth of her puppies grew closer, and there she would stay until her babies left.

Aw, look at the proud mama with her seven puppies – four boys and three girls. Leanne's favourite was the smallest female, the runt of the litter. She was shyer than the rest, quieter and more loving, content to cuddle rather than to play.

She leaned over the half-door, watching them for a moment before she went in. They were suckling and she didn't want to disturb them until they were done, so she listened to their little grunts and squeaks with an indulgent smile. They were simply too cute for words, and she wished she could keep them all. Her father flatly refused, of course. If they kept every puppy that was bred on the farm, he argued, the place would be overrun with dogs. Besides, these were working animals, bred for herding sheep; they needed to go to farms where they could do exactly that. He had already started their training in preparation for their new homes, but there were two babies who didn't cut the mustard, as he liked to say, and it was one of these, the rather timid little girl, that Leanne had her eye on.

When Bess had finally had enough of nursing her brood and the blissful look on her doggy face was replaced by a long-suffering expression as sharp little milk teeth made their presence felt, she scrambled to her feet. Shaking her pups loose, she jumped onto the raised platform above to escape them, and flopped down on the straw-covered wooden boards, her tail thumping a greeting.

This was Leanne's cue. Quickly she undid the latch on the bottom half of the stable door and slipped inside before any of the little blighters could escape. Then she dropped onto the straw and let herself be clambered over. There was nothing quite as lovely as being surrounded by a litter of milky smelling puppies, with their fat little tummies, soft paws and fluffy baby coats. The other thing that was wonderful about puppies was that they were always so delighted to see her. Stumpy tails waggling, they greeted her with little yips of excitement.

Oh, they were sooo sweet! She could spend all day in here being climbed over and nibbled at. The puppies soothed her nerves, and after a few minutes of wonderful doggy attention, her excitement over the news that she was through to the next round of the selection process abated a little, and she was able to think about it more dispassionately.

It was going to be hard and would mean a great deal of work, but imagine if she actually *won*! Calm down, she told herself. She had to get through the interview first, not to mention the televised rounds.

'Take it one step at a time,' she murmured, and Bess wagged her tail harder, as if agreeing with her. At nearly seven years old, the bitch was an experienced mum. She was also a brilliant sheepdog, which was why Leanne's father had bred from her. She had a lovely temperament and was happy enough to let people wade in among her little ones, although she kept a close eye on proceedings as Leanne scooped up the smallest puppy and held it close, feeling the beat of the little dog's heart. This baby had actually stolen a piece of her own, and she wished she was in a position to keep her, but she knew how much her dad disliked having pets around the farm. According to him, every animal should earn its keep, so the chances of Leanne being able to adopt the puppy were non-existent.

Her father had already picked out one of the males to train up to replace Shep, and he didn't intend keeping any of the others. Most of them were already sold, bought by farmers or shepherds. There were only two that weren't spoken for, and one of them was the little bitch.

Leanne had named her Nell. It was a mistake – not the name itself, but giving her a name at all. It would just make it that much harder when the pup left. But she hadn't been able to stop herself – it was a long time since she'd become so attached to one of the livestock. The last time it had been a piglet, bought to fatten up for slaughter; the enormous sow it had grown into had died of old age, because despite Leanne's upbringing and the fact that she knew what farm animals were all about, she had bawled her eyes out when it was time to send 'Grunter' to slaughter. Her brothers still teased her about it now, whenever their mum cooked roast pork for Sunday lunch.

Voices, one of them her father's, broke into her thoughts, and she gave the tiny dog a final kiss on its fluffy head before putting it down. Then she scrambled to her feet and backed into the corner behind the door so the newcomer could have a clear view of the pups. She peered through the crack between the door and the frame as the two men came into view. She found herself praying that the guy wanted a working dog and not a pet.

'There are a couple left, a dog and a bitch,' her dad was saying. 'I gotta be straight with you – the bitch ain't up to much. You'd be better off with the male. He's like his father, full of spirit and a bit cheeky.'

Leanne had to smile. Her dad was as honest as the day was long. He'd trained enough sheepdogs to know which were liable to become good ones, and even at this early age, he could usually tell. The way he was going, though, he'd never sell that pretty little girl, which was another reason why Leanne still had a smile on her face when the stranger leaned over the half-door for a closer look at Bess's pups.

'My, they're bonny,' he said, and she guessed from his accent that he wasn't local.

As the man studied the dogs, Leanne studied him, and what she saw made her heart flutter. He was gorgeous, in a rugged, outdoorsy kind of way. He had to be at least six foot, possibly taller, and had a decent pair of shoulders on him (Leanne had a thing for shoulders). Russet-coloured hair, slate-grey eyes and a proper man's jaw (she had a thing for jawlines, too) completed the parts she could see.

She brushed off her jeans and moved into his line of sight, conscious of his curious gaze turning towards her.

'Oh, hello, love,' her father said. 'I didn't notice you there.'

'Hi, Dad. He's right, you know,' she added to the stranger. 'The male is definitely the bolder, more confident of the two that are left.' She bent down to pick up the pup, who growled in protest.

The man laughed. He had a really nice smile, too, Leanne noticed.

'Isn't he a cheeky chappy? Is that the female?' he asked, pointing to Nell, who had climbed onto Leanne's trainer and was sucking on the end of one of the laces, content to let the rest of her litter-mates play boisterously around her.

Leanne looked down at her feet. 'Yes, that's Nell,' she said with a smile.

'You mustn't give them names,' her dad said. 'It just makes it harder when the time comes.'

'Nell, eh? Do you breed your dogs much, Mr Green?'

'Only now and again,' her dad replied. 'Shep, the father of this bunch, is getting on a bit and I need to start training a replacement. Bess,' he pointed to the bitch still lying on her platform, 'has had one litter before this one, so I'll probably not breed from her again – she's done her bit.'

Leanne was sorry to hear him say that. She loved it when there were puppies on the farm. There was nothing like the happy, non-judgemental welcome of a dog. Multiply that by however many were in a litter, and it was a recipe for paradise.

'I'm Leanne, by the way,' she said, deciding it was about time she introduced herself, and held out her right hand. The left still clutched the wriggling, squirming pup to her chest.

'Rex.' The man took her hand and shook it.

'Is that what you're going to call him?' Leanne asked, holding the pup up so the guy could get a better look at him. 'It's a good strong name for a dog.' Sheepdogs tended to have one-syllable names that could be easily shouted across a field.

Her father snorted. Leanne gave him a swift look, wondering why he was biting his lip and why his face was turning purple with suppressed laughter.

'Not the dog's name; *mine*,' Rex said. His smile was half apologetic, half resigned.

'Sorry. You must hear that a lot,' she said, wincing at her faux pas. Trust her to offend the only gorgeous man she'd seen around here in ages.

'What do you advise, Mr Green?' Rex turned to her father.

'Call me Geoff. It depends on what you want to do with it. The male will be more bolshie, the bitch will be calmer. Do you want it for a pet or for work? Because I have to be honest with you, that 'un,' he pointed to Nell, 'won't be any good around sheep. She's too people focused; she'll spend most of her time concentrating on you and not on her job. I know, I've seen it before.'

Leanne watched Rex's face, seeing a play of emotions scudding across it like clouds across the sky.

'A bit of both, really,' he said eventually. 'It'll have to come with me to work most of the time, and I expect to take it into schools and whatnot.'

'What do you do?' Geoff asked.

'I'm a park ranger.'

'Oh aye?' He nodded in approval. Both Leanne and her father knew how vital good management of the National Park was for its success. Her dad had a lot of respect for the rangers.

'I need a dog that won't be afraid of meeting new people, but won't get overexcited either,' Rex was saying.

Leanne had a feeling she was going to lose Nell, and to hide her dismay, she bent down to put the male pup back on the hay and picked the bitch up instead. It might be the last time she'd get to cuddle her. Nell snuggled into her neck, and she inhaled deeply. She didn't think she'd ever get tired of the smell of puppy, nor the feel of the soft little body in her arms. Nell licked her on the nose and Leanne laughed. This baby sure was a cutie!

'I take it you've owned a dog before?' her father asked cautiously. He was always careful to ensure that any dogs he bred went to good, knowledgeable homes.

'I lost my springer spaniel bitch a few months back,' Rex said. 'I thought I'd not be able to face having another dog, but I've come to realise that a house is too quiet without one.'

Impulsively Leanne took a step nearer to the half-door and thrust Nell into Rex's hands. She knew the puppy wouldn't be on the farm for much longer, regardless of whether he bought her or not, but it was the pain in his voice that made her mind up. If Nell had to go to anyone, then it should be to this man with love in his eyes and an ache behind his words. She would be well cared for, Leanne was certain of it. Although she didn't know a thing about the guy, she had a feeling he would adore the little dog as much as she did.

She watched his face anxiously. He blinked in shock for a second when the pup was shoved into his arms without warning, but his expression immediately softened as he gazed down at her.

Sad that the puppy would be leaving her but confident that she was going to the best of homes, Leanne unlatched the stable half-door. Hardly able to speak because of the catch in her voice and the tears pricking her eyes, she slipped through the opening and dashed back to the house, saying a silent goodbye to the little dog who had stolen her heart.

Chapter 4

'He's taken her, then?' Leanne asked her father at teatime, already knowing what he was going to say.

'Taken who?' That was Saul, the most annoying of her four brothers.

'I was talking to Dad,' Leanne protested.

'So? I can join in if I want.' Her brother reached across her for the tureen of mashed potatoes.

Leanne stuck her tongue out at him and slapped his hand away.

'Children, play nice,' their mother warned, and the pair of them subsided. Leanne might be twenty-nine and Saul thirty-three, but they still listened to Iris when she used that voice.

'Well, Dad, did he?' Leanne asked again, this time passing the tureen to Saul without being prompted.

'Did who do what?' Her father was busily tucking into his plate of lamb casserole. He loved his food, did her dad. Actually, they all did. Physical jobs combined with fresh air plus Iris's excellent cooking meant there usually wasn't much left over at the end of a meal.

'Did Rex take Nell?' Leanne persisted.

'Aye, he did. The pup's ready to leave now, so I thought he might as well. No point in delaying it. Anyways, Bess will be happy with one less mouth to feed.'

'Who's Rex?' Saul asked, around a mouthful of food.

'Some bloke who works for the Brecon Beacons National Park,' Geoff replied, clearly more interested in his dinner than in gossip.

'He's Scottish, he lost his dog a few months ago, he's tall and he's got auburn hair,' Leanne said, filling in the details.

'Fancy him, do you?' So far, Murray, another of Leanne's brothers, had been silent, but the thought of teasing Leanne had obviously proved irresistible to him.

'No!' she shot back. 'I'm simply observant.'

'Don't you mean nosy?' Saul clarified.

'Is he married?' Iris asked.

'How should I know?' Leanne retorted.

'You seem to know everything else about him,' Saul said. 'Where does he live?'

'I can answer that one,' their father interjected. 'He said he's got one of those cottages behind the high street.'

Leanne wondered whether she could see it from the rear of her shop. If not, then it was probably visible from upstairs. It was a pity the first floor was occupied by a firm of solicitors, because it would have made a great flat, she often thought.

She frequently considered moving out of her parents' house and finding a place of her own in the village, but so far she had yet to do anything about it. Stevie had offered her the flat above Peggy's Tea Shoppe, but Leanne hadn't taken her up on it, so instead Stevie had rented it out as a holiday let when she'd moved in with Nick, which had been around the same time as Tia, Nick's sister, had moved out of The Furlongs and into the downstairs wing of The

Manor with *her* fiancé, William. It seemed like everyone was moving on and moving out, except Leanne.

Maybe it was about time she thought seriously about her own space. It would be handy living just a few minutes' walk away from the flower shop instead of halfway up a mountain. On the other hand, she would have to do all her own cooking – unless, of course, she did what Saul and Murray did and came home each evening for dinner. She'd also have to do all her own washing and ironing, not to mention the cleaning. It wasn't as if she desperately needed her privacy either – she could barely remember the last time she'd had a boyfriend to need privacy for!

She knew she was spoilt living at home, but she kind of liked it. Besides, if she was going to take this competition seriously, she wasn't going to have that much time to play house, was she?

The competition!

'I've got news!' she shrieked at the top of her voice. How could she have forgotten something so important?

The noise around the table ceased. Even her brothers stopped bickering about football to listen. Seeing that she had her family's undivided attention, she took a deep breath and dived right in.

'I'm going to be on the telly, on a show called *Budding Stars*,' she announced.

Her family stared blankly at her.

'It's a new competition, like *Bake Off* or *Strictly*, and what's really cool is that the winner gets to design a display for the Chelsea Flower Show.'

She noticed her mother nodding – at least someone in the family knew what she was referring to. Iris loved watching both *Bake Off* and the televised highlights of the Chelsea Flower Show.

'How come *you're* going to be on it?' Murray asked.

'Gee, thanks for the vote of confidence,' Leanne drawled back at him. 'I never shot you down when you entered all those sheep-shearing competitions.'

'I didn't mean it like that,' her brother protested. 'I meant, *Bake Off* is for non-professionals. Surely this *Budding Stars* thing is the same?'

'No, it's not. It's to find the best all-round florist, whether they're amateur or not. The only stipulations are that you can't have won any kind of award, or have a qualification in floristry. Apart from that, anyone can enter, from a kid on work experience to someone who does the flowers in church every Sunday.' She paused to take a breath. 'I sent my application in weeks ago and I just heard back today that I'm through to the next round. I've got to go to London for an interview and stuff.'

'Stuff?' her mother asked. 'What kind of stuff? How long will you be there for, and who's going to look after the shop while you go swanning about?'

Leanne scowled. Thanks for all the support, she thought sarcastically. Not one member of her family had bothered to congratulate her. Placing her knife and fork down on her plate, she stood, pushing her chair away from the table. She was having difficulty holding back tears.

Then her mother was on her feet and there was the familiar feel of her arms around Leanne's shoulders. 'Don't think we aren't pleased for you, love, because we are. We're thrilled, aren't we, Geoff?'

Her dad nodded vigorously; even her brothers were smiling. Leanne gave a loud sniff, and her mother flinched.

'I was just being practical,' Iris pointed out. 'You can't be in two places at once.' She guided Leanne back to her chair. 'Finish your meal,' she insisted, 'and tell us all about it.'

Leanne sat, but she knew her mother was right. Iris couldn't be expected to step in, although she did help out if Leanne needed a break. But she wasn't getting any younger, and she had enough on her plate as it was, what with all the jobs she did on the farm. No one could say that being a farmer's wife was easy. Leanne knew from experience that there was always something that needed doing; right now, at this time of year, it was seeing to the orphaned lambs. So far there were five of them, all having to be bottle-fed several times a day, and the number was only going to rise, because lambing season wasn't over yet. Then there was the vegetable plot and the beehive — solely her mother's domain — plus the actual farmhouse itself, with all the cleaning, cooking and laundry to be done. Her mother was in charge of the farm admin and the accounts, too.

No, Iris had her hands well and truly full, and Leanne had no intention of adding to her burden.

'I'm going to take on an apprentice,' she announced, her eyes widening as the words slipped out of her mouth without any apparent command from her brain. She took a moment to think about what she'd just said. She had toyed with the idea when she'd been contemplating a life that didn't consist solely of working, eating and sleeping, so why not seriously consider the possibility now, when it was for a solid reason? After all, as her mother had just pointed out, she couldn't be in two places at once. If she was serious about this competition, then she'd have to make arrangements for when she wasn't going to be around.

But what if she didn't get any further than this next stage? she asked herself, before realising it didn't actually matter – she wouldn't have lost anything and would have gained an assistant, which would allow her a bit more time for herself.

Decision made, she set about wondering who on earth she could entrust her flower-shop baby to.

With her fork halfway to her mouth, she paused – actually, she knew just the person!

Now all she had to do was persuade her.

Chapter 5

Rex clambered out of bed, his eyes stinging and his body protesting, and rubbed a weary hand across his face, stubble rasping under his fingers.

If this was what having a baby was like, then no thanks.

Another mournful howl, followed by a series of pathetic yips, echoed up the stairs. After two nights of being separated from her mother and siblings, Nell showed no sign of settling down.

With a sigh, Rex trudged down the stairs and staggered blearily towards the kitchen, glancing at the clock as he did so. Two thirty. Great. He'd only been asleep for an hour, and this was the third time tonight he'd been forced to traipse downstairs to comfort the tiny dog. Despite his best efforts – soft bed, stuffed toys, a warm hot-water bottle – the puppy was having none of it.

The howling ceased as soon as he opened the door, and a pair of blue eyes peered up at him hopefully. He stepped inside and—

Bugger!

He hopped around, shaking his foot and cursing, because he'd only gone and stepped on one of the hard little chews he'd bought her. Then he cursed again as his non-injured foot trod in something cold and wet.

Great. The dog had managed to wee over the tiled floor, totally missing the puppy training pads he had placed around her bed.

He looked at them more closely and realised she hadn't missed them at all. A smelly little pile sat right in the centre of one of them, with brown paw prints dotted around it. Wonderful – she'd managed to tread in her own mess.

Very much awake now, he scooped up the ball of fluff and held her gingerly in one hand while cleaning up the mess with the other. When the astringent smell of disinfectant had replaced the less-than-aromatic smell of the little present she had left him, he turned his attention to cleaning the dog herself.

Thinking it was a game, Nell yipped and wriggled, trying to bite anything that came within range of her needle-sharp teeth, as Rex carefully wiped the pink pads of her paws, making sure to get between her toes. In order to keep her quiet, he let her nibble on his fingers, yelping himself once or twice when she bit too hard. Immediately the puppy was contrite, her tail wagging furiously as she tried to lick his face.

'I know, I know,' he crooned. 'You didn't mean to hurt me. You're only a baby.'

Nell whined back, still licking any and every bit of exposed skin she could reach, and he laughed when a wet pink tongue connected with his nose.

'Oi, stop it. Faces aren't for licking.' He chuckled, despite his tiredness. 'Now,' he said, putting her back in her basket, 'shall we try again?'

Nell sat on her haunches, staring up at him with liquid eyes, her tiny nose twitching, one ear cocked, the other flopping over. She looked so sad, his heart went out to her. He let out another deep sigh, which turned into a huge yawn.

'Night night,' he said. The dog continued to stare at him sorrowfully. 'You'll soon get used to it, I promise,' he added, praying it was true. He didn't know how many more nights of interrupted sleep he could handle. He didn't think his neighbours were too pleased with Nell's midnight serenades either.

He'd no sooner slipped back into bed than she started crying again.

Right, he decided, he was going to ignore her this time. If he went down to her every time she cried, she'd never learn to drop off on her own; although funnily enough, she had managed to sleep most of the afternoon yesterday, when he'd left her alone in the back of the Land Rover. He knew this because he'd been watching the little madam quite closely as he'd poked around in a pond, documenting the number of insect larvae and making notes on the variety of other wildlife he had spotted. It was a pity he couldn't have joined her for a nap, but someone had to earn enough to put dog biscuits in her bowl.

He covered his ears with his hands, but when that failed to do the trick, he tried a pillow instead. It made no difference – he could still hear her. Each mournful, drawn-out howl was followed by a yip; then when that failed to get him out of bed, she resorted to pathetic whimpering.

Oh God, he couldn't stand it. It wasn't just the not sleeping that was getting to him either; it was the total and utter desolation in her little voice.

Knowing he shouldn't relent, but unable to help himself, he slid out of bed once more and padded downstairs.

The pup looked so delighted to see him, as though he had been gone for hours rather than just a few minutes, that he had to laugh. She danced around his feet in joyous abandon, her little bottom wiggling from side to side with the force of her waggy tail. When Rex scooped her up and cuddled her into his chest, she buried her nose in the crook of his neck, her breath all warm and snuffly on his skin.

'OK, you win,' he said, turning towards the stairs.

He knew he'd regret it and that he was making a rod for his own back, but if he didn't get some sleep soon, he'd be a total wreck come the morning.

The last thing he remembered was the feel of a warm, furry body snuggling into his side as he finally drifted off.

Chapter 6

Leanne opened the door to Ken's wife with a broad smile on her face and hope in her heart. Mabel didn't appear nearly as happy to see her, and a frown creased her already wrinkled brow as she stood on the step worrying at her lip with her teeth.

'I don't know anything about flowers,' she announced as Leanne quickly ushered her inside before the woman could change her mind.

'That's OK, I can teach you,' Leanne said cheerfully, showing her into the storeroom behind the counter.

Mabel's eyes widened at the sight of the large metal door. 'Is that a safe?' she asked.

'Good Lord, no. It's a cold room. I keep the flowers in there so they stay fresher for longer.'

'I don't know anything about flowers,' Mabel repeated, 'and I'm too old to start learning new stuff.'

'You aren't old,' Leanne scoffed, hoping to reassure the other woman. Actually, she *was* rather elderly, being somewhere in her seventies. 'Anyway,' she continued, praying that it was true, 'you're never too old to learn new things.'

Mabel was understandably nervous, but Leanne was nervous too. Maybe this wasn't such a good idea after all, but she'd done it now and she couldn't take change her mind. Besides, she was running out of time: her trip to London was only a week and a half away. She needed to start training someone as soon as possible.

She knew money was tight in the Everson household. When she'd mentioned to Ken that she was looking for someone to help out in the shop, his eyes had lit up. She hadn't needed to persuade him to broach the subject with his wife – it was just a pity that Mabel didn't seem as keen as Ken did. Originally Leanne had thought her idea was an excellent solution. Ken was reliable and a good worker. Unfortunately, Mabel resembled a small child on her first day at school – worried, scared and a tiny bit excited, all rolled into one.

'You like flowers, though, don't you?' Leanne pointed out with false joviality. Maybe she should post an advert in the window and see what came of it. That was how Stevie had found Cassandra. Leanne wanted a Cassandra of her own – instead, she appeared to have landed herself with a reluctant pensioner.

'I'm not as young as I used to be,' Mabel insisted, still chewing on her bottom lip.

'You mightn't be,' Leanne countered, 'but you *are* a mature, sensible woman and I have every confidence that you can do this. You'll soon pick it up,' she added, more for her own benefit than Mabel's. 'Let me show you where everything is, I'll talk you through a typical day, then we'll have a cuppa. How does that sound?'

'OK.' Mabel's reluctance was tangible.

Leanne flicked a switch on the kettle and began to show the other woman around as they waited for it to boil.

'Let's see what you know and what you don't know, and we can take it from there,' she suggested, suppressing a sigh at Mabel's unwilling nod. She felt like saying, 'You don't have to do this,' but she reined herself in. She had a feeling Mabel *did* have to do this, both for financial reasons and to give her a purpose in life. On more than one occasion, Ken had mentioned that his wife had lost some of her get-up-and-go since she'd retired.

'You know what these are, don't you?' Leanne asked, pointing to a bucket of roses.

'Roses,' Mabel replied promptly. 'These are lilies, them there are chrysanthemums, and they're daffs...' She trailed off uncertainly.

'That's right! See, you *do* know your flowers.' Leanne was trying to be encouraging, but she was worried she was beginning to sound patronising.

Mabel looked slowly around the shop, nodding to herself. 'I recognise most of them,' she admitted reluctantly.

Over the course of the next hour or so, aided by two cups of strong tea and some digestive biscuits, Leanne saw a little confidence creeping into the older woman's face.

'I can't put them together in a bouquet, mind,' Mabel warned.

'You won't have to,' Leanne told her. 'I'll prepare the orders in the morning, and Ken knows what's what with the deliveries. All you need to do is man the shop and deal with the customers.'

'But what if they ask me something and I don't know the answer?' Mabel said, looking worried again.

'I'm not going to leave you totally on your own just yet, and when I do, it will only be for a day. Even then, my mother's on the other end of the phone.'

Despite the distance, Leanne planned to get up super-early on the day of the interview to drive to London, so that she could drive back the same evening. Surely Mabel could manage for a day?

The door opened and both women looked towards it, Leanne with a friendly, professional smile, Mabel with alarm on her face.

'It's only Stevie,' Leanne said.

'Thanks.' Stevie's voice was dry, but she was smiling.

'I mean, it's nothing for Mabel to be worried about,' Leanne said. She turned to Mabel. 'Stevie calls every other morning for fifteen flowers, one for each of her tables. Small flowers are better because they don't take up as much room. How about narcissi?' she asked Stevie.

'Perfect.' Stevie grinned as Leanne encouraged Mabel to pick out the required number of flowers and demonstrated how to wrap them.

Mabel handed the bunch to Stevie, then looked at Leanne for further instructions.

'Normally I'd tot up how much the customer is to pay,' Leanne explained, 'but Stevie has an account, so I just note it down in this book.' She showed Mabel the account book, then pulled a diary from under the counter. 'Orders go in this one here, everything from birthday bouquets to full-blown weddings. Have a look through and you'll see the sort of details I need.'

She left Mabel to it and walked Stevie to the door.

'How's she doing?' Stevie whispered. Leanne had confided in her friend about the competition but had asked Stevie to keep it to herself – she didn't want the whole village to know, just in case she didn't make it past the interview stage.

She pursed her lips. 'It's early days yet. She only started this morning, but I'm sure she'll be fine. She'll have to be, otherwise I'm never going to get to London.'

When the next customer came in, she showed Mabel how to work the till. 'You put the amount in here,' she said, pressing some buttons, 'and if the customer purchases more than one item, press the plus button and enter the new amount. When you're done, press this one here and it will total it up for you.'

Mabel didn't say a single word, and Leanne wondered if she had understood anything she had just said.

'Oh! The till roll has run out.' Worried that this new development might scare Mabel even further, she hastened to change it. Her surprise when the older woman proceeded to expertly flip open the holder, take the old till roll out and insert a fresh one was quite considerable. She closed her mouth abruptly, realising it was hanging open.

'Now this bit I *can* do,' Mabel said. 'Back in the day, I did a stint in a supermarket. That was before I joined Webbs.'

'What did you do at Webbs?' Leanne asked.

'I was the logistics manager.'

Webbs was an engineering firm in nearby Abergavenny, and although Leanne vaguely remembered hearing something about Mabel working for them (Tanglewood was a small place, and people generally knew what other folks were up to), she'd assumed she must have been employed on the factory floor. Once again she felt her mouth drop open.

That would teach her to make assumptions, she thought.

'Tills I can handle,' Mabel continued. 'Getting goods from A to B I can handle. But this,' she gestured around the shop, 'is totally new.'

'You'll soon get the hang of it,' Leanne repeated, meaning it this time. 'If you can run a big department in a company like Webbs, you can surely sell a couple of bunches of flowers.'

Mabel still looked dubious.

'How about you stick to what you're comfortable with and I'll sort out anything more complicated until you feel you're ready?' Leanne suggested. 'What do you say?'

Mabel held out her right hand. 'Agreed, but I'm not as young as I used to be; it might take me a bit longer to catch on,' she warned yet again.

Leanne took her hand and shook it. 'Welcome aboard,' she said, a flutter of excitement shooting through her.

Oh boy, London and the interview had suddenly become very real indeed.

Chapter 7

Nell squirmed inside Rex's jacket, her little paws scrabbling against the material.

'Not yet, young lady,' he told her. 'You can walk as soon as you've had your next lot of injections.'

In fact, that was exactly where he would be taking her in a couple of hours. But first he intended to call into the office to catch up on some paperwork.

'Ooh, what a cutie,' one of the admin staff cried, spotting the puppy's black and white head poking out from Rex's waterproof jacket.

'Aye, she is bonny,' he agreed. 'She's also a right wee madam when she puts her mind to it.'

The woman grinned at him. 'Just like all us ladies, eh? How old is she?'

'Ten weeks.' Rex shrugged his rucksack off his shoulders and brought out the dog's bowls, some toys, a blanket and a puppy training pad. He caught the woman watching him.

'I should imagine this is what it must be like taking a baby out,' he joked, placing the pup on the floor. Nell stood there uncertainly, nose twitching and tail quivering at the strangeness of the new surroundings.

'Believe me, kids are a lot worse,' the woman said. She bent down and made clicking noises with her tongue. Nell plucked up courage and padded towards her, tail going nineteen to the dozen. The woman giggled as the puppy licked her fingers. 'I should know, I've had three kids and I've got a couple of grandchildren too. When they're little, every time you step out of the door you feel as though you're taking your whole house with you.'

Rex decided he should buy another couple of bowls and other stuff to keep in the office to save carting everything around with him. He could keep some things in the Land Rover too, just in case.

He switched the computer on while trying to keep an eye on the dog. Although Nell seemed to be getting to grips with house training in the cottage, sometimes she forgot herself and widdled where she stood. He usually managed to anticipate her more substantial accidents though, because she tended to run around in frantic circles as if she couldn't decide on a suitable spot. He'd also noticed she tended to go not long after being fed, which helped to minimise the incidents.

Still, he kept a close eye on her all the same, because she had a tendency to chew anything that took her fancy, and there didn't appear to be any consistency in her choices. Puppies chewed shoes – everyone knew that – and he'd been prepared to have to move every pair he owned out of her reach. He vividly remembered his dismay when he'd caught Star eating his one and only pair of football boots. By the time he'd realised what she'd done, there hadn't been much left of them except for the studs and the laces.

Nell liked shoes. She *really* liked shoes. She also really liked telephone wires, skirting boards, chair legs and anything else she could sink her sharp teeth into. Except, that is, the things he had purposely bought for her to chew

44

on, which she ignored completely. So far, not one of the toys, balls or assorted chews he had purchased had caught her fancy.

After logging on to his emails and taking several minutes to read and answer each one because he kept having to jump up to either wrestle something out of the pup's mouth or remove her from whatever she was trying to destroy, he gave up.

Instead, he decided to check on how the repairs to one of the main hiking paths leading up to the main peak were going. Maybe some fresh air would wear the little tyke out.

The drive was a short one and he zipped the puppy into his jacket once more as he got out of his vehicle, leaving his hands free to lock the Land Rover. Being a ranger meant he had access to parts of the park where the general public's vehicles weren't allowed, and he'd driven as far up the track as he could before pulling over, leaving the Landy slightly skewed up a bank. Normally he'd hike up the track from the bottom, but he was conscious of not wanting to be late for Nell's injections.

He did take a moment to gaze at the view, though. Tanglewood lay directly below him, shining in the bright morning sunlight. From up here, it looked even more picture-postcard lovely, if that was possible, nestling in its wide valley with the river winding through it, and surrounded by trees, open fields and hedgerows. Beyond that lay the moors and the mountaintops. He took a deep breath of fresh, chilly air, thinking how lucky he was to live in such a beautiful, unspoilt part of the country.

The drone of a helicopter overhead shattered the peace, and he glanced up, smiling with satisfaction when he saw the payload of rocks dangling beneath it, destined to be dropped at some point further up the path.

There was a fine balance between protecting and conserving the National Park and allowing access to the countless pairs of feet that hiked the trails criss-crossing the mountains. That was where Rex, the other park rangers and the teams of volunteers came in. Today, some of them were laying stones over what was essentially a dirt track to try to reduce the erosion caused by the thousands of hikers, cyclists and walkers who visited the park every year. It took a lot of work to lay those stones, plus a great deal of organisation.

The only way to ferry a couple of tons of rock up a mountainside was by air, and several huge bags of blocks had already been placed at intervals along this particular path. Rex knew the copter would make several more flights today, if the weather held.

'Wake up, you,' he said to the puppy, who had fallen asleep in his jacket. A snuffle was her only response. Typical – she was fast asleep now, exactly when he didn't want her to be, which meant she'd be wide awake later when he was trying to eat lunch or do some paperwork.

Resigned to letting her sleep, he continued up the mountain until he reached the volunteers. There were four of them today, three of whom he'd met previously.

'How's it going?' he asked, after greetings and the inevitable cooing over the sleeping pup had been dispensed with.

'Grand,' one of the men replied. 'We've done about ten feet today. Hopefully we'll get another ten done before we finish.'

It was slow, back-breaking work, but essential to the health and well-being of the park, and Rex stopped to help for a while, taking his jacket off and placing it carefully in the heather with the pup still cocooned inside.

After an hour or so, he shared his flask of coffee with the volunteers and handed around a bag of doughnuts that he'd picked up from the bakery on the way, before heading back down the mountain thinking about the rest of his busy day. After Nell's visit to the vet, he was due to speak at a local primary school, and as he strode down the hill, an idea began to form.

It was all well and good telling the children about the importance of conservation in the park, but wouldn't it be better to show them? He didn't mean a series of PowerPoint slides, either. Maybe he could suggest to their teacher that they visit one of the more easily accessible places and do some painting. They could make a day of it, with Rex supplying the picnic (what did eight- and nine-year-olds eat? he wondered) and the art materials. The kids would get some exercise and fresh air, and have a chance to learn something new. At this time of year, there were tadpoles in the streams, new lambs frolicking on the hillsides and hundreds of nesting birds, as well as the lizards and grass snakes just coming out of hibernation. If they were really lucky, they might even get to see a slow-worm or a fox.

He wondered whether the paintings could be auctioned off, with half the proceeds going to the school and the other half to the National Park. Hoping his manager and the school would like the idea, he put the now wide-awake Nell into her travelling crate and drove to the vet, thankful that in a couple of weeks' time the

47

dog could be released from the confines of his jacket and walk beside him on her lead.

She was an absolute sweetheart as she was given her injection, only whimpering once, and as a treat he decided to take her to Peggy's Tea Shoppe for a spot of well-earned lunch.

He had his head down, concentrating on the little bundle snuggled against his chest, as he walked along the high street, so he wasn't aware of the person coming in the opposite direction until they bumped shoulders.

'Oops! Sorry,' a female voice said.

He looked down to see someone laughing into his chest. The young woman wasn't looking at him because she was too busy focusing on Nell, but he recognised her at once. Leanne, wasn't it? From the farm where he'd bought Nell.

'My, hasn't she grown!' she exclaimed, and he could see she was itching for a closer look at the dog.

He unzipped his jacket and handed the pup over. Nell whined ecstatically.

'She remembers me!' Leanne cried with delight.

'Of course she does. She's a bright little girl.' He watched as Leanne bent over the dog's furry head, and he knew she was inhaling the irresistible puppy smell.

'How's she doing?' she asked.

'She's really good. She's just had her second lot of injections today, and the house training is coming on a treat.'

'There's a good girl,' Leanne crooned, and for a second Rex thought he saw tears in her eyes.

It must be hard for her, he realised, to have a litter of puppies on the farm and not be able to keep the one she had clearly so closely bonded with. On impulse, he said, 'I'm going to grab a spot of lunch at Peggy's. Would you like to join me?'

He noticed her hesitation, and added, 'Only if you want to. I just thought you might like to spend a bit of time with Nell.'

'Oh, I do. It's just that Mabel, my new assistant, is on her own in the shop and I said I wouldn't be long.' She paused. 'Oh, why not? She'll be on her own for a whole day soon, so it won't hurt for her to get some practice in.'

'You own a shop?' he asked as they started down the high street towards Peggy's.

'Yes, the flower shop around the corner.'

He could see her as the flowery type, dressed as she was in a blouse with leaves all over it. A bright pink anorak and a pair of slim-fitting jeans completed the picture.

He opened the door and gestured for her to enter, catching a glimpse of her pert, rounded bum as he did so. Hastily he cleared his throat and followed her to an empty table, carefully averting his eyes. She was certainly cute, but he wasn't in the market for a relationship. Luckily she hadn't caught him checking her out.

'Look what I've got,' she sang, and Stevie hurried over. As they oohed and aahed over the little dog, Rex couldn't help staring at Leanne again.

With her upturned nose, brown eyes and ready wide smile, she was really pretty. He also had a feeling she'd be fun to be with and easy to talk to. He watched as she tossed her thick brown hair out of her face. It curled down to her shoulders and he had a sudden urge to run his fingers through it. Drawing his mouth into a firm line, he wondered where on earth that impulse had come from.

When Stevie finally remembered she had a tea shop to run and asked Rex what he wanted, his eyes were firmly on the menu.

'What's it like owning your own business?' he asked once Stevie had taken their order and Leanne finally sat down, the dog lying at her feet.

'Hard work, satisfying, exciting and boring, all rolled into one,' she said.

He cocked his head, encouraging her to go on.

'The hard work goes without saying,' she began, 'and the satisfaction comes from a job well done. I love seeing the look on my customers' faces when they pick up an arrangement I've made, or stop to look at the window display.'

She paused and leaned to the side as the pregnant waitress brought their drinks over and put them down on the table.

'When's it due?' Leanne asked her.

The waitress patted her stomach. 'A few weeks yet, but I've no idea how I can go on that long. Look at me, I'm huge.'

Rex looked, and had to agree with the assessment.

'Sorry, where are my manners?' Leanne said. 'Cassandra, this is Rex. He's Nell's new owner.' She turned to look at him. 'Thank you for keeping her name, by the way.'

'It suits her,' Rex replied truthfully.

'Rex, this is Cassandra,' Leanne carried on.

'Pleased to meet you,' Cassandra said. 'Although I've seen you in here before, several times.'

Noticing Leanne's questioning look, Rex explained, 'I'm not much of a cook, so Peggy's Tea Shoppe is a bit of a lifesaver.'

Once Cassandra had returned to the counter, he looked at Leanne. 'Did you say your assistant will be left on her own soon? Are you going away?'

Leanne laughed, and the way her nose crinkled as she did so fascinated him. It really was quite adorable. She had a nice laugh too, kind of tinkling, unlike the shrill giggle of some girls.

'Only for a day,' she explained, 'but I'm hoping it will be a regular thing.'

'Oh?'

She leaned forward and lowered her voice. 'I've entered a new TV show called *Budding Stars* and have got through to the interview.'

Budding Stars? Was it some kind of dancing or singing competition? he wondered. He had no idea what Leanne's singing voice sounded like, but he wouldn't be surprised to learn she was a dancer. She was quite graceful, except for when she bumped into people on the street.

'It's a competition for florists,' she explained. 'Like *Bake Off*, or that pottery show, *Throw Down*, was it called?

Rex stared blankly at her and she rolled her eyes.

'Don't you watch much TV?' she asked.

'Not really, but when I do, it's usually either the news, sport or a documentary.'

'Please tell me you've heard of *Strictly*,' she begged.

'No, what's that?'

Another roll of the eyes, this time accompanied by a deep sigh, but the smirk on her face told him she was teasing.

'Actually,' she said, 'if it was up to me, I'd probably not watch any of those programmes either, but my mum adores them, and as I still live at home...' She grimaced. 'How sad does that sound? I'm twenty-nine and still living with my mum and dad.'

'It's not sad at all,' Rex said. 'It must be comforting to have your family around you.'

Leanne's face fell, and she stuttered, 'I'm sorry, are your parents...?' She trailed off, her cheeks going a pretty shade of pink.

'Good Lord, no, they're still around. But they live in a little village in Scotland called Glenshona, so I haven't seen them since I moved to Tanglewood.'

'Feel free to borrow mine whenever you want,' she offered. 'I've got four brothers, to start you off, and two of them more or less still live at home. They've got their own cottage on the farm, but you'd never know from the amount of time they spend at Mum and Dad's. My parents should start charging them rent, or at least per meal. Dinner time at our house is like feeding the five thousand.' She giggled. 'I can't say anything, though, because I'm just as bad. Mum feeds me too. I really should get somewhere of my own, but with the way things are at the moment...' She ground to a halt.

Rex raised his eyebrows. Leanne was certainly a live wire, as his mum would say, and he found himself enjoying her company. He'd been right, she was easy to talk to – or should he say, she was easy to *listen* to, because she'd hardly paused for breath yet.

'The competition,' she added, as though that explained everything.

His eyebrows rose another notch. Resisting the urge to say anything, he waited for her to continue, guessing she would be unable not to.

'Look, I haven't told many people about it, and those who know have been sworn to secrecy. I don't know why I'm telling you all this, but I think I can trust you not to blab.' She paused to take a breath, and Rex found he was sucking in a lungful of air along with her, in sympathy. 'This competition is kind of a big deal for me, personally and professionally,' she carried on. 'I've got an interview and a demonstration, and if I get through those, then it's on to the actual televised programmes.'

She leaned forward again. 'It might mean I'm away for a fair bit. They said that each week's programme takes a whole day to film, and there are ten episodes. I know I mightn't get that far – I'll probably not even make it past the next round – but I really, really want to win.'

'Of course you do,' Rex agreed. 'What's the point of entering otherwise?'

'I suppose for some people it's the taking part that counts, but my eye is on the prize. That's what I really want.'

'What *is* the prize?' Rex found Leanne's excitement and enthusiasm infectious, and he leaned forward in his seat so their heads were practically touching.

'It's to exhibit at the Chelsea Flower Show.' Her face was alight, and she was positively glowing.

'That's fantastic,' he said. 'I really hope you win.'

'Oh, so do I. It'll be a whole new chapter for me, for my career.'

He watched with concern as her face suddenly fell.

'What is it?' he asked, hoping it was nothing serious, and wondering if there was anything he could possibly do to help.

'Nell has just done a wee on my foot,' she said.

Both of them burst out laughing.

Chapter 8

Had she remembered everything? Keys? Tick! Purse? Tick! Designs? Oh Lord, her designs!

Leanne dashed back up the stairs, feet thundering, and galloped into her bedroom.

Where were they? She was sure she'd left them on her bed.

'Is this what you're looking for?' her mother called from the hall.

She raced headlong back down the staircase before skidding to a halt as she spied Iris waving a wad of pages at her.

'Yes! Thank you! Where were they?'

'Right where you left them on the kitchen table,' her mother said. 'Sorry about the blob of marmalade – I've done my best to clean it off.'

Leanne grabbed the bundle of diagrams and hand-written notes, gave her mother a quick peck on the cheek, then sprinted for the door. If she wasn't careful, she was going to be late.

In reality, she was allowing herself plenty of time, but one never knew how the traffic was going to be, or she might get lost, or not be able to find anywhere to park. Oh dear, a hundred and one things could go wrong.

'You'll be fine,' her mother called as Leanne unlocked her car and threw her bag onto the passenger seat.

'Keep an eye on Mabel,' she yelled. 'I'll be back later tonight.'

'Be careful, and take your time,' Iris advised. 'And don't forget, as long as you do your best, you've got nothing to worry about.'

Of course Leanne had something to worry about! What if her best wasn't good enough? Or what if she made a silly mistake, or they didn't like her? Or what if she looked a total horror on screen?

Why, oh why, had she entered the stupid competition in the first place? she wondered as she manoeuvred her car down the narrow lane and pulled out onto the main road. She could be standing safely behind the counter of her little shop right now, preparing the designs for the Paisleys' wedding, rather than hurtling towards the motorway for a day of total and utter fear.

She knew this was the opportunity of a lifetime; if she didn't give herself a fighting chance, she would spend the rest of her life thinking 'what if' and beating herself up about wasting her chance, so she tried to shove the negative thoughts out of her mind. After all, she had nothing to lose except a bit of pride, and to be fair, getting this far was an achievement in itself. It wasn't as though many people knew, so if she was dropped at this stage, she'd only have to face the commiserations of her family and a few close friends.

And Rex.

Why she'd spilt the beans to a total stranger, she had no idea, but he'd been so easy to talk to, and there was no history between them to muddy the water. He didn't know that she'd once wet her knickers in assembly in primary school (and she had no intention of telling him, either); he didn't know she'd had a crush on Andrew Moreton, or that Handy Andy, as he was known, had kissed her behind the bike shed (what a cliché!) and had then asked Hattie Henderson out less than an hour later.

Leanne felt she had a clean slate with this newcomer to the village. He wouldn't judge her and find her wanting. That was the problem with living in such a small place – everyone knew everyone else; you couldn't keep a secret for toffee.

With the bright lights of the Big Smoke beckoning, she gathered her resolve and her courage and tried to focus on the day ahead. After only one comfort stop and a much-needed cup of coffee, she made it to the venue with plenty of time to spare, and she'd only taken a wrong turn once! Feeling immensely pleased with herself, she grabbed her bag and made her way to reception to sign in, nearly fainting when she saw the number of other people milling around. They couldn't all be there for the same reason, could they? She sincerely hoped not, especially when she spied one man holding what looked like shiny, professionally designed drawings in his hand. Crikey – it put her pencil sketches to shame. She wondered what sort of software he'd used and whether she could get hold of it.

Too late now, though, the deed was done. She'd simply have to make do with her scribbles and hope the organisers didn't ask to look at them.

The brief had been very brief indeed: *Design and produce a display suitable for a wedding.* There was no hint as to whether it should be the bride's bouquet, the flowers in the church, a table decoration or what.

Working on the premise that the bride's bouquet would be too obvious a choice, Leanne had chosen exactly that, praying that not many other entrants would go for it. After all, weddings were all about the bride; she had to look perfect. It was her day more than anyone else's and all eyes would be on her. Without the bride – and the groom, of course, but no one really noticed him except for his own parents – there would *be* no wedding.

She was also hoping that less was more. She was aiming for simplicity – the beauty was to be found in the perfection of the individual flowers themselves and not in the complexity of the creation.

Each contestant was allowed to explain the theory and thinking behind his or her design, and Leanne had toyed with various ideas: a spring woodland theme, a Caribbean beach wedding, a Christmas wedding and loads more. In the end, it was something that Rex had said in Peggy's Tea Shoppe the other day that had given her an idea. While cleaning up Nell's mess from the floor and Leanne's shoes, they'd talked about his job and how important it was to preserve the National Park for future generations, and she'd loved that he was so passionate about it.

Conservation, that was his thing, and hers too to a certain extent. Her dad had always made room for wildlife on the farm, long before it had become fashionable. He used to say that there was a place for everything, and everything deserved a place. He was particularly meticulous about the dry stone walls that were a traditional part of the Marches landscape, maintaining them with a fierce determination. The carefully placed stones provided a refuge for tiny lizards and a multitude of insects from beetles to bumblebees. Nesting birds used their crevasses, and he had always left small gaps at intervals along the base of the walls to allow easy access for hedgehogs, foxes and any other creatures that wanted to cross his fields.

Mum had a beehive at the bottom of her vegetable patch and a log store that provided a home for hibernating hedgehogs. Nesting boxes, which all the children in the family had helped nail together, hung from every tree on the property, and Geoff was careful not to disturb the swallows roosting in the barn, or the tawny owls that raised a brood of fluffy youngsters every year in the rafters of the tractor shed.

Conservation, recycling, reusing and eco-friendly were all buzzwords in today's world, but because the concepts had been drilled into Leanne and her brothers from an early age, they were second nature to her, instilled so deeply in the whole family that it was as though they were in their DNA.

Deciding on an eco-friendly theme for a wedding bouquet had been the easy part. Putting it into practice had proved to be much harder, especially when she'd only had a limited time to design, plan and source the materials.

Her biggest problem had been keeping the flowers in good condition. This bouquet wasn't going to be thrown away or tossed to the waiting guests. It was intended to be reused and repurposed, in the same way the top tier of a traditional wedding cake was sometimes carefully wrapped to be used as a christening cake for the happy couple's first child.

Leanne's bouquet would be a living reminder of the bride and groom's love for one another; she intended for it to continue to look vibrant and blooming long after a normal bouquet had turned brown and shrivelled up. Each and every piece of greenery and each and every flower would have its roots or bulb intact, and was intended to be replanted. Therefore the roots would need to be kept very moist. Each plant would need to be chosen with the utmost care, and not simply for its looks, either.

Mabel had watched in fascination as Leanne had spent hours perfecting her design, choosing a flower or a plant only to cast it aside in favour of another.

Finally it was finished, and she could do no more. She had put her heart and soul into this. If it didn't prove to be good enough, then so be it. At least she'd tried and had given it her best. Now all she needed to do was to reconstruct the whole thing during the interview.

Chapter 9

'So, Miss Green, what made you decide to enter this competition?'

There were three judges, and one of them – Jarred Townsend – was well known in the floral world. For some reason, Leanne hadn't expected the judges to be involved in this part of the selection process, and it had thrown her for a minute. She'd seen Jarred Townsend in magazines and on social media. He called himself a 'floral artiste', and everyone who was anyone went to him for their flowery requirements. He was quite a celebrity. She thought he looked rather forbidding and arrogant.

Someone cleared their throat, and she blinked. Ah yes, they'd just asked her a question, hadn't they – one she had been expecting and had prepared for. She tried to focus. 'I think I'm good enough to win. And of course, winning would be a feather in anyone's cap.'

The judges all nodded but made no comment. They must have heard the same answer a hundred times, and would probably hear it a hundred times more before the day was done.

'Have you always wanted to work in floristry?' asked one of the two female judges, Pauline Crowther. She was a small, elderly woman with severely cropped hair and a kindly smile, and Leanne had warmed to her immediately.

She had already given them some background on the entry form, and she could see they each had a copy in front of them, so they knew she wasn't an amateur. She decided to be honest.

'No, I fell into it by accident. I wanted to earn a bit of extra pocket money while I was at school, and when I saw an advert for a casual assistant in the flower shop in the village, I decided to apply. I remember thinking, "How hard can it be?"' She gave the panel a wry smile and was rewarded with several chuckles. Like anything of beauty, creating gorgeous displays was an art that had to be learnt and practised. Besides, plants and flowers tended to have minds of their own.

'When the owner retired,' she continued, 'she gave me first dibs at buying the business.' She didn't add that she hadn't had the necessary funds and her parents had stepped in, generously loaning her the money. Her repayments to them were built into her business plan, and in another couple of years, she would be free of the debt.

'What do you like most about being a florist?' Pauline asked.

'All of it!' Leanne replied promptly. 'I'm aiming for perfection, whether it be a simple corsage for a prom or a final goodbye to a loved one. No matter what the occasion, my customers deserve the best I can give them. Don't get me wrong, I love the big stuff too, like creating a design that makes people stop and look and marvel. I want them to love it as much as I do, and mourn when the flowers eventually die.'

'That brings us nicely to your wedding display,' Jarred said. 'I see you've gone for the bridal bouquet.'

He'd appeared to be the least friendly of the three judges when they'd been introduced to the contestants, and his tone confirmed Leanne's initial impression. Her heart sank to her smart new boots. Damn it, by going for the obvious, she'd clearly disappointed him. Heck, she had disappointed herself, after seeing some of the wonderful things the other contestants had created.

One of them stuck in her mind. It was a vast and enormously complicated depiction of a bride and groom, and it must have cost the guy who'd made it an absolute fortune. Tiny pale pink rosebuds, barely open, formed the bride's face, with deeper pink buds for the lips. White roses made up the dress, interspersed with white orchids to provide some detailing down the skirt. Black-dyed roses comprised the groom's suit, and Leanne marvelled at how the man had managed to acquire so many of them. To top it all off, the four-foot-high construction stood on a white pedestal entwined in ivy.

How on earth was she supposed to compete with that?

'Talk us through your design,' Jarred said, and Leanne could have sworn he sneered when he said 'design'.

For the next few minutes, she explained the reasoning behind her bouquet, trying to stress how nothing she had used would go to waste. Even the ribbons were strands of palm leaves, which could be composted.

'Thank you, Miss Green, you've been very informative,' the third judge said. Her name was Christel Lane, and this was the first time she'd spoken. Although she'd seemed friendly enough, she had spent far too much time glancing at her watch, and Leanne had the feeling she wished she was anywhere else but here, interviewing a jumped-up, two-bit, no-creative-flair person.

While Jarred and Pauline were well-respected florists in their own right, Christel was apparently a celebrity, although Leanne had never heard of her. Maybe she'd been on *Love Island* or *Big Brother*, neither of which Leanne watched, or perhaps she'd had a role in *EastEnders* or *Coronation Street* – Iris was an avid fan of both those soaps, but Leanne had only seen the occasional episode.

As she thanked the judges for their time and the opportunity, Leanne was convinced she'd bored one, and that another had found her sadly uninspiring. The only one she thought she might have impressed was Pauline Crowther, who was still smiling kindly at her. But then again, for all she knew, Pauline might do that to all the contestants, and underneath the smile she'd probably hated Leanne's entry too.

Despondently she followed one of the production team out into the hallway, and was surprised to be led into another room instead of being shown the exit. This one had a man with a camera in it. A really big camera, on wheels.

'Just a quick look-see, to get a bit of background on you. Nothing to worry about,' another man said, fiddling with a microphone.

'You're going to film me?' Leanne was shocked and more than a little put out. She'd not been expecting anything like that; her hair was a mess, her face was probably all shiny and she was convinced she had bits of palm leaves stuck to her blouse. She begged for a minute to nip to the loo, and as she stared at her reflection, she was dismayed at the image peering back at her. She looked beaten already.

That won't do, will it? she told herself sternly. Until they informed her otherwise, she was still in the running. She had to go out there and act as though she was in with a chance.

Pep talk over, she plastered a bright, confident smile on her face, squared her shoulders and marched to her doom.

Back in the camera room, she wriggled a little as the man with the microphone snaked a hand inside the top of her blouse to attach it. She found that somewhat disconcerting, but not half as disconcerting as his curt instruction to 'Begin.' Begin *what*?

'Er…?'

He sighed. 'Just say why you're here,' he huffed. 'Don't the runners tell them anything?' he asked the room in general, and Leanne guessed he wasn't expecting her to answer that.

'Hi, I'm Leanne Green, and I'm here to win?' she said. Damn, it had come out as a question, rather than the statement she'd meant it to be.

The cameraman was fiddling with buttons and dials and didn't look up.

'Excuse me, but are you checking that I look OK on camera?' she asked him nervously.

He lifted his head from the viewfinder. 'Good gracious, no. I don't care if you've got two heads and green scales. We need to get a sound bite from you for the introduction. We do that for everyone who's been selected.'

'Say again?' she asked.

Microphone man coughed loudly, and the cameraman's eyes widened. 'Forget I said that,' he said hastily, and the production assistant who'd shown her into the room gave him a frown.

Had she heard him correctly? Leanne wondered. She'd assumed that everyone went through this camera/microphone thing, but when she thought about it logically, she realised it would be a waste of time to film those contestants who hadn't been chosen.

'I'll take you back to the waiting area,' the production assistant said, and Leanne stumbled after her.

When they arrived at the area set aside for the contestants, she poured herself a coffee, sank onto a hard plastic chair and gazed around. There were only about thirty people left in the room; she had no idea where the rest of them had gone.

On impulse, she got to her feet, set her cup down on a nearby table and retraced her steps to the exhibition hall. Peering in through the door, she froze.

She counted the displays. Then counted them again.

Thirty-one remained. Of the rest, there was no sign. Hers was still sitting there in the same place where she'd left it.

As she stood there, a woman pushed past her, strode up to one of the displays, grabbed it and stalked back towards the door. As she drew closer, Leanne saw a hint of red in her eyes and a wobble to her chin.

She stepped to the side and watched as the woman headed towards the exit, and a tentative hope fluttered in her chest.

The next hour saw the number of entrants in the waiting room dwindle slowly, until only twelve remained, including herself.

Ten more minutes passed.

Fifteen.

The contestants spent the time eyeing each other speculatively.

No one uttered a word.

Then the door opened and the same production assistant stood there with a smile on her face. 'Can you follow me, please?'

She led them to the interview room, and they all lined up in front of the judges.

Pauline appeared to be the spokesperson. She had a smile on her face too, though Christel looked a bit vacant and Jarred was actually frowning. There was a long drawn-out pause as the contestants waited for someone to speak.

'Congratulations,' Pauline said. 'You've all been successful.'

For a second, there was a stunned silence, then the room erupted.

Leanne let out a squeal, as did a couple of the other women, and one guy yelled, 'Yes!' and fist-pumped the air. It was a few minutes before order was restored, and Leanne stopped hopping up and down and managed to catch her breath. She'd done it – *she was through!*

The remainder of the day passed in a blur of glossy booklets, instructions, reminders, rules and regulations, but hardly any of it sank in.

All Leanne could think about was that her chances of winning had risen from one in a couple of thousand to one in twelve.

She was still in the competition!

Chapter 10

'Nell, no,' Rex warned as the puppy danced on the end of the lead. The poor little thing looked as though she was trying to choke herself in her effort to escape the horrid piece of leather attached to her collar.

Nell didn't take kindly to being on a leash, no matter if clipping it onto her collar signalled that she was going outside and could actually walk by herself rather than being carried. She baulked and lay down, only to jump up and race to the end of the lead until she was pulled up short. Then she repeated the performance.

Rex couldn't remember Star acting this way, but then he'd been little more than a kid himself when he'd got her.

'You'll hurt yourself,' he said, trying again, as if the dog could understand him.

Nell sat on her haunches and refused to budge.

Rex hunkered down, bringing himself closer to her, and tried to encourage her with a small treat. At first she ignored it, but as he wafted the smelly morsel at her, her nose twitched and she rose onto all fours and took a tentative step towards him.

'Good girl. Who's my good, clever girl?' he murmured, encouraging her to walk a few more steps before he relented and let her have her reward.

She gobbled it up as though she'd not been fed for a week, then gazed up at him hopefully.

'You've got to earn it first,' he told her. He stood up and moved backwards.

Nell followed.

He gave her another treat.

Crossing his fingers, he repeated the action. This time, instead of walking towards him, the puppy pulled back and sat down.

Rex let out a long sigh. What was the saying, 'never work with children or animals'? It wasn't as though he had any choice in the matter, though, not if he wanted a well-behaved pet. He loved dogs, but ill-disciplined ones were a nuisance, and in his job, if his dog didn't do as she was told as soon as she was told to do it, she could become a danger to herself and to others.

Inside the house he'd managed to get her to sit and stay, and wait to be told she could eat, and come when called. Outside, it was a whole different ball game. She hated the lead and had no qualms about letting him know it. At this very minute, she was sinking her teeth into the leather and worrying at it, shaking her head furiously and emitting cute little growls.

'No,' he repeated firmly, bending down to free the lead from her jaws. 'Bad girl. Naughty Nell.'

Her ears drooped. Over the course of the past few weeks, her half-cocked, droopy ear had straightened up, but now both of them lay close to her head at her master's scolding. She knew what 'bad girl' meant, though Rex understood it wasn't the words themselves but the tone he used. She was very reactive to his voice, and was anxious to please.

She'd soon learn that having the lead clipped onto her collar meant new things to look at and new smells to sniff, and a chance to trot beside her pack leader. Eventually Rex would even allow her off the lead, but not for a good while yet; not until he could trust her to behave herself and come back when she was called.

There were lots of steps and hurdles in between then and now, and one of those was Nell's training with sheep. Her instinct was to herd, but that wasn't her job, and he had to be confident she wouldn't chase the flighty woolly animals before he let her run loose on the hills.

With that in mind, he was trying to head towards Leanne's shop – *if* Nell cooperated. The time for carrying her was gone, unless they were out for too long a walk for the pup's little legs to cope with, so he was determined she was going to make it around the corner and up the street without him resorting to picking her up. It was a perfect length for her first outing on her own paws, and he hoped she wouldn't disgrace herself and wee on the floor of the shop the second they were inside the door.

There were two reasons for the impending visit; three if he counted the lead training. The first was to ask Leanne if her dad would mind if Rex and Nell visited the farm for some essential training with a couple of Geoff's calmer ewes. The second was to see how Leanne had got on in London. He'd been rooting for her yesterday, hoping she had managed to take a step closer to her dream. If not, he was more than happy to provide a shoulder to cry on.

There was actually a fourth reason, which was to see Leanne herself.

'There's a good girl,' he said as soon as Nell walked a few paces next to him. Her nose was down and her tail was up, a clear indication that she was starting to enjoy the experience, and for a couple of yards she forgot she was being restrained. Then suddenly she remembered and started doing the mad capering dance once again as she objected to the leash.

Maybe she'd be more accepting of a harness, Rex mused, and decided to stop off at the ironmonger's on the way back. They had a good supply of pet stuff, so hopefully they would have something to suit a small puppy. Except she wasn't so small now. She was quickly leaving the adorable ball-of-fluff stage behind and was growing into a lanky teenager, all legs and very little coordination.

Tongue hanging comically out of the side of her mouth, she gazed up at him with expectant eyes. They were still blue, and Rex didn't think they were going to darken now, although they weren't as bright as they had been when he'd first got her.

'Come on, blue eyes,' he said, encouraging her with his voice as he tried to continue the short walk from his house to the flower shop.

With a series of jerky stops and starts, lots of praise and the odd treat or two, they eventually made it out of his road. Leanne's shop was only a hundred or so yards down the street, but by the time he pushed the door open and ushered the pup inside, he was exhausted. Who knew having a puppy could be so tiring? He'd clearly done all this before with Star, but he must have forgotten the sheer hard work it had taken. Or maybe he was simply getting old.

'Nell!' Leanne cried, rushing out from behind the counter and dropping to her knees as soon as she spotted the dog.

Rex watched her indulgently as she took the puppy in her arms and let Nell smother her with wet-tongued sloppy kisses.

'I can't believe she's old enough to be out for walks,' Leanne said. 'It was only yesterday that she fitted into the palm of my hand and her eyes were still closed. Oh, she's a darling, aren't you, little one!'

The dog squeaked a whimpering response and Leanne kissed the furry head. 'How is she doing?' she asked.

'Aye, good, thanks for asking. This is her first time on a lead, so she's a bit excitable.'

Several more endearments and kisses on both the dog's part and Leanne's followed before Rex managed to mention the favour he'd come to ask.

'Do you think your father would object if I brought Nell to the farm? I want to make her understand that sheep aren't for chasing. Of course, she's nowhere near ready for that yet,' he added, 'but give her a few weeks and she will be.'

'I don't think he'd mind at all,' Leanne replied, clambering to her feet. 'In fact he'd probably welcome it. I wish all dog owners were as responsible as you. You wouldn't believe the number of times an unleashed dog has gone after our sheep.'

Rex would; he'd been a ranger for long enough to know the damage even a small dog could do once it was consumed with the excitement of chasing livestock. That furry little ball of cuteness lying on the rug at home could quickly revert to its wolf ancestry if the situation presented itself.

'How did you get on yesterday?' he asked after Leanne had promised to speak to her father and get back to Rex with an answer.

He watched her face carefully and was relieved to see a huge smile spread across it. She could hardly contain her excitement as she told him her news, and was practically hopping from foot to foot.

'That's wonderful!' he exclaimed. 'I'm delighted for you.'

'Even if I'm sent home after the first round, it's still an achievement,' she said, but he could tell that if she *was* eliminated, she would be terribly disappointed.

'I'm sure you won't be,' he said. 'You can't think like that, either. Tell yourself you're going to win. I'm sure you wowed the judges.'

'I don't know about that. Jarred Townsend was a bit sneering and condescending, and he didn't seem to like me or my design.'

'I'm positive he did,' Rex replied firmly, 'and I'm sure he isn't as bad as you think he is.'

Leanne eyed him doubtfully. 'Maybe not,' she said, but she didn't sound convinced. 'He's one of the top florists in the country,' she continued, 'and I get the feeling he can be a bit of a diva. I suppose he's entitled to be, considering he does the flowers for lots of big names and top events, but I'm not sure I actually like him.'

'You don't have to like him,' Rex pointed out. 'All you need to do is to impress him.'

'I suppose,' Leanne said, then she smiled ruefully. 'But if you'd seen some of the other designs…' She trailed off. 'I still think Jarred doesn't like me, and I think he was outvoted by the other two. He's awfully young to be so successful – I think he's only a year or two older than me – and he's incredibly good-looking to boot.'

Rex was beginning to dislike the guy already, and it had nothing to do with the fact that Leanne seemed to have been quite affected by him.

'I've got something for you,' she said suddenly, and darted through the door behind the counter, emerging with a large pot full of flowers.

'That's kind of you,' he said, wondering what he'd done to deserve such a nice gift.

'If it wasn't for you, I wouldn't have come up with the idea for the task they set,' Leanne explained.

'And that was…?'

'A completely recyclable, reusable bridal bouquet.'

'I don't understand. Can't you compost the flowers anyway once you're done with them?'

'Yes, but this takes it a step further. Most brides throw their bouquets to their unmarried friends, and some keep the flowers and press them. Either way, most bouquets go in the bin eventually. My idea was to use living plants rather than cut stems, so they can be potted on afterwards. That way, the happy couple will have something to keep for a long time. All your talk about reduce, reuse, recycle had me thinking how wasteful even the floristry business can be, despite, as you say, being able to compost cut flowers. I just wanted to take it a step further.'

'It's lovely,' Rex said, regarding the pot with fresh eyes.

'It takes more time to prepare the bouquet and there are limits to the kinds of plants and flowers that can be used, but the judges seemed to like it. "Very on trend," was what Jarred said, although he didn't sound as though he meant it.'

There she was, talking about Jarred Townsend again, although why it should bother him so much, Rex had absolutely no idea.

'Have dinner with me tonight?' he asked abruptly. Crikey, where had that come from? He'd not arrived at her shop with the intention of asking her out, and he fully expected her to turn him down.

But he was delighted when she said yes, the expression on her face one of pleasant surprise.

And he found himself looking forward to the evening very much indeed.

Chapter 11

Leanne eyed the pile of garments strewn over her bed with dismay. How come she had so many clothes yet she had nothing to wear? She'd grown out of all her party gear – not that she ever went to that many parties – the stuff she wore to work wouldn't do (jeans, T-shirts and trainers; definitely not), and the few bits she did have that were presentable enough and grown-up enough to wear to go out for dinner weren't to her liking.

In fact, she couldn't remember the last time she actually had gone out to dinner. A quick meal down the pub after work with Stevie or Tia didn't count. They didn't care what she wore.

And Rex will? she asked herself.

Probably not, was her answer. He'd most likely only asked her out to say thank you for the planter, or because he'd thought she might want to celebrate her success at getting through the selection process with one of the few people who actually knew about it.

Eventually she decided on a pair of fitted black trousers and a floaty long-sleeved blouse in a pretty shade of blue. It was a bit officey-looking, but it would have to do. She seriously needed to invest in some new clothes, especially if she was going to be travelling down to London for the next few weeks – assuming she didn't get kicked out of the competition in the first round. She mentally crossed her fingers at the thought.

As she brushed her hair and pinned it up, she decided not to tempt fate by buying a whole new wardrobe, but to treat herself to one new thing now. If she was still in the competition after this round, then she'd buy some things for the next one. As long as she chose wisely, the clothes wouldn't be wasted, because she could wear them again.

She'd arranged to meet Rex at the Griffin, a gastropub on the outskirts of Abergavenny, renowned for its good food and excellent service. It even had a Michelin star, and thanks to Stevie, Leanne was well aware of what that star signified.

She pulled up outside the restaurant, where fairy lights added to the charm of the old converted farmhouse. Built of sandstone with a grey slate roof and a tiny door and windows, it looked more like someone's home than an upmarket restaurant.

There were several vehicles already in the car park, and when she saw Rex's Land Rover, she breathed a sigh of relief. Walking into places on her own was one of her pet hates. She always felt as though people were staring at her. At least she would be able to go straight over to her date and not have to wait for him.

She had only ever seen Rex in outdoor gear, but when she caught her first glimpse of him tonight, her breath caught in her throat. He looked gorgeous. His normally tousled hair was neatly brushed (apart from a lock falling down over his forehead, which only added to his good looks), and he was wearing a pair of chinos and a button-down shirt. He was the picture of casual sophistication.

'My, my, don't you scrub up well?' she teased, as he slipped off his stool by the bar to greet her.

The hug was totally unexpected, and as he wrapped his strong arms around her and pulled her close, Leanne couldn't resist breathing in his fresh, clean, manly scent. Wow, but he smelled nice! He felt nice too, but the contact was over all too soon as he released her and stepped back.

'So do you.' He grinned. 'It makes a change to see you without bits of foliage stuck in your hair.'

Self-consciously she reached up to pat her bun, and he laughed.

'Only kidding, you always look nice. Our table will be ready in a minute. Would you like a drink first?'

'I'll have a tonic water with a twist of lemon, please,' she said.

She could have done with a gin in it, but she had a tendency not to stop at the one, and she had work in the morning and a competition to prepare for. She noticed Rex had a soft drink too, although if he'd wanted something stronger, she'd have been happy to drive him home.

When she suggested it, he said, 'No thanks, I'll stick with orange juice. I'm going out with the Mountain Rescue Service tomorrow, so I'll need to keep a clear head, otherwise it might be me who needs rescuing.'

'I hope no one is in trouble.' Leanne knew full well that walkers sometimes came to grief on the mountains. Inexperienced hikers or those out for what they thought was going to be a pleasant stroll up a well-trodden peak were occasionally caught unawares. The weather could turn in an instant, and even those familiar with the trails could lose their way if they weren't careful, especially if an unexpected and often unprepared-for cloud crept up on them. A couple of people a year died in those very mountains.

'No, nothing like that, thank God,' he said. 'I'm joining them on a training exercise. They need all the support they can get.'

It was a good idea, Leanne thought. All the members of the Mountain Rescue Service were volunteers, and most had jobs, too. With Rex's growing knowledge of the National Park, and with public safety being part of his remit, he was in an ideal position to help them.

'Maybe you could train Nell to become a rescue dog?' she suggested.

Rex curled his hand around his glass and stared into space. 'You know what?' he said slowly. 'That's a brilliant idea.'

'Tit for tat,' she said, smiling. 'You gave me the idea for the wedding bouquet; it's only fair I repay you.'

'I thought the plant pot was my repayment?'

'Consider it a housewarming present, even if it is a bit late.'

'And here was I offering to take you to dinner as a thank you for the pot.'

'It's never going to end, at this rate.' Leanne laughed.

'I hope not,' he said with a slow smile.

She hoped not too; but now wasn't really the right time to begin a new relationship, not when she needed to focus all her attention on this first round of the competition. It wasn't fair on Rex. Maybe it would be better to be mates, she thought, although she did fancy him to bits. It was a pity he'd come into her life at just the wrong moment.

'Penny for them?' he asked, breaking into her thoughts. 'You look miles away.'

'Yes, I was. Sorry.' She decided that there was no time like the present to put the record straight. 'I'm going to be so busy over the coming weeks...' She trailed off, hoping he got the message.

Clearly he did. 'Of course you are, and if there's anything I can do to help, just let me know.'

'Don't worry, I will,' she reassured him. 'You're my ideas guy.'

'What are they asking you to do next?' he wanted to know.

Leanne breathed a sigh of relief as the conversation turned back to less complicated things (she ignored the treacherous little part of her that said it was a mistake to discourage him) and she told him about her next assignment.

'I've read the brief a thousand times,' she began. 'It looks like there'll be two parts to each round. The first is a sight-unseen task where you don't know what you've got to do until you're on set.' She laughed self-consciously. She was already picking up the jargon, and to her own ears she sounded a bit pretentious. 'The other task is one I get to work on beforehand. I'll be able to design it and practise making it. The only problem is, I haven't decided what I'm going to do. Filming starts the week after next, and I haven't got the faintest idea.'

'Run it past me — after all, you said yourself that I'm your ideas man. Maybe I can help.'

'It's a water-based theme. They're asking the contestants to come up with a display for an aquarium.'

Rex did a double take, which was actually quite comical, and Leanne laughed at his expression.

'What's an aquarium got to do with flower arranging?' he asked. 'I thought it was all about stems and leaves and those strange sponge things, not aquatic plants.'

'It *is* about all those things, but you'd be surprised what I get asked for. Only last week a customer wanted a Pluto arrangement.'

'Pluto as in the planet?' His confused frown was quite adorable.

'Pluto the dog, the Disney character. The guy's company was having a grand party to celebrate good end-of-year results, and one of the employees suggested a Disney theme.'

'But why Pluto?'

'No idea,' Leanne replied, 'but I do know they were having a Mickey Mouse cake, and a raffle with a family holiday to Disneyland Paris as first prize.'

'I think I'm in the wrong job,' Rex muttered, scowling, and Leanne giggled.

'Would you like to go to Disneyland?' she asked.

'Actually, no, I value my sanity too much. Give me the peace and quiet of the mountains any day. Right then, water-themed, eh?' He scratched his head. 'The seaside? That would fit in with an aquarium. You could do underwater plants and stick in a couple of plastic fish.'

Leanne threw him a disbelieving look. 'I hope you're not serious.'

'Or how about mermaids? In fact, you could dress up as one, to keep the theme going.'

'Now I *know* you're teasing.' Leanne shuddered. 'Have you *seen* those costumes? Besides, I wouldn't be able to walk with a fishtail.' She grimaced. 'I bet the bloke who did the bride and groom display will make a complete tank out of flowers, and he won't use plastic fish, either.'

'Seriously, stick with what you know,' Rex advised. 'You live in one of the wettest places in the UK. Think about how it looks in the Beacons after a heavy downpour – the gushing streams, the waterfalls.'

'I've got to be careful that I don't go too far down the landscape gardening route,' she said. 'The display should be all about the flowers, really. I'm surprised they actually let me through with my eco-friendly bridal bouquet – I don't want to get sent home after the first round.'

'How many varieties of blue flowers are there?' Rex asked.

Leanne blinked. 'Lots. Why?'

'Water,' he said, 'with white for the foam and green for lowlights and the plants growing around the sides of the stream.'

Leanne's eyes widened. He might be on to something. Aquariums weren't all about sea environments; there were freshwater fish and other creatures in those places.

'Do you know, it might work.' Her imagination was going into overdrive. 'Hang on, let me write this down.' She dug around in her bag for a pen and a scrap of paper and proceeded to scribble furiously.

When she was done – for the moment – she glanced up to find Rex looking at her, an indulgent smile on his lips. Her heart did a slow roll, and—

'Sir, madam, your table is ready,' the head waiter said, and for a moment Leanne couldn't actually remember where she was or why she was there. Her head was filled with ferns and heathers, and Rex's clear blue eyes. She had a strange urge to lose herself in their depths, then she pulled herself together and gave herself a mental shake.

But as she followed the waiter to their table, she couldn't help thinking that Rex had been looking at her in exactly the same way as she had been looking at him.

Chapter 12

'Tell me, what brings you to Tanglewood?' Leanne asked around a mouthful of shrimp. Stevie was right, the food here was delicious, and she had allowed herself one small glass of wine, although Rex was sticking to sparkling water.

'Work, first and foremost,' he said, spreading pâté on a thin slice of seedy toast.

'Haven't they got mountains in Scotland?' she quipped, and he raised an amused eyebrow at her.

'Ha, ha, very funny. They have, actually, quite a lot of them, and bigger than yours, too. You should go and see them.'

Leanne had never been to Scotland, but it sounded wonderful, she thought, as she listened to Rex describing Ben Nevis.

'It's a bit of a hike to the top,' he finished, 'but the views are worth it.'

'Is that where you worked, around Ben Nevis?'

'Ach, no, my range was the Trossachs and Loch Lomond. That was dramatic enough for me, and the Trossachs have a few high mountains of their own.'

'So why the Brecon Beacons?' Leanne persisted, and she saw his expression harden. 'I'm sorry, it's none of my business—' she began.

84

'It's OK,' Rex said, interrupting her. 'I suppose you could say I'm running away. A fresh start and all that. Although to be honest, the Brecon Beacons National Park was the first employer to offer me a job. I had applied for several others in Scotland and one in the Peak District. I could have hung on to see if any of those came to anything, but...' He ground to a halt.

'Wales is the furthest away?' Leanne suggested gently.

'Aye, it is at that. I do like it here, though, and the people are really friendly.'

'Do you think you might stay?' Leanne held her breath as she waited for his answer, torn between wanting to see him again – although she might well have wrecked her chances anyway by hinting that she was too busy for a relationship – and thinking it prudent not to start anything.

'I think I just might,' he replied, gazing into her eyes.

She wondered if there was anyone special back home. 'You've told me your mum and dad still live in Scotland. Do you have any brothers or sisters?'

'No, just me, and I did feel in sore need of a sibling or two when I was growing up. I envy you having so many.'

'Don't,' she said drily. 'My brothers are a menace, especially Saul. They used to tease me unmercifully. They still do.'

'Ah, but they're still your brothers. I bet if you needed help, they would be the first ones to come running.'

Leanne smiled. 'Yeah, they would. Now you've got me feeling sorry for you for not having any.'

'Good. I need all the sympathy I can get.' He looked so mournful, Leanne laughed. 'I have got a decent group of friends, though,' he added.

'I expect you miss them,' Leanne said.

'Yeah, Dean especially. He's a good mate. A bit daft sometimes, but I suppose you could say we're like brothers.' His expression clouded over.

'What's wrong?'

'Ach, it's probably nothing. I haven't really heard from him much since...' He hesitated. 'You know what men are like about keeping in touch. I bet if I went home tomorrow it would be as if I'd never been away.'

Leanne nodded, not knowing what to say. Poor Rex, he was clearly lonely and was missing his friends and family.

'When was the last time you visited?' she asked.

He looked sheepish. 'Erm... I haven't. I thought it best to give myself a wee bit of space.'

'Oh?'

'Jules, my ex-girlfriend, and I split up at around the same time I lost my job. And my dog. Star was my best friend, even more than Dean. I'd had her since I was a teenager and she went everywhere with me.'

'I remember you mentioning her when you came to buy Nell. She was a spaniel, wasn't she?'

'Aye, she was, and as daft as a brush. Nell is quieter, except when I try to make her sleep by herself. She's more needy, too, but I don't mind that. She can have all the attention she wants.'

It struck Leanne that Rex was far more forthcoming about Star than he was about his ex, and when he didn't mention her again, she didn't push it. After all, the girl was firmly in his past, and Leanne was beginning to harbour a tiny hope that she herself might have a place in his future, despite her vow not to get involved with anyone right now. In fact, the more she spoke to him, the more attracted to him she was becoming, although she suspected he might not feel the same way about her, because when the meal ended, instead of kissing her as she had hoped, he gave her a quick hug, then walked her to her car.

There was no mention of another date, either, so she bit back her disappointment, said a friendly goodbye and drove home with thoughts of him filling her head.

Chapter 13

Geoff had agreed to Rex's request, and today was the day for Nell's first encounter with some sheep.

'I thought we'd start her off with last year's hand-reared lambs,' Geoff said, after the two men had shaken hands. 'They'll be less skittish and not so inclined to run. I don't want to encourage her to chase them,' he added as they walked down the lane towards a nearby field. 'They're more used to dogs, and one of them is a right madam. With her around, Nell will be the one running away, not the ewes.'

Rex had Nell on the lead and she was walking calmly beside him, much to his delight. The training he was doing with her was finally starting to pay off, although she still had her moments.

He hadn't been expecting to visit the farm quite so soon, but Geoff had called and advised him to start Nell's familiarisation with the sheep sooner rather than later.

'Teach 'em young and they'll learn the lesson for life,' he had said, so here the three of them were, strolling down the lane with the sun on their backs and a variety of agricultural smells on the breeze, the predominant one being the pungent whiff of sheep.

Nell might be behaving herself at the moment, but Rex had owned her long enough to read her body language. The half-grown pup was positively vibrating with excitement.

'I hear you've been helping our Leanne with her flowers for the competition,' Geoff said.

'Not quite.' Rex rumbled out a laugh. 'I merely made a suggestion or two. I don't know the first thing about flower arranging.'

'That's as may be, but between the pair of you, you've managed to come up with a dilly of a design.'

'Oh?' Rex hadn't seen it, although he had bumped into Leanne once or twice since they'd had dinner.

He hadn't suggested another meal together, or anything else for that matter, because Leanne had made it perfectly clear that she didn't have time for a relationship. To be honest, he wasn't entirely sure he was ready to date again anyway, although he did have a sneaking suspicion he was only telling himself that solely because she wasn't interested in him.

'She'll be home in an hour,' Geoff said. 'Why don't you come back to the house and have a gander at what she's making? In fact, why don't you stay for tea? It's lasagne tonight.'

'Home cooked?' Rex pretended to think about it, even as his mouth was watering.

'My missus wouldn't have it any other way.'

'Are you sure?' Rex didn't want to intrude.

'I wouldn't have asked if I wasn't,' came the laconic reply. 'We've always got a houseful. One more isn't going to matter, and Iris will be delighted to meet you at last. Our Leanne hasn't stopped talking about you. It's Rex this, and Rex that.'

Really?

A soft glow spread through his chest for a few moments, but reality cooled it before it had a chance to warm his heart. She probably only talked about him because he'd helped her a bit, although he had no doubt she would've come up with the same idea as he had, given time.

For the next hour or so, Geoff and Rex worked with Nell and the sheep. Geoff had been right when he'd predicted the dog might be the one to run away, because after her first impulsive headlong dash at the peacefully grazing animals, she was brought up short when three pairs of eyes stared at her and refused to move an inch. The last straw for her had been when the boldest of the ewes had leapt forward on stiff legs and stamped her feet.

Much to the men's amusement, Nell had fled back to her owner with her tail between her legs.

'She's too timid to make a good sheepdog,' Geoff said. 'I could tell that from early on. But a dog is a dog is a dog. If an animal runs, it's in a dog's nature to chase it, and Nell here is no exception. It's best she learns now that it's wrong.'

The next time Nell approached the three yearlings, it was with considerably more caution and respect. No mad run at them; more of a slink, one paw at a time. The ewes allowed her to get close enough for a sniff, then went back to their grazing, totally ignoring the black and white pup at their feet.

'That's enough for one day,' Geoff said. 'It'll take more than one session to make her understand what's expected of her, so come back this time next week and I'll fetch a couple of ewes in from the main flock.'

The two men walked towards the farmhouse in companionable silence, Nell scurrying ahead of them, her nose to the ground as she investigated all the new scents.

'Put the dog in here,' Geoff said, opening one of the old stable doors. 'She can say hello to her mum. Bess, look who's here to see you.'

Mother and daughter greeted one another with wagging tails and twitching noses, and Rex could tell that they recognised each other immediately. Bess bowled Nell over and began to give her a good wash.

When he entered the cosy kitchen, the enticing aroma of garlic, herbs and onions made his mouth water, and his stomach rumbled loudly. An older woman, about his mum's age, stepped away from the oven to greet him, and after wiping her hands on a tea towel, she pulled him into a hug.

'I'm Iris, Leanne's mum. Lovely to meet you at last,' she said. 'I've heard so much about you.' She shot a look at an open door to Rex's right. 'We all have,' she added drily.

'Mum! I heard that!' Leanne's voice floated into the kitchen, making him smile.

'Geoff's been telling me,' he said, just as Leanne appeared.

'Dad!' She blushed, and Rex grinned widely when he saw her embarrassment.

She had a leaf stuck in her hair and her fingers were stained green.

'I've been told that your next fantastic creation is ready for viewing,' Rex said, just in case he was giving her the wrong idea and she thought he was there to see her.

The last thing he wanted to do was to make her feel uncomfortable in her own home.

She screwed her face up into a grimace. 'Not really. This is version twenty-six and I'm still not happy with it.'

'May I take a look?' he asked.

'Sure. Mum will give us a shout when tea is ready.'

Rex smiled to himself. Tanglewood had its own charm when it came to mealtimes. Breakfast was breakfast, lunch could be either lunch or dinner, and tea could either refer to a cup of tea or dinner, depending on the context. Not once had he heard it being used to describe tea and cakes in the afternoon, although Peggy's Tea Shoppe did serve a cream tea consisting of scones, cream and jam, or bara brith – a type of local bread – and Welsh cakes.

Leanne showed him into what might once have been a study but was now crammed full of half-completed waterfalls and buckets of flowers and greenery. Most of the blooms were in varying shades of blue or white, and there were drawings and sketches tacked to almost every bit of free wall space.

He studied her current effort, which was sitting on the table in the middle of the room. A computer and a printer had been relegated to the floor.

'I wish she'd bloody hurry up and win this competition,' Geoff said, walking past the open door clutching knives and forks in both hands. 'I want my office back.'

Leanne narrowed her eyes and poked her tongue out at her father. They had such an easy and loving way between them that Rex was abruptly flooded with longing for his own parents. He vowed to give them a ring when he got home.

'What do you think?' she asked him, and his attention was drawn back to the half-completed flower arrangement on the table. Then he scanned the others dotted around the small room. They were all slightly different, but each of them looked perfect to his untrained eye.

'I can't see anything wrong with any of them,' he admitted eventually. 'They all look good to me.'

'They don't capture the essence of the hillside streams,' Leanne said. 'Something isn't right. Take this one, for instance.' She pointed to a display on the floor near his feet. 'There isn't enough white for a tumbling brook.' She indicated another. 'It looks more like a fluffy cloud than water.'

Rex examined them, frowning. He could see what she was getting at.

'They should be drooping down,' he said abruptly.

'Oh, don't worry, a couple more days in Dad's stuffy office and they'll be drooping all right.'

'Not that kind of drooping,' he said. 'The flowers are facing up. They should be facing down.'

It was Leanne's turn to frown at her display, and she caught her lip between her teeth as she considered what he'd just said. He thought she looked quite adorable when she did that.

'You're right,' she said slowly. Then she let out a squeal. 'I could kiss you!'

She twirled around to face him, threw her arms around his neck and planted a big kiss on his cheek.

Automatically Rex's arms circled her and he pulled her close.

'Get a room,' a gruff male voice interrupted, and Rex let go of her so abruptly that Leanne almost stumbled backwards.

'Sorry, sorry... I... er,' he stuttered, reaching out to steady her before quickly releasing her once she had regained her balance.

'Bugger off, Saul, and mind your own business,' Leanne growled, but the twinkle in her eyes belied her tone.

For a second, Rex wanted to gather her into his arms again. She'd felt so damned good in them, and she'd smelled good, too.

He cleared his throat in embarrassment.

'Don't mind my brother. He's just jealous,' Leanne said, but Rex noticed that she didn't meet his eyes, and two spots of colour had appeared on each of her smooth, creamy cheeks. Was the rest of her skin just as creamy? he wondered.

Don't go there, he told himself. She's not interested in you.

'Jealous?' her brother scoffed. 'What, you think I want to give your boyfriend a hug? Hardly! He's not my type.'

Despite himself, for a second Rex couldn't help wishing that he, Rex, was Leanne's type, before he shut the ridiculous notion down.

But throughout the rest of the lively, delicious meal, the thought had an annoying way of popping into his head, and he was still trying not to think of it when he collected Nell and said his goodbyes.

He was still trying not to think about it when sleep finally claimed him.

Chapter 14

'Miss Green, we meet again.'

Leanne jerked her head up on hearing Jarred's smooth, slightly sarcastic voice. She'd been too busy concentrating on her very detailed notes and drawings to hear his approach. Besides, there was so much else going on that she probably wouldn't have heard a jet if it had landed right next to her. This was the first real round of the competition, the televised part, and she was determined not to mess it up.

For some reason, she'd expected to have her hair and make-up done, as she'd spotted the three judges being primed, primped and pampered. But it wasn't to be, and she'd had to dash off to the ladies at the last minute to pin her hair up and slap on some cosmetics, thankful that she'd had the foresight to stick her make-up in her handbag.

The only thing she'd had done to her was to have a tiny microphone attached to her shirt. She wouldn't have minded, but the fellow doing the attaching had stuck one hand down the front of her shirt and the other up underneath as he fiddled with it to make sure it was OK.

It also wouldn't have been so bad if he hadn't had terrible breath, and hadn't then shouted 'Next!' after he'd finished with her, as if she was on a production line.

Finally, all twelve contestants were shown into a vast hangar-like space, and Leanne stared around with her mouth open in awe. On telly, you didn't get to see the construction-site arrangement of scaffolding, lights, leads and cameras that went on behind the slick shows, and the sight fascinated her for far too long.

Willing herself to get used to it, she tried to focus on the forthcoming ordeal, but it was impossible when she was so nervous, and the environment was so new and disconcerting. She wondered if the other contestants felt as much a fish out of water as she did, and she smiled cautiously at the woman on the next bench.

There were two rows of six benches, and Leanne guessed that gradually they would be removed until only three benches were left. Dear God, let me still be in the competition when that happens, she prayed.

The contestants had all travelled to the venue last night, and had been treated to a hotel room and a lavish dinner. They'd been introduced to one another, and she'd tried to remember all their names, but it had proved beyond her. The only ones she could remember were a girl to her left – Fliss, which she assumed must be short for Felicity – and an older man, Raymond, to her right.

After more instructions and more fiddling with the equipment, the production team were finally ready to start. The contestants had already been told that they had an hour in which to produce a display (but not what it was), and that the various supplies were in a walk-in chiller to the rear of the set. To save any arguments – their words, not Leanne's – each contestant had been allocated a certain amount of supplies, and it was up to them how much or how little of them they used. There was also a bank of flowers and foliage from which they could take their pick.

Leanne stood behind her bench, her heart thumping and her palms damp, as the presenter, Rory, went through his spiel, the judges nodding sagely and smiling.

Finally it was time for the task to be revealed.

'Funerals,' Rory announced grandly. 'A time of upset and grief. A time when flowers can say what words cannot. You have one hour to prepare a floral display suitable to be placed on top of a coffin. Your time starts...' He paused dramatically, pretending to look at his watch, but in reality waiting for the producer, who was staring at the huge clock in front of the set that the viewers would probably never see, to give the signal. 'Now!'

As a group, the contestants charged towards the chiller, and there was a lot of argy-bargy as three of them tried to propel themselves through the door at once.

Leanne hung back, using the time to think. This task wasn't what she had anticipated at all, and she had to take her hat off to the people who had thought of it. To open the first episode of the very first show with something as sorrowful as funeral flowers was a stroke of genius.

Her mind whirled frantically, scanning through images of the wreaths she had made in the past before hastily discarding each one.

How about a cross? she wondered, then rejected the idea as being too trite, as was a traditional wreath shape. She wanted something more original, more personal, but everything that popped into her head was either tacky or had been done to death (she almost giggled at her little pun).

Realising she had to decide who the arrangement was for before she fixed on her design, she cast her mind around for a scenario.

A child?

No. Too awful.

A spouse?

Maybe…

How about an old lady who'd lived a life filled with love and laughter? Not so much mourning, but more of a celebration; thoughts of her own great-grandmother filled her mind.

Who would the wreath be from? Husband, son, daughter?

She'd got it! An old friend.

Decision made, she picked out a single floristry sponge and some old pink roses. As she did so, she noticed that the creamy calla lilies had been seriously depleted.

She tried to remember what her great-gran had been like. She'd died when Leanne was quite young, but she clearly remembered her lavender scent and the pearls she wore in her ears. She always used to have a lace-edged handkerchief about her person, too – handy for drying children's tears or dabbing at grazed knees.

Old English pink roses intermingled with alstroemeria would be lovely. Alstroemeria came in a variety of colours, and she was relieved to see some purply pink ones – she would use those instead of the lavender she would have preferred. They were perfect, because they symbolised enduring friendship. With a few pearls on long pins to provide the accent, and the deeper green of ferns giving a contrast, it should make for a heart-warming display.

She worked swiftly, her fingers sure and steady (unlike her heart, which was stuttering and thumping so hard she was sure the microphone must be picking it up). The presenter and the three judges were at the bench in front of her, but Leanne kept her head down. She knew they would make their way over to her eventually, but for now she was desperately trying to pretend that this task was nothing more significant than a rush order, and that she was behind her little counter in Tanglewood with the radio playing in the background.

'Hi, Leanne. This is... different,' Rory said, and Leanne gave a nervous laugh. She had deliberately tried not to look at what the other contestants were doing, otherwise she might be in danger of losing her nerve.

'You do know that it's supposed to be for a funeral, right?' he asked, the three judges loitering behind him.

Leanne giggled again, painfully aware that if she didn't do a good job, she'd be holding a funeral of her own for the death of her dreams in a couple of hours.

Taking her courage in both hands, she stopped what she was doing and stared into the face of the bemused presenter, trying not to look at the judges for fear of what she might see.

'I know funerals are sad occasions,' she began. 'It's awful to lose someone you love, but if that someone had a good long life, then surely that should be celebrated too?'

She risked a quick glance at Jarred, and saw a spark of what she hoped was genuine interest in his eyes.

'Take my great-gran, for instance. What I remember about her are her old-world manners, morals and attitude, and I've tried to replicate that with the roses. I would have used lavender too, if there had been any, because she used to wear the scent all the time, but the alstroemeria was the nearest I could manage in terms of colour, and its connotation means it's not out of place.'

'Friendship?' Jarred asked.

'Yes, this arrangement isn't from me; it would be from an old friend, someone who knew her well and wanted to honour her life.'

'What about the pearls?' Pamela asked.

'My great-gran always wore a pair of freshwater pearl earrings. I can't ever remember seeing her without them.'

'So this,' Jarred waved a hand at her display, 'isn't about death, but about love, friendship and memories?'

'Exactly,' Leanne said, pleased that he understood.

'Ten minutes!' Rory shouted, and she winced.

Where on earth had the last fifty gone?

The panel moved off and she breathed a sigh of relief, resenting the intrusion. It was necessary for the show and the viewers, but still…

It seemed like only a minute had passed when Rory called, 'Time's up. Step away from your arrangements. Peter, put that stem down.' His voice was teasing, but Leanne detected an undercurrent of caution. All the contestants had been warned not to take the mickey on the timings.

Everything stopped and a hasty clear-up took place. Leanne started to help, but was ushered away from her bench.

'We'll sort all that out, dear,' the kindly voice of one of the production staff said. 'You go and grab yourself a coffee.'

Leanne smiled her thanks and wandered into the refreshment area, needing something stronger than coffee. Gin would be nice. A bottle of it!

After coffee and cake, and a far-too-long wait, they were called back onto the set and told to stand behind their benches.

With all the debris of the task cleared away, Leanne saw her rivals' efforts clearly for the first time.

That cross was lovely, she noted — a mostly green creation, with one simple red rose at its centre. The rose said everything; there was no need for a background story.

Five of the contestants had chosen to do wreaths of varying sizes and colours. One had produced a single white lily, with fronds of delicate green grevillea. Another had chosen to do a plaque in yellow and white. Someone else had obviously run out of time.

Starting at Leanne's side of the room, the presenter led the judges from bench to bench, allowing each contestant to explain their piece, and once more Leanne briefly reiterated the rationale behind hers.

It sounded so trite when she said it out loud.

After the last contestant had been spoken to, the panel left to deliberate, and Leanne and the others were shepherded off set again.

To her surprise, they weren't called back straight away, but were told to have lunch first, then the second task would begin.

Too nervous to do much more than pick at the lovely buffet, Leanne put her barely touched plate down and made her way outside for some much-needed fresh air. Someone else was outside, but it wasn't the fresh air she was after.

'That was tough,' a little blonde woman in her thirties said, and Leanne recognised her as the contestant who had produced the single lily. 'You're Leanne, aren't you?' the woman asked, blowing a puff of smoke into the air.

'Yes. I'm sorry, but I can't remember your name,' Leanne replied.

'It's Dawn.'

'Oh yes, I remember now. I'm hopeless with names, sorry,' she apologised again. 'It *was* tough, wasn't it?'

'I loved your idea of making a funeral about life rather than about death,' Dawn said.

Leanne wanted to say something nice about the other woman's entry too, but she couldn't find the words.

'I'm not very good at being put on the spot,' Dawn was saying. 'I need time to think. I'm afraid my attempt was a bit too simplistic.'

'It certainly stood out,' Leanne said, and she wasn't lying. Among all the elaborate displays, Dawn's arrangement had actually looked quite inspired. Whether the judges liked it was a different matter, though.

Dawn stubbed out her cigarette and sighed. 'I'm not sure I'm cut out for this,' she said. 'It wasn't my idea to enter the competition, it was my mother's. She's always pushing me to do something, and this is her latest venture. She should have entered the damn thing herself if she was that keen. I think she just wants to boast to her friends that her daughter is on the telly.'

'I've kept it really quiet,' Leanne confided. 'Only my family, a couple of close friends and...' She hesitated, wondering how she should refer to Rex. She could hardly call him her boyfriend, unless by that she meant that he was both male and a friend.

She let it go and said instead, 'I think everyone will know soon enough when the programme is shown on TV.'

The second half of the day passed much like the first had done, except everyone was now working from their own designs and knew what they were doing. Sort of. Judging by the frantic racing around, the muttering and the head-scratching, most of them, including Leanne, seemed to have forgotten everything.

When Rory called, 'Put your secateurs down,' Leanne obediently stopped primping her waterfall and stepped back from the bench.

Once again, a clean-up operation took place while the contestants had a well-deserved break, and then they were called back on set. A similar procedure took place, with the judges approaching each bench and the contestants explaining the thinking behind their designs.

Then came the part Leanne had been dreading – the verdict.

With the contestants lined up like a row of naughty schoolchildren in front of the head teacher, Rory played up to the cameras, stringing it out until she wanted to scream at him to get on with it.

Each judge would award each task a mark out of ten, and the contestant with the lowest mark would go home. In the case of a tie, it had been explained that the judges would cast a vote.

The highest score was awarded first, and although Leanne knew it couldn't possibly be her, she still couldn't help hoping it might be.

It wasn't.

That accolade went to a scrawny little man with slicked-back hair and a goatee, wearing a dicky bow – he of the foliage cross with the single red rose. He'd been awarded the highest mark for the sight-unseen arrangement and the second highest for his aquarium design of coral and exotic flowery fish.

As the scores were read out in descending order, Leanne's nerves started to get the better of her. She wanted this so badly that if she had to go home now, she'd be devastated.

'Seventh with thirty-seven points is…' Rory paused, and the camera panned across the remaining contestants who were yet to be informed of their fate. 'Leanne Green! Congratulations, Leanne – the judges especially liked your waterfall arrangement. Jarred? I know you wanted to say a few words about this one.'

Jarred gave Leanne a professional, polished smile. 'When you explained what you were designing, I had my doubts,' he said. 'I didn't think a Welsh waterfall had any place in an aquarium, but the result convinced me. As did your passion.'

Did he just wink at her?

No, she must have imagined it, surely? And if he had, so what? She didn't care, because *she was through to the next round*!

Chapter 15

According to his mother, it had been three months and five days since Rex had left Scotland for a new life in Tanglewood, so it really was about time he went back for a visit.

His mum had been nagging that she hadn't seen her favourite son in months (ha, ha, very funny, he thought, considering she only had the one child!), and now his father had been badgered into nagging him as well.

'Can't you spare your mother a few days? Surely you can't be that busy?' he grumbled over the phone.

Rex could, and he wasn't. He had a few days' holiday he could take, but although he very much wanted to see his parents and he longed to return to the place where he'd grown up, he was reluctant to risk coming face to face with Jules. He wasn't quite ready for that yet.

Jules hadn't exactly broken his heart when she'd told him she was leaving – how could it break when the pair of them had been drifting apart for so long? – but the separation had been painful all the same.

'I'll see what I can do,' he promised, hoping it would serve to placate his mother for a while.

'You'd better,' his dad warned. 'You're not the one who has to listen to her complaining about it every five minutes.' His tone softened. 'She misses you, son. We both do.'

And he missed them too, but playing the guilt card simply wasn't fair of them.

'Let's just settle on a date,' his father was saying. 'If she knows when she's going to see you, she might stop whingeing.'

His mother never whinged, Rex knew. That was simply his dad's way of saying that he wanted to see Rex too but wasn't going to admit it. He never did, and Rex smiled fondly. It had always been the same – Dad blamed everything on Mum, but not in a mean way. 'Your mum will go mad if you don't tidy your room,' he'd say, meaning 'I want you to tidy your room.' Or, 'How about giving your mum a cuddle?' knowing full well that Rex would hug him too.

Rex was quite surprised that his dad had actually admitted he missed him. He must really, really be missing him to say it out loud.

Feeling incredibly guilty for not making an effort sooner, he agreed to travel back to Glenshona in a couple of weeks.

'I'm warning you, I won't be on my own,' he added.

But before he could explain what he meant, his dad jumped in with 'You've got yourself a girlfriend?'

He sounded a little off, as if he was disappointed that Rex had found someone new. He knew his parents had liked Jules, but honestly, it wasn't as though they'd been married. Besides, she'd left him, remember?

He was about to point that out when his dad continued, 'Are we going to meet this new girl of yours, then? Are you bringing her with you?'

'Er… yeah. But Dad—'

His father interrupted him. 'I don't think it's a good idea, son. Your mum hasn't seen you for ages, and it might be best if you came alone.'

'I've got to bring her – her name is Nell and she's a Border collie. I can't leave her on her own. Is that OK?'

'Oh, I see, of course it is,' his father said, and Rex could have sworn the older man sounded relieved.

The thought of travelling almost five hundred miles with an excitable puppy in the car didn't fill Rex with much enthusiasm, but he'd promised now, and he wasn't going to go back on his word. Despite his misgivings about returning to the small town where he and Jules had lived together, he found he was actually looking forward to it.

It was just a pity he didn't have a real girlfriend to take with him, and unbidden, the image of Leanne popped into his mind.

Chapter 16

'Well?' Stevie hissed in a loud whisper as she swept into the shop to collect her usual flowers.

'I'm not supposed to talk about it,' Leanne said, 'under pain of death or something.'

'Huh! We'll know soon enough if you leave Mabel in charge for a couple of days next week,' Stevie pointed out. 'You may as well spill the beans now.'

'I could be off enjoying a few days' holiday, for all you know,' Leanne protested.

'Not on your life! You don't do holidays. You haven't had one since I moved to Tanglewood.'

'That's because I've never had anyone to look after the shop except Mum, and I didn't like asking her all the time. Now that I've got Mabel, I might just decide to go to Barbados for three weeks.'

'Not you, you're a workaholic, except when you're getting me too drunk to stand up. Remember the last time?'

'The only time, you mean. You haven't been out for a proper drink with me since.'

'Can you blame me?'

Leanne giggled. 'Not really, although you are a bit of a lightweight. You only had four glasses of wine.' In fact,

Leanne hadn't had a proper drink since either. She was turning into a lightweight herself.

Stevie tutted. 'You still haven't answered my question,' she said, and when Leanne's face broke into a huge grin, despite her brain telling it not to, Stevie let out an ear-piercing scream.

'I knew it! I bloody knew it! Well done, girlie.' She threw herself at Leanne and gave her a massive hug. 'I'm so proud of you.'

'Anyone would think I've won the damned thing already,' Leanne muttered, but she was delighted all the same. 'Anyway, what about you? How are the wedding plans coming along?'

Stevie's smile almost split her face in two. 'I've found the most wonderful little wedding shop. It's called Moira's and I didn't even know it existed until last week.'

'Oh yes, I keep forgetting about it too. It's because it's so out of the way.' The shop was situated under a cobbled archway between two buildings, just off the high street, and really was quite unassuming. It didn't help that there wasn't any signage for it either. Unless you already knew about it, the odds of discovering it on your own were quite slim.

'It's a wonder they do any business at all, and that Moira woman who owns it is a bit stuck up, but they've got the most gorgeous dresses I've ever seen,' Stevie said. 'You're going to have to come and have a look, especially since you're going to be wearing one of her bridesmaid dresses. I know it's not for ages yet, and there's Tia and William's wedding first, but you have you plan these things well in advance. Will you come with me when I try a few gowns on?' she added. 'I'd really value your opinion.'

'When were you thinking of?'

'Whenever you're free and whenever Karen can make it. I'll get back to you with some dates, if that's OK?'

It certainly was. Leanne had never been a bridesmaid before, and she was really looking forward to it. She loved weddings! She knew that both Stevie and Tia would make the most beautiful brides.

She was sure she'd have no trouble getting Mabel to manage the shop for her when the time came. The older woman was doing a grand job as it was, filling in for her when she went to London.

She still couldn't believe she'd got through to the next round. She also couldn't believe she only had a week – less than that now; six days, to be exact – before she was expected to do it all over again. The next theme was 'The Office'. What on earth was she supposed to make of that? When she thought of offices, the only planty image to come to mind was a huge pot with a dusty palm or ficus in it, maybe with a scattering of pebbles on the surface of the soil for a bit of added interest as well as to keep the moisture in.

With Mabel having today off, Leanne didn't have much time to worry about the task until she closed the door on her final customer of the day and sank against the glass, weary to the bone.

The thought of having to go home and spend the evening frantically coming up with an arrangement that was good enough to keep her in the competition filled her with dread. She'd not had a minute to herself since this whole thing started, and what was worse, she had no one else to blame. She'd got herself in this position; it was up to her to deal with it. The ancient Chinese proverb of being careful what you wished for came to mind.

She was walking slowly back to her car when she heard her name being called, followed by, 'No, Nell! Come here!'

Looking over her shoulder, she was just in time to see an overexcited Border collie racing across the road.

Without stopping to think about the consequences, she launched herself towards the dog in a mad dive. She hardly heard the squeal of brakes, or Rex's horrified cry, before she was knocked off her feet.

Stunned, she lay on her side, not daring to move. She wasn't dead – at least she didn't think she was – and nothing seemed to hurt. *Yet.* That was a good thing, wasn't it? Or maybe she was in shock, and the pain would hit her like a train in a minute or so.

The blasted dog licked her face, practically lying on her head, and all Leanne could think about was that Nell was safe. Thankfully, the car had hit her instead of the puppy.

'Oh my God, are you all right? Leanne, speak to me. Are you hurt?'

'She stepped out right in front of me!' a man cried. 'I didn't stand a chance. I've killed her, haven't I? I've killed her!'

Leanne saw a pair of anxious faces peering down at her as she tried to squint around a blanket of excited dog.

Someone else said, 'I saw it all, mate. There was nothing you could have done. Has anyone called an ambulance? And the police?'

'Oh shit, that's Leanne Green. Her mother will be devastated,' another person said.

'Lea, Lea, speak to me.' Rex sounded frantic.

Leanne made a feeble attempt to push Nell away. She couldn't breathe with all that fur on her face. When she felt the dog being dragged off her, she blinked owlishly.

'She moved. Her eyes moved. Did you see that? She's not dead.'

Leanne thought it was Sid the butcher who had spoken, but she couldn't be certain, because from this angle all she could see was legs. Except for Rex. She could see him all right, because he was on his hands and knees in the middle of the road, his face inches from hers, and horror was written across every inch of it.

'I'm not dead,' she croaked, but it came out as a wheeze as she tried to catch her breath.

'If anyone's to blame, it's that dog of yours,' someone said. 'It should be on a bloody lead, it should.'

'Lea.' Rex's voice was more controlled. 'Stay with us. An ambulance is on its way.'

Leanne had absolutely no intention whatsoever of staying there. She had to go home and find some ideas for the next task. Besides, she'd only had a sandwich all day and she was starving. Cautiously she tried to push herself into a sitting position, but a firm, strong hand held her down.

'Don't try to move. Goodness knows what you might have broken. Oh God, if anything happens to you, I'll never forgive myself,' Rex groaned.

She tried to speak again, this time with more success. 'I'm fine,' she croaked. 'Winded, but fine. Nothing is broken either, see?' She wiggled her fingers and toes.

She guessed the car must have almost been at a standstill when it clipped her, knocking her off her feet rather than smashing into her. She might have a bruise or two come the morning, but she suspected the main injury was to her pride. How could she have been so stupid?

'Is Nell OK?' she asked, once again struggling to sit up. This time, instead of forcing her back down, Rex helped her.

'She's fine, thanks to you. But you're not,' he said.

'I am,' she insisted. 'Honestly. You can stop fussing, and could someone please let the ambulance know it's not needed?' She felt such a fraud; although to be fair, if the driver hadn't reacted so quickly, things might have been very different.

She got to her feet with a little help from Rex and stood, wobbling slightly, flexing first one leg, then the other. Her hip was rather sore where it had collided with the road, but apart from that, everything seemed to be working just fine.

'Are you sure you're OK?' Rex demanded, the anxious expression still on his face.

'Stop fussing. Nothing is broken. I'm just glad Nell wasn't hurt.'

They both looked down at the dog, whose tongue was lolling out and whose tail was wagging, and burst into laughter.

'It's not bloody funny,' the driver said. He'd gone from worried to irked in the space of a minute, and Leanne didn't blame him. He must have had one hell of a fright.

'No, you're right, it isn't,' she said, suddenly contrite. 'Let me give you my details. If there's any damage to the car, call me and I'll pay for it.'

She rooted around in her handbag, which had miraculously managed to stay on her shoulder, found one of her business cards and handed it over.

'This is you, is it?' the man demanded, squinting at her suspiciously.

'It's me,' she confirmed. 'I own the flower shop around the corner.'

'She does,' Rex tried to reassure him. 'I can vouch for her.'

'And who might you be?'

'Rex McMillan. That's my house over there.'

With some muttering and a couple of dark looks, the driver was eventually persuaded that Leanne wasn't trying to rip him off, and got back in his car. She watched his incredibly slow progress to the junction, and gave a sigh of relief when the car turned the corner and was finally out of sight.

'I'll drive you home,' Rex offered.

'Thanks, but I'll need my car to get to work tomorrow, and anyway, I'm fine.' If she had to say she was fine one more time, she thought she might scream.

'I'll follow behind you,' Rex insisted.

Although there was absolutely no need for him to do so, Leanne was quite touched. He really was very sweet and thoughtful. She gave in, realising he probably felt guilty, and phoned ahead to warn her mother that he would be joining them for tea again.

When they arrived at the farmhouse, Rex tried to reverse out of the yard, but she wouldn't take no for an answer, insisting that he stay to eat with them.

'Anyway, I want to pick your brains.'

'Oh?'

'Let's talk about it after tea,' she suggested.

Thankfully, he only had to put up with Murray this time, because Saul had found himself another victim

(Leanne really should stop referring to his girlfriends like that, but her brother was so much fun to tease), and Murray, being the quieter of her siblings, actually behaved himself without Saul's bad influence. Her father had raised an eyebrow and given her a pointed look when she'd strolled into the kitchen with Rex, but apart from that, no one made any comment. She could tell that her mother was itching to say something, though, which was why Leanne hurried Rex out of the house as soon as they'd finished eating, and was now leading him past the vegetable garden and into the field behind the farm.

The evening was a fine one, the sun dipping behind the western edge of the mountains, leaving tendrils of orange and pink across the sky.

Puffing a little – she couldn't remember the last time she'd hiked up the slopes – Leanne explained her predicament.

'An office?' Rex scratched his head, causing his hair to stick up as his fingers rippled through it. 'I don't do offices much,' he said. 'I don't think I can help you with that. The only ones I'm familiar with are in the park centre, and those awful big ones you see on the TV. You know, where employees are shoved into little boxes with only a partition between them. Oh, and there are those big director's offices, with board tables in them. Maybe you can...' He ground to a halt.

Leanne had also ground to a halt – a physical one. He'd said something about partitions... For a second, she forgot he was there, and when she came back to herself, it was to see him staring at her with that anxious look on his face again.

'What? Are you OK? How's your head? Did you bump it when the car hit you? Oh God, you might have concussion.'

'No concussion,' she reassured him, 'but I have got an idea. Thank you!'

She threw her arms around him and stood on tiptoe to give him a kiss on the cheek, but something went a little awry with the plan, because Rex turned his head at exactly the same moment so that instead of kissing him on his slightly stubbly cheek, her lips met his mouth full on.

Her heart stopped.

The kiss was feather-light at first, then he pulled her into him, tightening the embrace, holding her in a cage of solid muscle.

Without conscious thought, she closed her eyes and melted into his embrace, the rightness of being in his arms sweeping her away and filling her senses. Nothing and no one existed except him. His mouth claimed hers, the firm insistence of his lips making her go weak at the knees, until the only thing keeping her upright was his arms. Her legs trembled, her heart thumped and fluttered, and she was suddenly breathless.

Oh my – she'd never been kissed quite like this before.

As she gave a small cry, her lips parted and his tongue slipped into her mouth, finding hers. The taste of him, the smell of him, was all she could think about.

Then, as quickly as it had begun, it was over.

Rex broke the connection, abruptly dragging his mouth away, and Leanne felt lost and abandoned even though she was still encircled in his arms.

She opened her eyes. He was staring at her in confusion, breathing hard. His eyes had turned a dark blue, almost navy. Although she could see the hunger in his expression, he was clearly regretting what had just happened.

'Oops,' she said inanely, desperately searching for a way to cover her embarrassment. 'Oops' didn't do it, but it was all she could think of.

A sudden chill went through her when he released her and took a step backwards. He'd been so warm, so vibrant... she'd enjoyed the encounter far too much for her own good.

Rex focused on a spot over her right shoulder and cleared his throat. 'Your idea?' he reminded her, and it took Leanne a second to gather her scattered thoughts. What idea? What was he talking about?

'Oh yes, the idea. Um... partitions,' she muttered, her lips tingling and her voice somewhat hoarse. Her own gaze was on a clump of celandine at the side of the path. Absently she noticed the fresh green leaves and the beginnings of newly forming buds. Their eventual bright yellow flowers would be a welcome treat for her mother's bees. In fact, there was one of the little insects now, not long out of hibernation, hoping to find a quick meal of nectar before bedtime.

'Partitions?' Rex sounded brisk, almost businesslike.

Damn it, she thought. That kiss should never have happened. Now she'd jeopardised their new and fragile friendship, and all because he'd turned his head at the wrong time.

It was a mistake, that was all, an accident; nothing but an unfortunate touch of lips.

So why had it felt like so much more?

Chapter 17

Rex couldn't sleep. For a long time he lay there listening to the diminishing sounds of a Tanglewood night, until no more noises could be heard except for the occasional car engine on the main street.

At one point he thought he heard a fox bark and got out of bed to investigate, tugging the curtain to one side to peer out into the dark and earning himself a disgruntled grizzling from a sleepy Nell.

Her complaining continued when he returned to bed. Unable to keep still, he tossed and turned until the dog shuffled over to the far side of the mattress and settled down again with a huff.

'Sorry,' he whispered, and saw the faint gleam of an open eye. 'Anyway,' he added, 'I don't know what you're complaining about – it's all your fault. None of this would have happened if you hadn't slipped your lead.'

Maybe 'slipped' wasn't a totally accurate description. Rex had been trying to do three things at once – lock the car, hoist his rucksack onto his shoulder and wrap Nell's lead around his hand – so he had to take some of the blame.

He shuddered at the thought of what might have happened. Things could easily have been a great deal worse, and if Leanne had been seriously hurt, he didn't know how he would have been able to live with himself.

'It's all your fault,' he repeated to the dog, getting a half-hearted wag in return. But he wasn't just talking about the accident – he was also talking about the kiss. There had been an inevitability about it, as though Nell slipping out of his grasp was fated to end in him grabbing Leanne and forcing himself on her.

'Forcing' was a bit strong, but his attention clearly hadn't been all that welcome, as her cry of dismay when his tongue had found hers had shown.

Then she had let him off the hook and made a bit of a joke about it by saying 'oops'. Except there'd been no 'oops' about it. He'd known exactly what he was doing when she threw her arms around him.

The turn of his head had been totally and utterly deliberate.

He'd not stopped to consider the consequences. He'd acted purely on instinct; on a desire to taste those full, luscious lips and to feel her body close to his.

What *had* he been thinking?

Clearly he hadn't been thinking at all right then, but he was certainly thinking now, and was desperately hoping he'd not scuppered their fledgling friendship.

But she'd felt so good in his arms.

Stop it this very second, he told himself. Don't go there. She doesn't want you except as a friend.

Feeling a right idiot, he threw in the towel and got up.

Two cups of coffee later, he was still restless and out of sorts, so he decided to go for a walk – anything to take his mind off his churning thoughts.

As soon as Nell heard the jangle of her lead, she leapt off the bed, going from an apparently deep sleep to excited watchfulness in the blink of an eye and dancing around his legs uttering excited little barks.

'Behave yourself this time,' he warned her, clipping the lead onto her collar, then he opened the door and they disappeared out into the night.

The river was a different place in the wee hours, he noticed, unlatching the gate and making Nell wait for him to go through first. He took every opportunity to instil manners into the dog, and he didn't see why a midnight walk should be any exception. Once the gate was safely closed behind them, he made her sit and wait while he let her off the lead.

'Go on,' he said in a low voice, and she took off at a rate of knots, nose down, tail up. 'Don't expect this every night,' he warned, although he supposed that if he saw much more of Leanne Green, this wouldn't be the last walk he and his dog would be taking in the middle of the night.

The river was up, recent rains swelling it, and the gurgle of the water and the sound of the wavelets lapping the bank went some way to soothe his troubled soul.

As Nell cast back and forth, sniffing out rabbits and chasing down interesting smells, Rex tried to stay focused on the dog's antics, especially when the squeak of a small rodent had her charging into the undergrowth, but he found he couldn't get Leanne's stricken expression out of his mind. Nor the way she'd leapt at the chance to pretend nothing had happened between them. At least he'd managed to help her with her next task, albeit unwittingly, so some good had come of the evening.

Partitions was a good idea. He could picture it now: walls of living plants instead of plastic and metal separating the various work areas. It was a proven fact that people felt better when surrounded by greenery – maybe it had something to do with the increased oxygen levels in the air, besides providing something inherently pleasing and calming to look at.

He knew Leanne would instinctively choose slow-growing plants that needed the minimum of care, and he hoped the idea was good enough to get her through to the next round, as he knew how much it meant to her.

There was only one problem, though: if she got through to the end and actually won the damn thing, she'd probably be gone from his life for good.

And he had no idea how he felt about that.

Chapter 18

Concentrate, Leanne told herself for the umpteenth time that morning. She was in the shed, trying to construct a partition and not making a very good job of it. She blamed her lack of focus on the constant bleating of the newborn lambs and their mothers coming from the lambing shed, but in reality she knew it was because whenever she thought about her design, Rex's face was superimposed upon it.

'Whatcha doing?' Saul strolled into the shed, bringing with him the pungent, unmistakable smell of sheep.

'Go away, I'm busy.'

'I can't, not until I find the wire cutters.' He rooted around in the massive toolbox, disturbing her concentration even further. 'Anyway, shouldn't you be working?' he asked, making more noise than a JCB on a construction site. That was Saul, she thought. You always knew when he was around.

'I *am* working. This,' she pointed to the half-completed wood and chicken wire ensemble, 'is work.'

'It doesn't look like any flower arrangement I've ever seen,' her brother said, his hands on his hips as he eyed the contraption. 'What are you trying to do?'

She told him.

'That's not going to work,' was his ill-considered verdict. Ill-considered because Leanne was sorely tempted to throw the hammer she was holding at his stupid head.

'It will,' she insisted. 'It's an excellent idea.' Although she said it with a degree of certainty, she was actually far from confident. She couldn't even get the basic structure right, for goodness' sake.

'It needs to be on castors, for a start.'

'Castors?' Leanne scowled at him. What a daft thing to say.

'Those kinds of offices that have partitions are a movable feast,' he explained, ignoring her surliness. 'The whole idea is that they're fluid and can be arranged to suit the circumstances.'

It was Leanne's turn to put her hands on her hips. 'What do you know about offices?'

'I dated a girl who worked in a call centre in Hereford. She showed me around once.' He grinned and waggled his eyebrows, so Leanne guessed there'd been more to it than a simple guided tour. She rolled her eyes in disgust; her brother was incorrigible. Her mother despaired of him ever finding a nice girl to settle down with. Leanne didn't care if he did or didn't. She just wanted him to explain his castor thing.

'If the partition is on lockable castors, it can be moved a lot easier than if it's static,' he continued. 'It's going to be a fair old weight, what with the structure, the soil and plants, not to mention the water. I think we've got some around here somewhere, from when we took the butcher's block out of the kitchen.'

A few years ago, their mum had insisted on having a new kitchen installed. However, true to farmers everywhere, nothing went to the skip. The old dresser had been sanded down and repainted, and now had pride of place in the dining room, adorned with their great-grandma's china. The cabinets had found their way into the feed barn, where they held various bowls, buckets, scoops and ladles. The butcher's block – minus the castors – was used as a workbench.

Saul found the wheels and insisted on fixing them on. 'You do know you need some kind of irrigation system?' he said to her, standing back to admire his handiwork.

'Duh! I know.' Leanne pointed to several lengths of hosepipe.

'Right then, let's get started,' he announced.

Leanne was shocked. When they were children, Saul had always made the best constructions out of Meccano and Lego, but he'd never offered to help her. More than once he had stated that girls were as capable as boys at that kind of stuff, but if he helped her, she'd never learn. She used to think it was because he couldn't be bothered.

Brother and sister worked side by side for the next couple of hours, bending metal tubing and attaching wires. Saul dug out an old enamel trough, one of the smaller ones, and together they secured it to a plinth. They even found an old pump that had once been part of a water feature.

Finally the whole thing was ready for planting. Leanne had initially thought to use climbers, but understood quite quickly that it would be too simplistic, so she attached small plastic pots all over the structure and filled them with compost, ensuring that each one was rigged up to the irrigation system. Then she filled the trough with water, connected the plug to the mains and switched on the pump.

For a moment, she thought it wasn't going to work, but after a pause, the motor roared into life and she let out a whoop.

Saul bumped her shoulder. 'Will it do?'

'Will it ever! It's brilliant. Thank you.'

'You can repay me when you're rich and famous,' he said with a laugh.

She put her arm around him. Annoying big brothers could come in handy sometimes, she decided. They stood watching the water drip for a while before Leanne turned the pump off.

'It'll only need switching on for a few minutes every day,' she said, 'and depending on the time of year and the temperature, you could probably get away with checking the reservoir about once a week.'

'What's next?' Saul asked.

'I've got to do the planting, and I need to find some kind of lid for the reservoir.'

'You do your planty thing, and I'll make the lid,' Saul suggested. 'We've got some marine plywood somewhere.'

When Leanne showed him what she wanted, he set about his task with enthusiasm while she went off in search of her plants.

By dinner time, she was finished, and she stood back to admire the display. She'd aimed for year-round colour, and had interspersed the body of green foliage with spring, summer and autumn flowering plants. At the moment, it was resplendent with late-flowering primroses, the last of the dwarf narcissi, tiny nodding Spanish bluebells and hyacinths.

She surveyed it for a long time, walking around it, scrutinising it critically, adjusting and fiddling as she went. Several scribbled notes later, she felt she was as ready as she could be.

She also made a mental note to take the plants she'd used today to the local nursing home, as she did with all the flowers that had gone past their prime. Thankfully for her profit margin, she didn't have a great deal of wastage, but she always took a few bunches over to the home regardless, never letting on that some of the flowers were actually prime stock.

It was only when the display was in bits that she wished she'd taken a photo and sent it to Rex.

Ah well, too late now. It was probably for the best anyway – she didn't want him thinking she was chasing after him or anything.

Chapter 19

'Show me your shoes,' Rex instructed.

Eleven little feet waved in the air, the children they belonged to hopping unsteadily on the other.

'Great! Show me your backpacks.'

Eleven little bodies turned around in unison.

'What have you got in them?' Rex shouted. 'Hands up. You?' He pointed to a cutie with blonde pigtails.

'Gloves,' she lisped.

'Hands up if you've forgotten your gloves.' He stared at each child in turn. All shook their heads. 'What else?' he cried.

'Hat,' another child called out.

'Who's forgotten their hat?'

No one put their hand up. He could see that every pupil had a waterproof coat on, so he didn't need to check that.

Miss Harding, the Class 3 teacher, had brought a selection of spare clothes as instructed (he knew from experience that at least one small person would fall in the stream), and Rex had persuaded the National Park to fork out for cake and nibbles to supplement the pupils' packed lunches. He'd also supplied paper, pencils and paints.

It was promising to be a fun day out. They were in the car park below one of the reservoirs, and the plan was to walk for about half a mile until they reached a stream that fed into it.

He'd chosen this stream because it was shallow and not particularly fast-flowing —although if it rained, that could quite quickly change — and he knew that some of the tiny rivulets leading into it contained tadpoles. The stream itself was alive with brown trout and insect larvae, and if the children were quiet enough, they might catch a glimpse of a wagtail or a nightjar.

Ravens, skylarks and red kites were a given, as were the ever-present sheep, although only last year's youngsters were out on the hills now. If they were really lucky, the pupils might spot one of the tiny herds of semi-wild Welsh ponies that roamed the park. At this time of year, one or two of the mares might even have a foal at foot.

With Rex leading the way, Miss Harding by his side and a learning support assistant chivvying the stragglers, the little group made their way past the reservoir and towards the stream.

Rex gave the children plenty of time to stop and look, explaining as they walked and pointing things out they might otherwise have missed.

'Can we have our picnic now?' one little boy asked.

'Later, Cameron,' Miss Harding replied.

Rex had to smile; clearly the thought of eating his lunch outdoors was far more exciting to the child than the trip itself.

Gradually the path became steeper, and the excited chatter trailed off a little as the children panted and puffed up the hill. Rex sneaked a look at the woman walking next to him. She didn't seem at all out of breath.

'Are you a hiker?' he asked her.

'Yes. I love it, and I'm so pleased you approached us. I've been wanting to take the children out ever since I started.'

'Have you been at the school long?'

'Since September. I'm an NQT.'

Rex had no idea what that meant. She must have seen his expression, because she explained, 'Newly qualified teacher. This is my first proper year of teaching. I only graduated last summer.'

'Do you enjoy it?'

'Oh yes! There's nothing so satisfying as shaping these little minds. You wouldn't believe it, but some of these kids have never been into the National Park.'

Rex did believe it. Despite living in a rural area, many children led rather sedentary lifestyles. He found the teacher's enthusiasm quite endearing. Reading, writing and arithmetic were essential, of course, but learning about the natural environment and your place in it was important too.

It took him a while to realise that Miss Harding was flirting with him. She kept bumping into him, for a start, and glancing at him out of the corner of her eye. She asked him loads of questions too, and when she learnt he was single, her efforts intensified.

Under any other circumstances Rex might have been flattered. He might even have reciprocated by flirting himself, but he was working. It wouldn't be at all professional. Besides, they had twelve pairs of curious eyes watching their every move, and he didn't fancy an audience.

But the real reason, and one he was only just admitting to himself, was that he wished the woman at his side was someone else entirely.

Chapter 20

Was it her imagination, or was Jarred Townsend flirting with her? Leanne wondered.

For once, two of the judges were having dinner with the contestants, and Jarred was seated next to her. Throughout the meal he'd been very attentive, wanting to know where she came from – even though he already knew everything about her, having read her application – and they had chatted almost to the exclusion of everyone else.

Conscious of the rest of the entrants giving her less-than-happy glances, Leanne tried deflecting his attention onto the others, but every time she attempted to include someone else in their conversation, he shut the other person out. He wasn't obvious about it, but Leanne could see what he was doing.

To her surprise, after a while she realised he was easy to talk to, and not the pretentious, up-his-own-butt git she'd originally thought he was.

'I understand you still live at home?' he was asking her.

She grimaced. 'Yes, it's easier that way, and I'm too lazy to cook for myself.'

'I'm sure you're not,' he said with a twinkle.

'I'm sure I am,' she retorted. 'I can't cook for toffee. I suppose I'll have to learn one day, but...' She let the rest of it hang, allowing him to think what he liked.

'I'm quite a good cook,' he said. 'I make a mean Moroccan meatball tagine. I'll have to cook it for you sometime.'

Definitely flirting. Leanne didn't know what to say, so she just smiled and played with her food. She was too full of nerves to have much of an appetite, but although the pressure was increasing with each shoot, at least she knew what to expect this time, so that when the next day arrived, she felt a little more confident that she'd be able to cope with the following few hours.

The unseen task for this week was called 'The Chameleon' – a double-sided display that looked totally different on each side. Leanne opted for a hot/cold arrangement, using greenery to shield the opposite side from view. To be honest, she didn't consider it much of a challenge, and wondered if that meant she hadn't done a good enough job.

A quick buffet lunch followed where she tried her best to mingle and make friends, then it was on to the next task.

When Rory called time at the end of the day, Leanne had a good look at everyone else's work and was horrified to see that she was the only one who'd gone for such a large display with her office partition. Any confidence she might have had disappeared very quickly, and she took her place on the set feeling like a Christian being fed to the lions, and convinced she'd be going home tonight, never to return.

'Leanne,' Rory said when he came to her, and she stood straighter, hoping the camera didn't pick up the wobble in her knees. 'The judges thought your unseen task wasn't creative enough. Pauline, you wanted to say something about this, didn't you?'

'We did think it wasn't your best work,' the judge said diplomatically. 'Jarred especially thought you were capable of so much more.'

Leanne thought she might be about to cry — she had guessed it wasn't as good as some of the others, but she'd been hoping she might have scraped by.

'However,' Pauline said, holding up a finger, 'you redeemed yourself with your prepared task. I love the idea of a living wall, and once again you've proved you can think outside the box.'

Leanne's emotions were all over the place; criticism and praise, one after the other. She didn't think she could take any more. Just give me the verdict and put me out of my misery, she wanted to yell, but all she did was give the panel a solemn nod. If by the remotest chance she wasn't sent home today, she fully intended to take the advice on board. She knew she had let herself down.

When the scores came, she lifted her chin and gazed over the judges' heads, not daring to look at her fellow contestants for fear of crying. She prayed she could hold her tears in until the cameras were off her, not wanting half of Britain to watch her lose control in glorious red-eyed, swollen-faced technicolour. Ugh, no thanks. If she was going out of the competition today, she wanted to do it with dignity.

She didn't achieve top marks, nor second or third. When it came down to the last two and she still hadn't been given her result, she resigned herself to her fate.

'Leanne, Tara... one of you is going home today,' Rory said. 'Before I announce who it is, I want you both to know that getting this far is a great achievement. You should be really proud of yourselves.'

Leanne didn't feel proud at all. She felt terribly disappointed and very, very upset. She willed her eyes not to fill with tears, and took a deep, steadying breath.

'Tara, I'm sorry, my darling, but you're leaving the competition,' Rory announced, and the tears that Leanne was trying so desperately to hold in check trickled down over her cheeks.

Without thinking, she turned to the other woman and gave her a big hug, the rest of the contestants crowding around to offer their sympathy.

It was when she was packing up her things – not that she was likely to ever use the living partition again, but she could hardly leave it here – that Jarred strolled back onto the set. The judges usually disappeared pretty swiftly, so she was surprised to see him. She was even more surprised when he sauntered over to her workbench. She could see the few contestants who still remained shooting her filthy looks as he did so, and she frowned, wondering if these sorts of competitions were all the same – bonhomie and camaraderie while the cameras were rolling, and narrow-eyed stares and animosity when they weren't. Or was it just for her? Did the other contestants think there was something going on between her and Jarred?

'You did a good prepared task,' he said when he got closer, causing Leanne to receive more filthy looks.

134

'Thanks,' was all she said, not wanting to encourage him.

'I like the way you can see the environment the flowers sit in, and not just the blooms themselves.' He nodded slowly at her while he spoke.

All Leanne could manage in response was a nervous smile.

'Do you have to rush off?' Jarred asked when she'd finally got everything packed ready for one of the runners to take out to her car.

'Er… yes, I've got work tomorrow.'

'Work? Ah, you're the contestant with her own florist's business. You do know that some of the others believe the competition should only be open to amateurs, don't you?'

Leanne didn't, but it wasn't really a surprise. She'd thought the same thing herself.

What did surprise her, though, was that Jarred had chosen this moment to mention it. Why say anything at all? For a second there, the obnoxious Jarred was back, and she wondered whether she'd imagined the other, nicer one. But then, with disconcerting speed, he was back to flirting again.

'It's a pity you have to leave. You could have sampled my cooking,' he said, all twinkly-eyed and as smooth as melted chocolate once more.

'Another time?' she suggested hesitantly, meaning 'never' but not wanting to upset him. There was no point in alienating one of the judges – possibly the most influential judge – when she could just play nice and keep things friendly.

'There's always next week.' He smirked as a parting shot, and with relief she watched him go.

The relief didn't last long, however, as one of the other contestants, a plump woman in her fifties, muttered out of the side of her mouth as she was passing, 'There's nothing like sleeping your way to the top, is there?'

She swept past Leanne, leaving her with her mouth hanging open. Had the woman really said that? More to the point, did everyone else think the same thing?

Oh bother!

Never mind, she thought, she would probably go out in the next round anyway, so they could believe what they bloody well liked.

Chapter 21

Leanne didn't go out in the next round, nor in the one after that, and now there were only eight of the original twelve left and things were starting to get serious.

Which was why she had accepted the offer of a night out with Stevie, Tia and their respective partners. She felt she needed to unwind for once. Ever since she'd entered the competition, it had been all work and more work. Play simply hadn't come into it.

'Bring Rex,' Stevie had suggested. 'It will even up the numbers.'

'You sound like Julia Ferris.' Leanne laughed. Julia – or Lady Tonbridge as she was also known – would shortly become Tia's mother-in-law and was a bit snooty, to say the least.

'God forbid!' Stevie screwed up her nose. 'I've nothing against Julia – she's actually quite nice – but I'm not used to such poshness. Anyway, you know what I mean about bringing Rex.'

'I have no idea what you're talking about.'

'Oh yes you do, lady. Don't act all coy with me. You never stop talking about him.'

Leanne's eyes widened. 'I hadn't noticed,' she protested. 'It's just that he's got some great ideas.'

'Yeah.' Stevie chuckled. 'So you keep telling us. Look, if it makes you feel better, it can just be us girls.'

'No, it's OK. I haven't seen Nick in ages. It'll be good to catch up.'

Rex, to her surprise, had sounded delighted to be invited, and Leanne wondered if he was lonely. It must be hard to move to a completely new part of the country and not know anyone, she thought, resolving to try to include him more. Maybe Saul could be persuaded to have a pint with him. After all, they'd seemed to get on OK on the two occasions they'd met. And Rex had appeared to hold his own when confronted with the madness that was her family.

Now the six friends were in the Duke's Arms enjoying a quiet Friday night drink, which probably wouldn't end up as quiet as it started.

'Gin?' William asked Leanne as he got the first round in.

'Sparkling water with a twist, please,' Leanne replied, and Tia nearly fell out of her wheelchair in shock.

'What's wrong with you?' she asked. She turned to Rex. 'You do realise she normally drinks like a fish, don't you?'

'Oh?' He grinned at Leanne, who pretended to ignore him.

She'd been so pleased – too pleased, actually – when he'd said he'd come that she continually had to tell herself to behave, especially when he was being so teasing and slightly flirty. It didn't help that he looked gorgeous tonight in faded jeans and a plain black T-shirt. The colour set off the bronze highlights in his hair and—

Oh shit. There she went again, thinking romantic thoughts about him. She'd been OK until she'd kissed him... or had she? Maybe not, she admitted to herself, but the kiss most definitely hadn't helped.

Rex, however, had seemed to have forgotten all about it. There wasn't a hint of the discomfort Leanne felt. Although she was convinced everyone could tell what had happened just by looking at the pair of them, in reality she realised Rex was showing no undue interest in her whatsoever. Any fancying was strictly all on one side – hers.

'Sparkling water?' William repeated, and Leanne realised everyone was still staring at her, waiting for a response.

'I've got work in the morning,' she replied, remembering the last time she'd used that excuse. She recognised that it *was* an excuse, because having to get up at a ridiculous hour the following day hadn't stopped her previously. In fact, the real reason she wanted to keep a clear head this evening was because it wouldn't do to get squiffy and make a total prat of herself, not with Rex in such close proximity.

'How are the wedding plans going?' she asked Tia, as much to change the subject as because she had a genuine interest in the answer.

'Ugh. His mother wants to invite half of England – the more influential half, of course – but William and I just want it to be a few close friends plus the necessary relatives.'

'Who's winning?' Nick asked.

'His mother is. She only went ahead and sent out the invites without checking with us first.' Tia shuddered. 'Sorry, Will, but sometimes she's insufferable.'

'Only sometimes?' he joked.

Leanne could see Rex trying to make sense of the conversation and took pity on him. 'Will's parents are Lord and Lady Tonbridge,' she said, then noticed Rex's blank expression and explained further. 'They own Tonbridge Manor, that big white mansion just above Tanglewood. You must have seen it,' she insisted.

He nodded. 'You can't miss it.'

'And Nick is a famous showjumper,' she carried on.

'Really? Nick...?'

'Saunders.'

'I thought I recognised the face,' Rex said.

'Don't be so modest,' Leanne told Nick as he bowed his head. 'You should be proud of yourself.'

'And so should *you*,' Stevie interrupted. 'You've all heard that Leanne is still in the competition?'

'Shh, I'm not supposed to say anything,' Leanne pointed out.

'You can hardly keep it quiet in a place this small,' Tia argued. 'I think everyone already knows. By the way, I hope you've set aside some time to do our wedding flowers?'

'Of course. I'm honoured that you trust me.'

'*Trust you!* Julia can't wait to tell everyone that her son's bridal flowers are being done by none other than the florist who will be designing a display for the Chelsea Flower Show!

'I've got to win first,' Leanne replied.

'You will,' Stevie assured her, and everyone nodded. Their faith in her was touching, even if it was somewhat misplaced.

A few more drinks later, everyone had begun to relax. Except for Leanne, who was strung tighter than a washing line, her nerves only increasing as the night wore on.

To give herself some breathing space, she decided to nip to the loo, but the hoped-for respite didn't happen as Tia followed her in.

'You fancy him, don't you?' were the first words out of her friend's mouth.

'Who?' Leanne washed her hands, refusing to meet Tia's gaze.

'Rex, silly. Who else?' Her friend paused. 'Or *is* there someone else?' She manoeuvred her chair until she was next to Leanne.

'Of course not!' Leanne protested.

'Lea, don't try to deny it. You look like a lovesick calf.'

Leanne frowned. Whatever that was supposed to look like…

'If it's not Rex, it must be someone you've met in London,' Tia insisted.

'Hardly. Four of the other contestants are women, and of the men, one's in his sixties, one is gay and the other is very definitely married.'

'OK, how about someone working on the show?' Clearly Tia wasn't going to let this lie. 'A cameraman? Editor? Key grip?'

'What's a key grip?' Leanne wanted to know.

'I've no idea, but if you watch the credits on any film, there's always someone called that.'

'No, no and no. None of those.'

Tia leapt on the remark. 'So if it's none of *those*, that means it's someone else.' She stared at her reflection, brushing her fingers through her hair. 'It can't be that Rory guy, because he's gay too, so it must be...' She clapped her hands. 'I've got it! It's Jarred What's-his-face, isn't it?'

'No!' Leanne protested, wishing she'd kept her mouth shut about meeting Jarred Townsend. She was beginning to wish she'd never said anything to anyone about the show at all.

'I knew it! You've got the hots for Jarred,' Tia crowed.

'I haven't!' Leanne most definitely didn't, despite his continuing pursuit of her. She'd begun to avoid him, trying not to make it obvious, but it wasn't easy.

'Well I never,' Tia continued, oblivious to Leanne's discomfort. 'What's he like in real life?'

Leanne tried to be diplomatic. 'He knows his stuff,' she began, as the pair of them made their way back to the table.

'I should bloody well hope so, considering he's one of the judges,' Tia interjected. 'I'm not interested in the professional stuff. What's he like as a person?'

'Confident, very sure of himself. Good-looking.'

'I can see that for myself; he's always in the gossip columns,' Tia said. 'Tell me something I don't know.'

'He's a good cook.'

Tia's eyes became as large as the beer mats their drinks rested on. 'Aren't you a sly one?' she said as Leanne slipped into her seat.

'What's she up to now?' Stevie wanted to know, and before Leanne could shush her, Tia said, 'Leanne has been seeing Jarred Townsend.'

'Really! Ooh, what's he like?' Stevie asked.

'He's a good cook,' Tia said.

'He is?' Stevie raised her eyebrows.

'I don't know,' Leanne admitted.

'You just said he was,' Tia protested.

'He hasn't actually cooked for me, so I've only got his say-so to go on.'

'But you'd like him to, right?' Stevie insisted.

'Not really,' Leanne said, but her face felt hot, and she knew she was blushing.

While the others fired questions at her – questions she was unwilling or unable to answer – she noticed that Rex wasn't joining in.

As she tried to turn the conversation away from her imaginary love life, she came to the conclusion that maybe it was best if he did believe she was interested in someone else. At least then he wouldn't think she had the hots for him, when he so obviously wasn't interested in her.

Chapter 22

Rex couldn't get Leanne out of his mind, and he was seriously annoyed about it. Forget about her, he told himself as he stuffed a pair of waterproof trousers into his rucksack. She was seeing someone else, someone far more interesting than him. Someone who could offer her much more than a mere park ranger could. Someone who knew his daisies from his marigolds.

Wondering what else he'd need for today, he became even more annoyed as he couldn't remember what he'd already packed. See, that was another reason why he should stop thinking about Leanne Green – she made him lose concentration at a time when he needed to focus. He was joining the Mountain Rescue team for another training exercise, and as he crossly checked the contents of his rucksack, he tried once more to think about something else.

Catching Nell's expectant expression, he immediately felt guilty he wasn't able to take her with him.

As usual when he went out without his dog, he ensured she had plenty of water, that her biscuit bowl was full and that a selection of toys and chews were scattered across the floor to keep her happy. But he knew she wouldn't be truly content until he returned. She wasn't old enough to begin her rescue dog training yet, so he had no choice but to go to the session today on his own. Reluctantly, because he hated leaving her by herself for any length of time, he closed the kitchen door on her reproachful little face.

He took the road to Brecon and then onto the A470, which would lead him to the Storey Arms, an outdoor centre at the base of Pen y Fan. On a rainy Monday, the car park near the centre was only half full. The fair-weather walkers didn't usually venture up the highest peak in South Wales on days like today, and only a few diehards would be out, so it was perfect weather for a search-and-rescue practice mission.

Clouds hung low, obscuring the upper slopes of the mountains, and fog was coming in fast, scudding like dragon's breath along the valley floor. The temperature wasn't much above freezing; at these altitudes it was common to have severe frost or even snow around Easter, whereas nearer the coast it could be a balmy twelve degrees Celsius and sunny. It was the changeability of the weather and the deceptive ruggedness of the terrain that Rex especially enjoyed, and he was really looking forward to today.

The other team members greeted him like an old friend, and he realised how much he'd missed this kind of camaraderie. The awkwardness he'd felt last night with Leanne and her friends – although they'd done their best to include him – dropped away. Here he was in familiar territory, with like-minded people, in the mountains he was beginning to love; he felt instantly calmer, as if nature herself had thrown a comforting blanket over his shoulders.

While the rescuee went off to find somewhere to hide, Rex and the rest of the team loitered near the tuck van in the car park, enjoying cups of builder's tea and stuffing their faces with bacon butties smeared with HP sauce while they waited for their cue.

The usual scenario for a real rescue was that the team would have a location or a 'last seen' to work towards, and today they intended to replicate that situation. As soon as the casualty radioed she was ready, they set off.

Rex stayed towards the back, observing everything carefully, especially the search-and-rescue dog. The English springer spaniel's tail hadn't stopped wagging from the moment Rex had set eyes on it. The dog repeatedly dashed to the end of its lead, casting around for a scent. Every now and again it would stop to cock its head, its nose twitching, then it was off again, dragging its handler up the track.

Rex had read up on search-and-rescue dogs, and he knew they could accomplish the work of twenty to thirty humans with their boundless energy, their incredible sense of smell and hearing and their better night vision. They especially came into their own in the mountains, when it was so easy for walkers to become disorientated in low cloud and wander off the path. It didn't take long for someone to develop hypothermia up here, and time became even more critical if that person was injured.

Rescue scenarios varied immensely, and the team tried to practise for all eventualities. A typical one was receiving a report that someone hadn't made it home when they were supposed to, which meant the dog had to track by scent. But today they were practising an accident situation, and having been told over the radio that the 'casualty' had fallen off Corn Du, a sister peak to Pen y Fan that was notorious for its steep, rocky drops, especially on its western flank, the team left the path and headed out through the tussocky grass and clumps of heather.

There, the going was harder. Familiarity with the terrain didn't necessarily prevent a misstep, which could result in a twisted or broken ankle. No one wanted to be a casualty for real, so the pace slowed accordingly.

The dog became more focused as the hikers on the path behind them faded from view, and although his tail still wagged nineteen to the dozen, it was clear to see he knew the real work had started.

They'd travelled only two hundred yards or so from the path, and already it could no longer be seen. They were in the clouds and the going became even slower, the team leader stopping every so often to check his GPS.

The casualty had been given instructions not to shout for help, thus making it harder for the dog, and Rex guessed that another twenty minutes or so went by before they reached her approximate location. She should be around here somewhere.

He watched in fascination as the dog handler unclipped the lead from the spaniel's harness and let him loose. It was too dangerous for the rescuers to wander around so close to the treacherous slope, but once they had a firm location, they could clip together and make the descent. Setting the dog free was a wise move. The canine was much more sure-footed than any human, and could cover three or four times the distance in the same amount of time.

Rex quickly lost sight of the spaniel and waited anxiously until it reappeared. Trained to cast out and come back repeatedly, the dog didn't seem to tire; when it failed to return after the seventh attempt, however, he began to worry. Not even dogs were invincible.

A faint bark reached them and everyone paused to listen.

'He's found her,' the dog handler said, but when Rex began to move off in the direction of the noise, the man added, 'Wait. Blue will come back and guide us in.'

Indeed, he'd no sooner finished speaking than the dog emerged from the mist and halted, one paw lifted, his head cocked to the side. He barked again.

'Lead us to her, boy,' the handler said. 'Find, Blue, find.'

Blue found, dashing ahead then returning to the group until eventually he led them to the casualty, who was lying immobile in the grass pretending to be unconscious. Not an inconceivable situation.

Rex watched as the dog raced over to the woman and lay down beside her, crawling as close as he could and waiting for his handler to tell him what a good and clever boy he was.

The spaniel received his reward – a favourite toy – and as the team assessed the 'injured' woman and made pretend calls to base, the dog and his handler stepped aside, their work for the day done. Rex studied the way the woman was lifted onto the spinal board, then he took his turn carrying her down the mountain. They had to be extremely careful not to cause her any more damage, since there was no knowing just how badly injured she was, so the hike back down wasn't nearly as easy as he'd assumed it would be.

Every so often the casualty would tell him he needed to keep his end of the spinal board up, to hold her as level as possible in case of back or neck injury. By the time they crossed the wooden bridge over the little river that ran alongside the car park, his shoulders and arms were on fire.

Bloody hell, that had been hard.

'You did good, mate,' the team leader said, clapping him on the back. 'A couple more of these and you'll be ready to go out with us for real. Coming for coffee and cake?'

It was a bit of a tradition after a rescue or a training session, and as Rex slid behind the wheel of his car, he felt he was really becoming accepted as part of the community. It felt good.

Now all he had to do was to forget a certain pair of brown eyes and he could be content.

Easier said than done, though, wasn't it?

Chapter 23

It was no good, Leanne couldn't forget the feel of Rex's arms around her, the taste of his lips on hers or the smell of his aftershave. No matter how hard she tried, she couldn't get him out of her head.

She'd not seen him since the evening with Stevie and Tia last week, and it wasn't as though she'd spent a great deal of time in his company prior to that, but she missed him, darn it. Not just because of his ideas, either – although she could certainly use his unique take on things right now.

Should she give him a call? She could use the excuse that she wanted to pick his brains... or maybe not, because he might think the only time she contacted him was when she wanted something.

Perhaps she could suggest dinner, or drinks, or even a coffee. Would he accept, and if he did would he be agreeing simply out of friendship and inherent good manners? Or would he give her some lame excuse and refuse? She didn't know which would be worse. Besides, he wasn't interested, so she'd only be torturing herself, and she'd told herself more than once that she needed to focus on the competition; everything else was a distraction.

Desperate to get away from the shop for a couple of hours, she left the increasingly competent Mabel in charge and nipped to the bank.

With the business stuff taken care of, and not wanting to return to work just yet, she decided to call into Peggy's. Stevie was level-headed and could always be counted on to give good advice. *If* Leanne decided to confide in her, that is.

To her disappointment, Stevie wasn't there and neither was Cassandra. Betty was in charge and loving every second of it.

'Cassandra's gone into labour,' she announced with excitement when Leanne asked about her friend. 'Stevie's taking her to the hospital.'

'What about Aiden?'

'They can't get hold of him. He's probably in his workshop with that noisy saw of his going full blast. It's a girl,' Betty added.

'Oh, she's actually had it, has she?' Leanne asked.

'Not yet.'

'How do you know it's a girl then?' Leanne knew full well that neither Cassandra nor her husband wanted to know the gender of the baby. 'Or do you think it's because she's carrying it low, or high, or something?'

'Pish, all those things are old wives' tales,' Betty said dismissively.

'So how do you know? Crystal ball?'

Betty's face closed up and she heaved a sigh. 'Summat like that,' she muttered as she stomped back to the counter to fulfil Leanne's order of a pot of tea and a scone.

Leanne smiled. Betty had a reputation for being slightly eccentric, and making comments like that only served to play to her audience. She was as daft as a box of frogs, but there wasn't any harm in her. In fact, if it hadn't been for Betty, neither Tia nor Stevie would be arranging their weddings right now.

When she returned to Leanne's table with her order, the old woman was wearing an entirely different expression. 'That ranger man was in here earlier,' she said.

'Oh?'

'He's nice.' Betty plonked her skinny frame down in a chair and stole a bit of Leanne's scone, chewing noisily.

'Yes, he is,' Leanne agreed politely, careful to keep her face blank.

'You'd make a perfect couple,' the old woman said, 'if you can sort yourselves out.'

'Excuse me?' Leanne paused in the middle of spreading jam on a scone.

'It's cream first, then jam,' Betty pointed out. 'Everyone knows that.'

'I like jam first, and it's *my* scone.' Leanne playfully slapped Betty's reaching fingers away. 'Get one of your own.'

'It's the last one,' Betty said. 'I'd make some more but my rheumatism is playing up summat awful.'

'Oh, sorry. Here, you have it. I'll have something else.'

'Don't want it now you've done it wrong. Cream first, then jam.'

Leanne rolled her eyes.

'It's that kind of attitude that will drive your young man away,' Betty stated.

'I haven't got a young man.'

'Ah, but you have, if you only knew it.' Betty's eyes twinkled.

'I haven't. He's not interested.'

'You think?'

'I know.' Leanne put down the knife she had been wielding, her appetite suddenly gone.

'How do you know? Has he said?' Betty asked.

'No, but look, I've no idea why I'm discussing this with you.'

'Oh, I think you do,' Betty replied calmly. She hauled herself to her feet and Leanne assumed the bizarre conversation was at an end.

No such luck. Betty returned with a cup and saucer, and proceeded to pour herself some tea. Leanne watched in fascination as the old lady transferred half the contents of her cup into the saucer, blew on the liquid, then proceeded to suck it up, smacking her lips in appreciation as she did so. She wondered why Betty had bothered with the cup in the first place.

'Right,' Betty said when she had drained her saucer. Actually, the slurping noises she'd made sounded remarkably like a drain themselves. 'You like him, he likes you. What's the problem?'

Leanne pursed her lips. 'For one thing, I don't like him. I mean, I do,' she amended hastily, 'but not like that. Two, Rex doesn't like me. *Like me* like me, I mean.'

'How do you know?' Betty asked again.

'Women know these things,' Leanne replied loftily.

'Pah! That's a load of old tosh if ever I heard it. You're too young to know your arse from your elbow. Wait until you get to my age, then you can say you know things. You clearly don't know anything.'

Leanne finally lost patience. 'Look, he kissed me, OK? Then he regretted it.'

'Did he *say* he regretted it? What sort of kiss was it? Did he—'

'Hold it there, Betty. I'm not going to discuss Rex McMillan's kissing technique with you.'

'Oh dear, it was that good, was it? You've sure got it bad, my lovely.'

'No. I. Haven't.' Leanne gritted her teeth so hard she thought it might take her dad's crowbar to prise her jaws open.

'If you like him that much, do something about it,' Betty said.

'I don't like him that much. He's not too keen on me either, not in that way... Wait a minute.' Leanne leaned forward and put her elbows on the table. 'How do you know how he feels about me? Has he said something?'

Betty examined her empty saucer. 'He might have.'

'What's he said?' Leanne demanded.

'That would be telling.'

'Betty...' Leanne's growl sounded remarkably like Nell's doggy ones.

'Are you going to eat that scone, or are you just going to look at it all afternoon?' Betty asked.

'Have it.' Leanne pushed the plate towards the old woman, who dived on it like a gannet who hadn't seen a herring for a week. 'And stop trying to change the subject. You started this, you're going to have to finish it.'

Through a mouthful of baked goods Betty retorted, 'I could say the same about you.'

'What do you mean? I didn't start anything. *He* kissed *me!*'

'He doesn't *like you* like you, but he kissed you anyway?' the old lady gloated. 'Explain that.'

'I can't. It was a mistake, an accident. I could tell he regretted it straight away.'

'Was that before or after the tongues bit?'

Leanne shook her head. The woman was incorrigible.

'If he didn't say he didn't like it, how do you know he didn't enjoy it as much as you did?' Betty continued relentlessly.

'Because he pushed me away.'

'So?'

'Betty, you're not making sense.'

'Is he married?' Betty asked.

'No.'

'Got a girlfriend?'

'No.'

'Then he's not feeling guilty and he doesn't want you just for sex, either.'

'Betty!'

'Well, he doesn't. If he did, he'd have got on with it, and it would have been wham, bam, thank you, ma'am, can we do it again sometime?'

Despite herself, Leanne barked out a laugh. She simply couldn't hold it in. Betty was a hoot, even if she didn't have a clue what she was talking about.

'I bet he'd take the sex if it was on offer, though,' the old lady was saying. 'Have you tried that tactic?'

'No, I most certainly have not.'

She let out a grunt. 'It's probably wise. There's no point in supplying him with all the milk he can drink if you want him to buy the cow.'

'You're too much!'

'And you're not enough. A man kisses you passionately and makes you go weak at the knees...' Betty held up a

155

hand when Leanne tried to interrupt. 'Then you get the idea in your noggin that he's not interested in you. Of course he bloody well is.'

'So why hasn't he bothered with me since?' Leanne couldn't believe she was having this conversation with a mad octogenarian baker.

'Have you bothered with *him*?' Betty countered.

'No, but—'

'It works both ways, my dear. Maybe he thinks you're the one who isn't interested.'

'I'm not.'

'There you go, then. You've been sending him bugger-off signals. No wonder the poor bloke doesn't know whether he's coming or going. You need to decide whether you want him or not. To do that, you've got to listen to your heart, not your...' Betty trailed off.

'Betty!'

'Your *head*, I was going to say, before I lost my train of thought. You're already thinking with your...'

Leanne shook her head in disbelief. But something Betty said stuck with her until the evening, and was still on her mind the following morning.

Maybe Rex did think she wasn't interested. After all, she'd made it fairly plain that she was focused on winning *Budding Stars*, and Tia had insinuated there was something going on between her and Jarred Townsend.

But the Jarred insinuation bit had occurred after the kiss. Although to be fair, she might have given the impression she had no time for romance right now.

That's because you don't, a little voice in her head said. *What's the point of starting something you might not be able to finish?*

Go away, she told it. If she worked on that premise, then she would never have applied for *Budding Stars*, because there was no guarantee she wouldn't go out next week or the week after.

So concentrate on the competition, and if you don't win, take a crack at Rex, the voice said.

Take a crack, indeed! That little voice really did need to shut up now. Anyway, who said she couldn't do both?

You did, remember?

Oh, go away!

The voice finally fell silent and Leanne was left to decide whether she should follow her heart or her head.

Chapter 24

'Hi, it's me, Leanne.' A nervous giggle followed.

Rex hoped it *was* nerves; for all he knew, Jarred Townsend could have been tickling her feet with a feather. Although that wasn't very likely given the rest of the message.

'Um, do you fancy going out sometime? For a meal or a drink or something? Like a date?' She paused.

Like a date, or an *actual* date? Rex wondered, for the ninth time. Yeah, he'd listened to the message that many times already.

'Anyway, call me if you do. I'm free every night except Wednesday – I'll be in London, you see. Please, please, please don't think it's because I want to pick your brains again. Although it would be great if I could run something past you. Oh, that still sounds as if I only want you for your mind. Oh shit, now you think I want you for your body.' Another pause. 'I mean, I do, but… Oh bugger. Look, if you fancy going out sometime, phone me, or text me, or… Damn. Scratch that, I'm sounding desperate.' Another pause was followed by another nervous laugh. 'Anyway, if you don't, I'll completely understand. Er… bye.'

Could she really be interested in him? His heart gave a little lurch and he made the decision to text her.

How about tonight?

Tonight was only a couple of hours away – it was already five o'clock. Maybe it was too short notice for her.

Great! Where do you fancy going? was the instant reply.

He had no idea. *Up to you,* he responded lamely.

A long wait followed, which he filled by making a coffee and checking his phone every few seconds with the obsession of a teenager hoping for likes on Instagram.

How about if you come to mine for a meal? he suggested when the wait became too much. Then he worried he was being overly forward and she might jump to the wrong conclusion.

I thought you couldn't cook? she texted back.

He couldn't – unlike Jarred bloody Townsend. *Take-away? The Chinese is good.* He knew that from first-hand experience, having had a meal from there at least once a week since he arrived in Tanglewood.

OK. 7?

Great. Rex put the phone down, a huge grin spreading across his face, only for it to disappear as quickly as it had arrived as he gazed around his living room.

He spent the next hour or so frantically tidying up, emptying the bin in the kitchen and giving the bathroom a quick clean.

A knock twenty minutes later made him jump, and he scrambled to pull a clean T-shirt over his head. Barefoot, he padded downstairs to open the door.

She looked amazing, and for a moment he was speech-less.

'Are you going to let me in?' she joked. 'Or are we going to eat on the garden path?'

'Sorry.' He stepped to the side, inhaling her perfume as she came close. Bloody hell, she smelled almost good enough to eat!

He watched her walk ahead of him into the living room, admiring the sway of her hips and the curve of her bum in her tight jeans. She was wearing a pretty turquoise top that left her shoulders bare, and he had an insane urge to kiss the smooth, tanned skin it revealed.

He coughed and cleared his throat, tamping down his libido. Leanne wasn't here to be ravished the minute she walked in the door; she was here for dinner, and although he would have loved nothing better than to sweep her into his arms and carry her off to bed, he reined himself in. She clearly liked and trusted him, or else she wouldn't be in his home; he didn't want to do anything to jeopardise that. Maybe, after a few more dates, she'd let him kiss her again.

Deep in thought, he didn't realise she'd stopped suddenly until he walked into her, nearly knocking her over. He made a grab for her, only to find that his arms went around her waist of their own accord. Then his nose was in her hair and she was half turning to him, and without conscious thought his mouth found hers.

The kiss was soft at first, a brush of lips, the hint of her breath on his cheek, the tantalising taste of her. He let out a small groan and crushed her to him, his mouth claiming hers fully, his tongue slipping between those delectable lips.

It took everything he had to gently disengage himself, common sense gradually winning over desire. He consoled himself with the fact that she seemed as eager as he did. Could he really begin to hope she'd enjoyed it as much as he had?

Her cheeks were flushed and her lips were parted as she gazed up at him with an inscrutable expression.

He held his breath, waiting for her to slap him or run away.

She did neither. 'How about we order?' she suggested, and he noticed that her voice was as shaky as he guessed his would be.

Slow down, Rex my boy, he told himself, and the realisation that his internal voice sounded exactly like his dad's killed the mood instantly. There was nothing like imagining your father looking over your shoulder as you held a beautiful girl in your arms to dampen your ardour.

Actually, he was quite thankful for that.

'I'll fetch the menu,' he said, releasing her and stepping back. He indicated that she should take a seat. 'What would you like?'

'I eat most things,' she said, and laughed. 'You can't accuse me of being fussy. When I was a child, I had to get in there fast, otherwise my brothers would polish off the lot.'

While they waited for their meal to be delivered, they chatted easily.

'Did you enjoy growing up on a farm?' Rex asked her.

'It was the best,' she said, then added, 'Most of the time. It was great when I was small, though it got a bit harder when I had to keep begging Mum and Dad for lifts as a teenager. I couldn't simply pop down to the river on a Saturday evening for a sip of stolen vodka like my mates did. I had to rely on someone to give me a lift, then pick me up afterwards. After a while, I got a bit cannier and tried to get one of my brothers to fetch me. At least they didn't lecture me if they knew I'd been having a sneaky drink or two.' She smiled.

'On the other hand,' she continued, 'I learnt how to drive a tractor as soon as my legs were long enough for my feet to touch the pedals. I used to love nothing better than helping around the farm. My parents didn't object to a bit of free labour either, and I didn't get special treatment just because I was a girl. Actually,' she giggled, 'I'm still a girl, in case you hadn't noticed.'

Oh, he'd noticed all right. How could he fail not to when he'd kissed those luscious lips not once, but twice? And when she was sitting next to him on the sofa, with her shoes off and her pink-tipped toes curled up beneath her. She was even doing the girlie thing of hugging one of the cushions to her chest. He wished she was hugging him instead.

Thankfully, their meal arrived at that exact moment, so he was able to concentrate on setting it out on the table rather than on what he'd really like to do – kiss her.

He watched with amusement as she ate. There was no delicate picking or playing with her food like his ex used to do; Leanne set to with gusto, and even though he'd ordered enough to feed a small army, she made an admirable attempt to clear her plate.

His appetite matched hers – a day spent on the mountain used up a considerable number of calories, and he was surprised to discover just how hungry he was.

'That's it, I'm stuffed,' Leanne announced, putting her fork down and leaning back in her chair.

Bless her, she offered to help clear everything away, but she was his guest and he wanted to impress her, so he insisted she stayed put while he made them both a coffee, glad he hadn't suggested opening the bottle of white wine that was chilling nicely in the fridge. He didn't want her to think he was plying her with alcohol just so she wouldn't be able to get home.

When he walked back into the living room with a mug of coffee in each hand, Leanne was sitting on the floor tickling Nell's tummy.

'You wanted to keep her, didn't you?' he asked.

She shrugged. 'I always want to keep them, and not just the puppies, either. I used to bawl my eyes out whenever my dad sent one of the hand-reared lambs to market.'

'Didn't you want to be a farmer yourself?'

'Not really. It's such hard work, and you have to arrange for someone to look after the farm if you want to go on holiday. Which is why we never went anywhere when we were kids. And if you're ill – tough. The animals still need seeing to. I can't remember my mum or dad ever taking a day off. The only time we went anywhere was to the Royal Welsh Show, but that was still classed as work. I'll have to ask my dad to show you the trophies and rosettes he won.' She smiled fondly. 'What about you? What was Glenshona like?'

He shrugged. 'It's a small village, with the sea on one side and mountains on the other.'

'You must find Tanglewood very different,' she said.

'Not really. I've still got the mountains and I love my job.' He went on to tell her about taking a class of children into the Beacons, and about the painting competition. 'It was great fun,' he finished, 'seeing all those inquisitive little faces.'

'Do you want kids one day?' she asked him.

'Oh yes. Two, maybe three.'

Looking back later, he could pinpoint that this was the exact moment when the atmosphere between them changed. The easy-going chatter stopped abruptly, and the air became charged.

He stared into Leanne's eyes; she stared back, the depths of hers drawing him in.

This time, when their lips met, it was more tender than passionate, and he scooted closer, his arms reaching for her.

She sank into them as though she belonged there, and he tightened his embrace as her own arms snaked around his neck.

When they finally came up for air, there was no embarrassment or awkwardness, only the knowledge – on Rex's part at least – that this was the start of something new and wonderful.

And as he watched her get into her car and drive away, many kisses later, he understood that he would never be the same again.

It was too soon to say if what he felt was love, but if it wasn't, it was pretty damn close!

Chapter 25

Leanne's concentration was shot to pieces. When she should be focusing on the unseen task, all she could think about was blue eyes smiling down into hers and that delicious mouth hovering inches from her own.

It was five days since she'd seen Rex, and every one of them was proving to be longer than the last, which was ironic considering there was so much going on in her life right now.

She kept thinking back to the other night. They'd got on so well (snogging aside) and she felt as though she'd known him for ages. After their meal, they'd spent the rest of the evening cuddling on the sofa, listening to music. She smiled as she recalled teasing him about his penchant for heavy metal from the 1970s when he'd inadvertently clicked on a Deep Purple track, before he'd found some Ed Sheeran to listen to – much more suitable for snuggling. They'd parted with a date fixed for this coming Sunday, when he'd promised to take her to a secluded spot to watch beavers. Who knew there were beavers in the area? William did apparently, because they'd been released onto his family's land, and Rex had asked whether he could see them.

Leanne couldn't wait, but she wasn't entirely certain it was the beavers she was excited about. She had an inkling it was more to do with the hunky park ranger who'd be accompanying her.

Right now, though, she shouldn't be thinking of beavers or Rex – she should be focusing on her unseen design.

The brief was to design a 'Picture of Flowers', and so far she was stumped.

Then it came to her – lilies!

What was more perfect than a painting that featured flowers? She could do a living version, if only she could remember what Monet's lily painting looked like in the first place. Or poppies maybe – that might work, but she didn't think she'd spotted any of the scarlet blooms in the chiller.

Putting all other thoughts out of her head, she set about making her display. But every so often an image of him would appear in her mind, and every time it did, she couldn't help smiling to herself.

'You seem happy today,' Jarred said in her ear, making her jump.

She did a quick scan of the set, just to make sure that none of the cameras were pointed directly at her. There were three mobile ones, plus another two up in the metal rafters that were operated remotely; she knew those were running at all times, so she couldn't do anything about them, but at least there wasn't one right in her face picking up every word.

She caught one of the other contestants, Desiree, shooting her a filthy look, but she ignored her. They were down to seven now, including herself, and she thanked her lucky stars she was still in the competition.

'I am happy,' she replied, conscious that Jarred was waiting for her to say something. 'I'm just pleased to still be here.'

'And why wouldn't you be? You're a talented floral artiste.'

Floral artiste? She'd never been called that before. It sounded a far cry from a simple florist. She was aware that even if she crashed out of the competition now, just having got this far would do wonders for her career and her business.

'Have you thought any more about letting me cook dinner for you?' Jarred was asking.

'Er... sure. I mean...' She hadn't – not at all.

'No pressure; I'd like to get to know you better, that's all,' he said. 'How about tonight? After filming?'

Dear Lord, what was she supposed to say to that?

'Is it allowed?' she asked, hoping the answer would be no, giving her a get-out clause.

Jarred shrugged. 'No one has said it isn't.'

Which was how Leanne came to find herself perched awkwardly on a stool in a penthouse apartment, watching Jarred Townsend throw an assortment of vegetables into a wok and wondering how she'd allowed herself to be talked into this.

To be fair to Jarred, he hadn't actually made a physical move on her, and he was quite a good cook too, she discovered after he placed a sizzling dish in front of her.

To her surprise, and despite her trepidation about what was to follow, she devoured the lot.

Eventually, with the meal finished and a glass of chilled sparkling white wine in her hand, Jarred made his move. But it wasn't the sort of move she'd been expecting.

'I want to offer you a job,' he announced.

Leanne, having just taken a sip of her drink, spluttered, dribbled some down her chin, then broke into a coughing fit.

'A job?' she managed to squeak when she got herself under control.

'Yes. A job.'

'What kind of job?'

'The sort where you work for me and I pay you for it,' he teased.

It might be the wine, but suddenly Jarred didn't look as predatory as she'd originally thought.

'Doing what?' she asked.

'I want you to spearhead my new venture.' He leant forward on the breakfast bar, steepling his hands under his chin. 'You gave me an idea the very first time we met,' he went on. 'As you know, the flower industry is quite resource-intensive and the growing season in the UK is very short, which is why we have to import so much from the Continent or grow them under greenhouse conditions. It all costs money and it's no good for the planet.'

Leanne had to close her mouth, which was hanging open. She'd never in a million years have taken Jarred Townsend for an environmentalist. His next sentence proved her correct.

'It's the way forward, the future; everyone is trying to show that they're doing their bit. The florist industry must follow suit, and I intend to be at the head of the game.'

'Oh? *Oh.*'

'Everyone who's anyone is trying to reduce, reuse and recycle. Take the big supermarkets, for instance – all of them are rushing to exchange plastics for more environmentally friendly products.'

'But flower arranging is hardly in the same league,' Leanne protested.

Jarred gave a little moue. 'It's not,' he agreed, 'but we have an obligation to make it not such a throwaway industry. Yes, our customers can compost their bouquets, their bunches of carnations and their buttonholes, but I want to take it further, much further, and I believe you're the woman to help me do exactly that. Your reusable wedding bouquet was genius; so inspired.'

He didn't actually look all that pleased about it. In fact, Leanne thought he seemed positively annoyed that he hadn't come up with the idea himself.

'You don't need me for this,' she argued, aware that she might be talking herself out of one of the most exciting jobs she could ever imagine being offered.

'Oh, but I do,' he replied. 'You're already getting a reputation in the field – Pauline and Christel have both remarked upon it. You'll be the perfect face and brains for the venture. With your ideas and my name and resources, it can't fail.'

And if it does, Leanne thought, hearing the words he wasn't saying as well as the ones coming out of his mouth, he can walk away from it with his reputation intact, and leave me to pick up the pieces.

Risk aside, though, it was a very exciting prospect indeed.

'Are you on board?' he asked.

'Can I think about it? I'd like to get the competition out of the way first.'

'Of course. Whether you go out before the final or not, the offer still stands. I think we could do glorious business together.'

Leanne thought back to some of the winners of shows like *Bake Off*. One woman had gone on to do great things and was now an established celebrity with a column in a national newspaper, but Leanne was never going to be in the same league as Jarred Townsend.

'What will the winner say? Or the viewers?' she wanted to know. 'Especially if I go out in the next couple of weeks.'

Jarred waved a hand dismissively. 'Who cares? What I do with my own business is exactly that – my own business. It won't detract from the winner in any way.'

Leanne thought it might, but she didn't say anything. If he'd made the same offer to someone else and Leanne had won, she might feel a bit miffed that she hadn't been handed such a wonderful opportunity.

'Think about it, take your time,' he continued. 'I want you to work for me, and if you do, you'll have a glittering future ahead of you.'

Yes, she would, wouldn't she? She could take him up on his offer right now and her future would be assured. But first there was something she wanted to do.

She wanted to win!

Chapter 26

'Where exactly are we going?' Leanne asked as she followed Rex's broad back along what was little more than a steep track.

'You'll see,' he said.

Leanne had thought she knew her patch of the Brecon Beacons quite well, but she'd never been along this particular valley before. Mind you, she didn't normally venture onto Lord Tonbridge's land that often, either.

They'd been walking for nearly an hour now, following a stream, and were deep in woodland. Birds sang in the trees, and every so often a clearing would reveal a spread of nodding bluebells, the sunlight dappling through the canopy of leaves like spotlights in one of nature's finest theatres. Even if they didn't get to see the elusive beavers, the scenery alone made the whole trip magical.

Then, without warning, the trees opened up and a still, calm pond appeared.

'Is that what I think it is?' Leanne whispered, pointing at an untidy pile of branches, rocks and mud at the edge of it.

'A beavers' dam, yes.'

'Oh wow!' A trickle of water emanated from the dam's base, and the gurgle mingled with the birdsong.

'It's a little late in the day,' Rex said. 'William told me that beavers are more active in the early morning, but I didn't think you'd appreciate hiking through the woods in the dark.'

The sun hadn't quite risen yet, but it had been light enough when they set out for them to be able to see where they were going without the need for torches. It was still early, and the peacefulness of the little pond and its clearing was definitely worth getting up for.

Rex led her towards the hide and they slipped inside.

'The beavers probably know we're here,' he whispered, 'but if we're quiet, hopefully they'll show themselves.'

He had packed two pairs of binoculars, and he handed one to Leanne.

'See those stumps over there?' He pointed to the far side of the pond. 'Notice how the edges are raw? That's typical beaver work.'

'They look like badly sharpened pencils,' Leanne answered softly, and she saw Rex biting back a laugh.

'They gnaw all around the base of the tree, then let gravity do its work. Once the tree is felled, they slice it up into manageable lengths, drag it to the water's edge, then let the current carry it downstream to the damn. The smaller branches, the ones with loads of leaves on, are used for food.'

'I always wondered what beavers ate,' she said. 'For some reason I thought it was fish.'

'You're thinking of otters. I'll take you to see some of those next time. There's a holt further up the River Usk, and I've heard they've got kits.'

'I'd like that.' It was amazing – she'd lived in the area all her life and thought she knew most of the wildlife.

Clearly she was wrong. She'd never been lucky enough to see an otter, but she had seen plenty of other things, such as foxes, rabbits, herons and kingfishers. Otters, though? And beavers! Wow. Just wow!

She wished she could capture the magic of the scene in her work, and she suddenly understood where Jarred was coming from. To be able to bring even a tiny piece of this wonderland into people's homes, offices, churches and function rooms would be special indeed. While Jarred might be looking at the commercial angle – the profit to be made and the bottom line – Leanne would be looking to bring nature inside. Together they could make a formidable team.

But – and there was a very big but indeed – there was no way she could work out of her little flower shop in Tanglewood. It would mean moving to London.

Hang on, wasn't that what she wanted? Why else had she entered *Budding Stars* in the first place? She recalled her restlessness at the start of the year, the feeling she had of needing something more and the excitement she'd experienced when sending her entry off.

Wasn't that what she was working towards – new horizons, new challenges, new experiences? Not to mention a new outlet for her creative talent.

So why was she suddenly feeling reluctant at the thought of leaving all this behind?

'Look.' Rex nudged her arm, bringing her out of her thoughts.

A ripple radiated across the still water. Then another. A brown head broke the surface, a chevron of wavelets following it.

Leanne held her breath, her eyes wide with wonder, as the beaver trundled onto the bank like a shaggy tank. It was smaller than she'd imagined.

'There'll be another one nearby,' Rex said. 'William told me this is a breeding pair.'

'Which is this, the male or the female?'

'No idea. But I do know that the female rules the roost, so this is probably the male, dispatched to bring his lady some breakfast.'

'Ha, ha!'

They watched as the beaver rooted around in the undergrowth before disappearing from view.

'Do they have any natural predators in this country?' Leanne asked, fearful for the beaver's safety so far away from the pond.

'The adults don't, but any beaver kits would be a tasty morsel for a fox. I bet a stoat or a weasel wouldn't say no, either. Which is why beavers build a dam in the first place. The lodge is in the deep water in the middle. See?' He pointed to a bunch of branches in the centre of the pond, and Leanne focused her binoculars on what she had originally assumed was a pile of driftwood.

'The only access is underwater, so the kits are really safe in there,' he explained.

'I wonder if there are any babies in there now?' she mused.

'William said something about putting cameras inside the lodge next year,' Rex told her, and when Leanne had the disconcerting realisation that she probably wouldn't be around to see them, disappointment swept over her once more.

Don't be daft, she told herself. It wasn't as if she was emigrating. She could come home as often as she wished. She was already travelling back and forth to London every week, although the strain was beginning to tell on her.

Thinking about Jarred's offer led her to thoughts of her flower shop. Would she still keep it on? She had no idea, but it was something else she had to consider.

They watched for a while longer, but when the beaver didn't make a second appearance, Rex put down his binoculars and opened his rucksack.

Croissants and coffee – how marvellous! Leanne was starving, and she ate every morsel before leaning back against the wall of the hide, cradling a plastic mug of coffee in her hands.

'What's your next task?' Rex asked.

She told him about the previous Thursday, and that she was still in the contest (*round seven, squee!*), but she'd yet to discuss Jarred's offer with him. Actually, she didn't know if she was going to mention it at all until she'd made up her mind. She had to get everything straight in her head first.

When Rex gently removed the mug from her hands and pulled her close, burying his fingers in her hair, kissing her until she was breathless, she was even more determined not to say anything until she had some definite news.

She was starting to fall heavily for this lovely man and she hoped he felt the same way about her. Until she'd actually decided if she was going to accept the job, there was no point in telling him that the most he could expect was a long-distance relationship.

She sank into his embrace, and for a while neither the competition nor Jarred's offer crossed her mind.

Chapter 27

Rex squinted at the number on his phone. It was a number he recognised but hadn't expected to see again.

'Hello?' His voice was tentative, almost reluctant. Why on earth was Jules calling him? Everything to do with the house had been settled a few weeks ago, and he'd received a bank transfer for his half of the property, but he hadn't wanted to know if she'd sold it or simply bought him out. He had simply been relieved that the ties between them were finally severed. As far as he knew, she didn't have any reason to contact him. Unless she'd heard he was going to visit his parents tomorrow and fancied meeting up for old times' sake.

He frowned, not fancying the idea.

'Rex? Is that you?'

'Jules. Hi.' Her voice was so familiar, his heart gave a small lurch. They'd been good together, once.

'I… um… We need to talk,' she said.

'We do? What about?'

There was a long pause. 'I'm pregnant.'

Oh. He hadn't been expecting that, and he wondered who the father was and why his ex-girlfriend felt the need to phone to tell him—

Oh hell.

'Whose is it?' he asked. His voice was hoarse and he felt as though he'd just been kicked in the stomach. 'Is it mine?'

There was a silence on the other end.

'Jules, please, you've got to tell me,' he begged. He staggered to an armchair and slumped into it.

When she finally answered, her voice was barely above a whisper. 'I don't know.'

'You must know!' Rex was stunned. How could she not know? He closed his eyes, then slowly opened them again.

'I'm sorry—' she began.

'*Sorry?*' he yelled, then stopped and took a deep breath. Shouting wouldn't do any good, no matter how much he felt like it. 'Tell me,' he said, in a slightly calmer tone of voice.

'I don't know where to start...'

Rex pictured her standing by the living room window in the house they'd once shared, staring out at the street, nibbling her finger. She often used to stand in that very spot when she was on the phone.

Oh God.

'The beginning?' he suggested, trying to keep calm.

'When we were still together, I... um... fell for someone else.'

Rex swallowed. He knew things hadn't been brilliant between them, but he hadn't expected *this*.

'We... I didn't mean for it to happen, but it did. I didn't want to hurt you, neither of us did.' She hesitated.

Rex began to feel sick.

'Me and Dean—' she said, but Rex didn't let her get any further.

'You and *Dean*? My *best friend* Dean?' He didn't believe it. He *couldn't* believe it. How could they do that to him?

'I'm sorry.' She sounded close to tears.

'You were sleeping with both of us at the same time?' His voice was rising again, but he couldn't help it.

'Yeah, I'm sorry.'

'So you keep saying.' He took a ragged breath and cleared his throat. 'How far along are you?'

'Seven and a half months.'

He counted back. Damn and blast. 'Why have you left it this long to tell me?'

'I wasn't going to tell you at all,' she said, and Rex heard the tears in her voice. 'But in all conscience, I can't keep it from you – you've got a right to know if the baby's yours.'

He rubbed his free hand over his face, a terrible sinking feeling in his stomach. He'd worked so hard at getting his life back together, and now it was falling apart around him. What the hell was he going to do? He buried his face in his hand and said through his fingers, his voice muffled, 'Can't they do a DNA test or something?'

'Not until the baby's born,' she said, sniffling. 'Both you and Dean will have to be tested.'

Nearly two whole months to wait for the verdict. He didn't know how he'd get through them, or how he'd get through the weeks and months after that if he turned out to be the baby's father.

How was he going to cope? Where would he live? He couldn't stay in Tanglewood, that was for sure, not if he was to have any part in the child's life.

He sat up and squared his shoulders. He knew what he had to do, what the decent, moral thing was, and he was determined to do it. If the baby was his and fatherhood was going to be thrust upon him, then he'd do his best for the little mite.

He'd be a proper father to him or her, move back to Glenshona and support the baby in any way he could.

He didn't see that he had any other choice.

Chapter 28

The drive to Glenshona and his parents' house was a long one, giving Rex plenty of time to think and brood. Too much time.

'Balls,' he muttered, and Nell let out a whine from the back seat.

'It's OK, girl,' he said, not meaning a word of it. He had an awful feeling that things wouldn't be OK again for a very long time indeed.

He knew he was all bitter and twisted, but damn it, he felt entitled to be. It was one thing him and Jules growing apart; it was another thing entirely being cheated on – and with his best friend, as well. She had even fed him the old chestnut of 'it's not you, it's me' and he'd swallowed it whole, like the gullible prat he was. No wonder Dean had been cagey and distant on the few occasions they'd exchanged texts since he'd moved to Tanglewood, and never answered his phone when Rex called. Rex hadn't thought anything of it; neither he nor his friend had been great communicators, preferring to do their talking over a pint in the pub.

To think that Rex had even blamed himself for him and Jules splitting up: the fact that he worked odd hours sometimes, often at weekends; that he hadn't been paying

Jules enough attention; that he was preoccupied with Star's illness... The list went on.

But he hadn't been to blame after all.

Not this, please not this, he kept pleading silently. Not when he'd moved on with his life. His sense of betrayal and disbelief was vast. He thought he'd known Jules inside and out – he'd championed her, supported her, loved her, once. But now it seemed like he'd not known her at all. How could she do this to him? And what about the poor little bairn she was carrying?

He wasn't looking forward to telling his parents, but they had a right to know. He didn't want to leave it until the baby was born and the paternity test had been done. If it was positive, the shock might be too much.

Breaking it to them gently and in person was the kindest thing to do. Then he'd go to see Jules.

He wasn't looking forward to that, either.

Glenshona was just the same as when he'd left. This was swiftly followed by the thought that everything looked different. Or maybe it was Rex himself who was different. He'd grown up in this village, had been born here, and at one point he'd thought he'd never leave it.

But a desire to escape his failed relationship, plus needing to find another job, had driven him to apply for the ranger's job in Wales – as if by leaving Scotland he could leave his past behind.

Unfortunately, his past had tracked him down, and dragged him kicking and screaming back to his former home. He wondered how many other people in the village knew about the situation. Like Tanglewood, in Glenshona everyone knew everyone else's business. He just hoped that his parents hadn't already found out.

He planned on taking a more circuitous route through the village, not wanting to pass the house he and Jules had once shared, but when he arrived at the outskirts, he almost took the wrong road and had to give himself a mental shake. His mum and dad had moved to a little bungalow on the edge of Glenshona a couple of months before his life had fallen apart. It wasn't just because they were getting on a bit, they'd been quick to reassure him when they'd told him; they'd felt it was the right time to downsize. He could tell they'd been thinking ahead to their retirement and the years to come. His dad would have far less DIY to do in a single-storey place, and the garden, although considerably smaller, was still large enough to allow his mother to potter.

It felt strange, though, not to be pulling up outside the family home, and he wondered if he'd ever get used to his parents' new place.

As he switched off the engine and said a few reassuring words to the dog in the back, he scanned his surroundings, seeing his mother's touch in the pretty planted tubs and the nodding flowers in the raised beds. The bungalow was freshly painted and everything looked spick and span.

He inhaled deeply. Even from a mile or so inland, he was certain he could smell the sea, and he realised how much he'd missed it. His boyhood had been spent trawling along its shoreline looking for washed-up treasure, or pretending to be a pirate, or snorkelling off the rocks and turning blue with cold then running back to his mother for a dry towel and a flask of hot chocolate. With the mountain range behind the village and the ocean in front of it, he'd had the best of both worlds growing up.

He'd only just unclipped Nell's harness when his mum flew down the tidy little drive to greet him. He wrapped his arms around her, feeling about eight years old again, and breathed in her familiar scent. Ever since he could remember, she'd smelled of Chanel and baking, with a faint undertone of bleach. His mother had a fetish for bleach; Rex wondered, not for the first time, if she bathed in the stuff. Saying she was house-proud was like saying the Atlantic was big.

A movement caught his eye, and with a muttered oath, he released his mother and shot off down the road after Nell, who'd become fed up of sitting obediently at his feet and had decided to explore.

When he returned, puffing a little, with a chastened Nell in tow, it was to find that Dad had joined his mum on the drive and they were both laughing at him.

'You've got your hands full with that one,' his mother pointed out, as she linked her arm through his free one to steer him into the bungalow. 'Fetch Rex's bag, would you, Dougie,' she called over her shoulder.

'Yes, boss,' his father replied with a wink and a tug at an imaginary forelock.

The comforting smell of hotpot greeted Rex as soon as he stepped into the compact hall.

'I've made you your favourite,' his mum said, finally letting go of him and stepping back to give him a good once-over. 'You've lost weight,' she announced accusingly. 'Haven't you been eating properly?'

'No, I haven't, and yes, I have,' Rex replied, filling a bowl of water for the dog before opening the door to the garden in case she needed to go out.

'Well, you look skinnier,' his mum retorted. 'Sit down and I'll dish up. You could do with some more meat on your bones.'

With one eye on the excited Nell as she scuttled from one new scent to another, Rex let his mother spoon out an enormous portion of hotpot and plonk a plate in front of him. There was no way he was going to manage all that, but he was determined to do his best, realising that feeding him was her way of showing how deeply she cared. It wasn't as though he needed feeding up, he thought. His active lifestyle meant he burned a considerable number of calories, and he was probably in better shape now than he'd ever been, as the way he'd helped bring the 'casualty' down off the mountain had proved. His belly was flat, his chest firm and muscled; he wouldn't describe himself as 'ripped', but at least he could wear a pair of bathers in public without feeling too embarrassed.

After he'd made a valiant attempt at finishing his meal, he plucked up the courage to break the news to his parents.

'Mum, Dad, there's something I need to tell you,' he began, before grinding to a halt. How did you tell your parents something like this?

His mum removed his plate and gave him a sharp look, but didn't say anything.

'Mum, come and sit down.' Rex patted the seat of the chair next to his.

'We already know, son,' his dad said.

Eh? Rex blinked at his father. 'You do?'

'You can't keep a thing like that quiet in a place like Glenshona, especially with Jules starting to show a few months ago.'

'And you didn't think to tell me?' Rex demanded.

Neither of them would look at him, but his mother did find the courage to say, 'It's not the sort of thing we wanted to tell you on the phone, which is why I've been nagging you to come back for a visit all these weeks.'

'Jules called me yesterday and told me.'

'Oh Rex...' His mother's face was a mask of pity.

'The baby might be mine,' he blurted.

'We have heard the rumours.' She glanced at his father, then back at Rex.

'Yeah, she told me she was sleeping with both me and Dean before we broke up. She doesn't actually *know* who the father is. Apparently we have to wait for it to be born, then Dean and I have to have a paternity test.'

'Oh love.' His mother sat down next to him, reaching for his hand. 'What a mess.'

He shrugged. It was, but there was nothing to be done about it now.

'What if the baby is yours?' his mother wanted to know.

'I'll do what's right,' he said, 'and try to be a proper father.'

'Just when you were getting your life back on track, too. It's lucky you only brought a dog with you,' his dad said. 'You had me going on the phone the other day – I thought you'd found yourself a new girlfriend.'

Rex had thought he had too.

Oh God, Leanne... She'd been on his mind the whole journey.

He couldn't drag her into this – he simply couldn't.

Chapter 29

There was something wrong with Rex, Leanne sensed it. He'd not responded when she'd sent him a text last night saying she was missing him. And when she'd sent him another one this morning asking if everything was OK, all she'd received was a curt reply saying, *Fine. See you when I get back.*

He was probably out with his old mates, partying or something, she reasoned, but she had an awful feeling that in returning to his roots, he might be regretting his decision to come to Tanglewood. She just hoped he wasn't regretting his relationship with her, too.

She decided to try contacting him again. After all, he might simply be busy. Relatives had a habit of demanding your attention, and with Rex being an only child and living so far away from his parents, it was only natural if they wanted him to spend every minute with them.

But surely a quick text to say he was missing her wasn't too much to ask?

Unless he wasn't, and it was.

Before she could second-guess herself, she called him.

She could hear a customer in the shop, but she let Mabel deal with them and went into the storeroom for some privacy.

'Rex? Hi, it's me, Leanne.'

'Hi.'

Her heart sank. He didn't sound at all pleased to hear from her. In fact, he sounded quite put out.

'How are you?' she persisted.

'Good.'

It was like talking to a stranger, and her eyes pricked with the sudden sting of tears. Didn't she mean anything to him?

'Can you talk?' she asked.

'Not really.'

Ah, maybe that was it. She wouldn't want to be all lovey-dovey over the phone with her parents in earshot either. 'How are your mum and dad?' she asked.

'Fine.' A pause. 'Look, I've got to go. I'll give you a call later.'

'Oh, OK. Bye.'

The phone went dead and Leanne looked at it disbelievingly.

He'd not even said goodbye.

He hadn't sounded anything like the Rex she was falling in love with, and a tide of jealousy rose up, threatening to swamp her. She had a nasty suspicion that he might have bumped into his ex and wanted to get back together with her.

In the space of a day or two, Leanne had gone from being happy and eager for what the future might hold to being thoroughly miserable.

Budding Stars was down to five contestants now – there were only two more rounds, then the final. She should be excited, but all she felt was numb.

What had got into him?

What had she done wrong?

Chapter 30

Rex ended the call before he said something he would regret, like 'I love you.'

There was no way he could talk to Leanne, not right now. He needed to get his head around the situation first, to think things through. What if the baby *was* his? He wanted to be a proper father to him or her; if that meant moving back to Glenshona, then so be it. How could he carry on a relationship with Leanne when he was so far away?

Would it be fair to drag her into all this when he might have the sudden responsibility of a child to consider?

'I'm going to speak to Jules,' he said, grabbing his car keys off the table in the hall. 'Then I'm going to give my so-called friend a piece of my mind.'

'Do you think that's wise?' his mum asked worriedly. 'Douglas, tell him…'

Rex ignored her. He knew he was being unreasonable, and that his parents were only doing what they thought was best, but he couldn't help blaming them for not telling him sooner. It was always going to be a shock, whenever he found out, but if they'd told him a few months ago about the rumours floating around, then he would have known the truth sooner and wouldn't have let things go as far as they had with Leanne.

He'd started to have deep feelings for her; hell, he thought he loved her.

If only his mum and dad had told him about the baby earlier, he wouldn't be suffering now.

Well, not as much, he conceded. The problems would still be there, the feeling of betrayal, the hurt, the knowledge that his life was going to be irrevocably changed, but at least he wouldn't have a broken heart to contend with at the same time.

He imagined the look on Leanne's face after he'd ended the call so abruptly, and his heart ached. He hated himself for doing this to her, but he couldn't face speaking to her right now, trying to pretend everything was OK when it so clearly wasn't.

He didn't bother to get out of his car when he pulled up alongside his old house. A woman with a toddler was digging in the flower beds, the child joining in enthusiastically. He didn't recognise either of them, and he realised Jules must have sold the place after all.

Dean lived a few streets away, so Rex made his way there. If his former best friend had also moved, then he would simply pay a visit to Dean's mum to ask her where he was living now.

Dean's pride and joy – a Golf – was on the drive and Jules's Fiesta was parked next to it. Rex narrowed his eyes, taking a deep breath. He wasn't looking forward to this, not one little bit, but it had to be done.

He probably knocked harder than he needed to, but he couldn't help himself. He felt like punching someone. Dean would be a good start.

But it was Jules who opened the door; a very pregnant, glowing Jules.

The glow swiftly faded when she saw who was standing on her doorstep. She put a hand on her swollen stomach and Rex's gaze was immediately drawn to it.

That was possibly his child in there. *His!* He wasn't quite sure how he felt about that.

'Rex,' she said.

The word spoke volumes – surprise, fear, regret, defiance. Or was Rex simply reading too much into it?

'Hello, Jules.' His own voice was flat and hard. 'Is Dean in?'

'No. Football.'

Dean loved his football, Rex remembered bizarrely, recalling how a group of them used to kick a ball around when they were kids, pretending to be this player or that. It all seemed such a long time ago now.

Jules backed away from the open door. 'You'd better come in.'

He agreed. He had no intention of airing his dirty laundry in front of the prying eyes and ears of Glenshona. The village would know about this visit soon enough, but he refused to add further grist to the gossip mill.

Dean's house showed evidence of a feminine touch. Rex recognised a few pieces from the house he and Jules had shared – the mirror above the fireplace, the scatter cushions on the leather sofa. He could even remember buying them with her, and the memory stabbed at him.

He didn't want her back, he didn't actually want anything to do with her, but the thought of his child being brought up in this house with one of his best mates playing dad made him feel physically sick.

'It's a mess, I know—' Jules began, but recoiled when Rex all but growled at her.

'You can say that again.'

She lowered her bulk into a chair, using her hands to support her weight, and as she sat down, he noticed how swollen her ankles were.

She saw him looking. 'Being pregnant isn't all it's cracked up to be,' she said.

'You should have thought of that before you shagged my best mate,' Rex retorted, then immediately wished he hadn't as he saw her shrink back as though she'd been slapped. 'I'm sorry,' he said. 'It's the shock. You should have told me sooner.'

'You're right, I should have done. You had every right to know, but I was so confused.' She hesitated. 'I still am.' Another pause. 'For a while, I thought about pretending it was Dean's. No one would ever know. But I couldn't live with myself. Dean says he'll love the baby no matter whose it is, and I know he'll be a good father, but the longer it went on, the more I realised it would be wrong not to tell you. You, Dean and the baby all deserve to know the truth.'

'But you were already three months pregnant when you left me, and you didn't think to mention it then?'

She stared at the pale grey carpet. 'I only found out the day before we split up.'

'You still should have told me.'

'Yes, I should have, but I didn't want you to think we were going to get back together just because there was a baby involved.'

'You must have been sleeping with Dean for ages before you gave me the elbow,' Rex said conversationally, but it didn't make him feel any better when he saw the stricken look on his ex-girlfriend's face.

'Don't start,' she warned. 'It's not good for the baby.'

Rex rolled his eyes. 'What isn't good for the baby is having a mother who doesn't know who the father is,' he retorted.

'Dean will be his father.'

'His? The baby's a boy?'

She nodded.

Oh my God, Rex thought. A son. It took a moment for the idea to sink in. This was real. He was going to be a father.

Or not.

Jules was struggling to her feet, and automatically he stepped forward to help her, but she brushed his hand away.

'Whoever Lyall's biological father is, Dean will be his dad,' she said firmly. 'But so will you – if he's yours, and you want to be.'

Who the hell is Lyall? was Rex's first thought, quickly followed by the realisation that Jules meant the baby. She had already given his child a name, and not one he had helped choose either. He felt oddly cheated, and more than a little sad.

So this was how it would be. If the child was his, he'd have little say in his upbringing. All he would be able to do was provide for Lyall financially, and beg as many visits as Jules was willing to allow.

He already knew it wasn't going to be nearly enough.

'I want to be part of Lyall's life,' he said. 'If he's mine, I want to be a real father to him.'

'You can be as much of a dad to him as you want; you can be as involved as you want.' She let out a small gasp and clutched her stomach. 'He's kicking. Do you want to feel it?'

Rex bit his lip. Did he?

This was so new, so surreal, but if this baby was indeed his, he knew he'd regret not taking this opportunity. He nodded.

Jules caught hold of his hand and placed it on her swollen tummy.

When he felt the baby move, Rex was filled with a sense of wonder, and a sudden desperate sorrow that it wasn't Leanne he was sharing this magical moment with.

Oh God, what a sodding mess.

Chapter 31

Leanne had never set foot inside Moira's wedding shop before; in fact, as she'd told Stevie, she had more or less forgotten it existed. As she trotted underneath the old archway and into the little cobbled square beyond, she was expecting something dusty, old-fashioned and rather run-down.

She was in for a delightful surprise.

The square itself was tiny, with just a couple of cottages and the wedding shop, which had been converted from an old stable block. The archway had been where the horses and carriages had ridden through after they'd delivered well-to-do ladies and gentlemen to the public house at the front.

The pub had long gone, although the building remained, having been transformed into a quaint antique shop filled with the most wonderful things; there was also a shop selling hand-made soaps, candles and other gorgeously scented items, and a beautician's, which was a new addition to the village. Leanne hadn't tried it out herself, but a few of her customers had, and had recommended it. Maybe she'd treat herself before the wedding, have one of those facials she'd been harping on about.

She gazed with a critical eye at the little window boxes and the pots blooming with spring flowers standing next to each cottage door. It all looked charming.

Moira Carrington's shop was tiny but lovely. There was a plush seating area just as you walked in, with squashy armchairs and a sofa, a coffee table set with little china cups and saucers and a vase of fresh flowers, and not a dress in sight.

Stevie and her friend Karen were already enjoying a cup of tea and discussing tiaras.

Stevie stood up to give Leanne a hug, then resumed her seat, leaned back and narrowed her eyes. 'Are you OK?'

'Yeah, why?' Leanne sat next to her.

'You look... I don't know... a bit anxious?'

Leanne shook her head. 'I'm fine,' she protested.

'Is it the competition?' Stevie persisted. 'If you need any help, just shout. We're all here for you.'

'No, really, everything's good. Honest,' she added when Stevie continued to watch her beadily. 'Have you decided on a colour scheme?' she asked, to change the subject.

Actually, she wasn't all right. Not really.

She couldn't shake the feeling that something had definitely been wrong with Rex last night. There wasn't anything she could put her finger on, but he'd given her the impression he didn't want to talk to her. He'd sounded preoccupied, and had been keen to end the call.

Giving herself a mental shake, she realised she was probably being silly. He'd been busy, or Nell had just had an accident on the rug, or he might have been in the middle of eating his supper – anything.

But then again, why hadn't he explained to her why he had to go?

She quickly checked her phone.

Still no text, and no missed call, either.

'What do you think?' Stevie's voice roused her from her vague sense of worry.

'Eh? Oh, that's lovely. Why don't you try it on?' Leanne said, looking up to see Mrs Carrington (no one would ever dare call her Moira, despite the name above the door) holding up a mass of champagne tulle with a pretty appliqué neckline.

'Not for *me*, for you and Karen,' Stevie said, and Leanne saw Mrs Carrington roll her eyes.

'Aren't we here to get you kitted out with a dress?' Leanne pointed out.

'We are, but when I saw this, I thought it would suit both your colouring.'

Leanne was brown-haired and brown-eyed, and Karen had dark, almost black hair, with chocolatey eyes. Leanne knew which of them would look better in the dress, and it wasn't her. But then compared to Karen, she was always going to come second. Oh well...

'Edie, bring out the Stardust dress in ivory and nude,' Mrs Carrington called over her shoulder.

While the three girls waited, Leanne sipped at her slightly tepid tea and surreptitiously checked her phone again.

'Excuse me, but I don't allow photos,' Mrs Carrington said. 'These are all one-off designs. I can't have them copied. I'd be grateful if you'd put it away.'

Sheepishly Leanne switched her mobile off, dropped it in her bag and placed her hands demurely on her knees, feeling as though she'd been told off by a headmistress. Crikey, but the woman was scary.

Stevie was trying not to snigger, and Karen was staring determinedly at a print on the wall.

When Mrs Carrington turned away for a second, Leanne elbowed Stevie in the ribs and hissed, 'Are you sure you want to buy the dress of your dreams from *her*? Oh...' She breathed out slowly as a girl came out from behind a curtain, holding up the most gorgeous creation Leanne had ever seen.

'Bring it here, girl,' Mrs Carrington ordered, and her assistant stepped forward, holding the dress as high as she could to show off the fall and flow of the fabric.

'It's got an off-the-shoulder neckline and a fit-and-flair skirt,' Mrs Carrington said. 'Can you see how the nude silk underneath the lace complements the champagne colour of the bridesmaid's dress I've just shown you? You've got the figure to carry this off,' she added, running a critical eye over Stevie.

'It's wonderful.' Stevie had teared up, and Leanne reached for a handily placed box of tissues on the coffee table (did many brides cry? she wondered) and passed her one.

'Try it on,' Karen urged. 'I bet it'll look fabulous.'

Leanne thought so, too. She couldn't wait to see her friend in it – she'd be the most stunning bride ever.

'Edie, take Miss Taylor into the fitting room. I'll be in shortly.'

'Edie? Edie Adams? Is that you?' Leanne cocked her head to one side. 'Don't I know you from school?'

'You were in the year above me,' the girl said, shooting an anxious glance at her boss.

'I thought so. How are you?'

'Great, thanks. Excuse me, but I need to get Miss Taylor undressed.'

'Call me Stevie,' Stevie said. 'Everyone else does.'

'Not everyone, *Miss Taylor*,' Mrs Carrington said. 'Now, if you don't mind, I have another bride in an hour...'

Oops. 'Sorry,' Leanne mouthed at Edie, suddenly very glad indeed that she was her own boss. She'd hate to be spoken to the way Moira Carrington spoke to little Edie Adams. Which was another reason why she'd have to seriously consider this offer of Jarred's. She wasn't sure she could work for anyone else after running her own business for such a long time.

Then there was Rex, and her growing feelings for him. Why, oh why, did life have to be so complicated?

Chapter 32

Rex put his head in his hands and gave a huge sigh. Next to him, Nell whined, pawing at his leg, and he reached out absently to ruffle her ears. She sensed his unhappiness, bless her, but there was nothing she could do. Nothing anyone could do. Not until he knew for sure whether his life was about to be turned upside down.

He knew he wasn't being fair to Leanne by not speaking to her, but how could he? What was he supposed to say: 'Hi, I think I'm in love with you, but my ex-girlfriend may be pregnant with my baby, and if it is mine then I'll be moving several hundred miles away and probably won't manage to get to see you more than once a month'?

He couldn't, could he?

But she had to be told at some point. He couldn't keep avoiding her calls. She deserved better than that from him.

Oh God, he wasn't looking forward to this one little bit.

Gathering his resolve, he picked up his phone to call her before he had a chance to change his mind.

It rang once, twice.

He hung up before she could answer.

I'll tell her in person, he decided. It would be better than trying to explain over the phone.

Yes, that was what he'd do. He'd speak to her as soon as he got back to Tanglewood, face to face.

It did occur to him that he was putting it off, but the relief he felt at not having to give the woman he was falling in love with the news that their relationship might be on the rocks before it had hardly got started was immense. He was back in Tanglewood on Monday – he'd tell her then, and let her choose whether she wanted to keep seeing him. If she decided it was too complicated, then at least he'd given it his best shot.

–

Damn and blast! She knew it! She simply knew it! The minute Leanne had been incommunicado, Rex had called. Sod's law.

But when she tried to ring him back, he wasn't answering. Typical.

Crossly she stomped back to the shop to relieve Mabel, not even the thought of the wonderful bridesmaid's dress cheering her up. There was far too much happening between now and Stevie's wedding to begin to get excited about it.

If only Mrs Carrington hadn't made her turn her phone off…

Oh grow up, she told herself once she was safely ensconced behind her counter and back in control once more. He'll ring again. Or you'll call him. One or the other. It didn't matter if they went for a day or so without speaking to each other, did it? They didn't exactly live in each other's pockets, and neither of them was obliged to tell the other what they were up to every minute.

She really did want to speak to him, though, just to check that everything was OK between them. Common sense told her there wasn't any reason for it not to be, but nevertheless, a frisson of unease travelled down her spine, making her shiver.

Chapter 33

Leanne checked her watch again. Barely ten minutes had passed since the last time she'd looked at it. Rex had been gone nearly three whole days, and she'd hardly heard from him. She'd tried to call him back a couple of times, without success, and now the whole non-contact thing was starting to get to her.

She let out a long, heavy sigh. It was gone ten o'clock and another sleepless night stretched ahead.

Should she call him again?

Yes.

No.

Oh hell – she'd been having this argument with herself for days, and each time she came to the conclusion she should wait for him to call her. She didn't want to come across as a stalker. She'd already done enough chasing; it was his turn to make the next move.

But what if he didn't? What should she do then?

Carry on as before, she told herself. After all, nothing much had happened, had it? A few kisses – she deliberately tried to push to the back of her mind just how wonderful those kisses had been – and some (marvellous) embraces, that was all. It wasn't as though either of them had declared their undying love for the other, was it?

Maybe she should give him another call, ask him straight out if there was something wrong.

Bad idea; she was bordering on stalking again.

But she had to know, one way or the other.

Then again, maybe she was reading too much into the whole thing. As that thought flitted through her head, she began to wonder exactly what it was she had been reading too much into – their romance, or his lack of contact?

She groaned. Her head hurt with all this thinking.

She made a conscious effort to think of something else; anything would do – the price of lamb (always important for the farm's financial health), how Mabel was doing in the shop (fine, actually), whether Rex was cooling off—

Bugger, she was at it again, thinking about Rex.

Try again, and this time focus, she told herself sharply. She should be concentrating on the most exciting thing to have happened in her life so far – *Budding Stars* – and not on a man. She was so close to winning, she could almost taste it. Five of them left. *Five!*

Three more rounds. When she said it like that, it was quite frightening.

It was Monday already; she only had a day and a half to perfect her latest design, so why was she wasting time thinking about Rex?

She checked her watch again. Eighteen minutes past ten. Still no call from him. He should be back in Tanglewood by now. She was positive he'd told her he was coming home today.

He could still be on the road, though. If he was, she didn't want to distract him.

A blast of noise from her phone made her jump, and she scrambled to retrieve it from the bedside cabinet, her heart thumping, her mouth dry.

A swift look at the screen confirmed her hope – it was Rex.

'Hello?' She hated that her voice sounded so high and reedy, and more than a little nervous.

'Hi. Look, can we meet tomorrow? There's something I need to talk to you about,' he said.

'Um… OK.' Leanne's heart sank to her fluffy pink bed socks, and her stomach turned over. He didn't sound as though he'd missed her, as if he loved her and was longing to take her in his arms again. His tone was grim, and she guessed what was coming. 'On second thoughts,' she said, 'say what you've got to say now.'

'I think it would be better face to face.'

'I don't. Just tell me.' Praying she was wrong about the whole situation, she held her breath.

'I like you; in fact I more than like you—' he began, but before he could say anything further, Leanne burst out laughing.

It came out shrill and slightly manic, and she bit her lip to prevent another cackle from escaping. She'd *known* it; she'd had a feeling he was going to end it, and here he was doing that very thing. Tears gathered in the corners of her eyes and she blinked them away. She had no intention of letting him know how much she was hurting right now.

'It's just that… There's this…' he tried again, and Leanne shook her head, her chin wobbling.

This was too painful for words. If he didn't have the guts to come out with it and end it, then she would. There wasn't any point in delaying things – he was clearly trying to break up with her, so she'd put them both out of their misery and try to reclaim some self-respect while she was at it.

'I should never have kissed you,' she said, before he could say anything else. 'I'm sorry, Rex, but this can't possibly work, me and you.'

A slight pause, then he said, 'It can't?'

'Good, I'm glad you realise it too. I'll see you around, yeah? Take care.'

She ended the call, and this time when her eyes filled with tears, she let them fall. That would teach her to read more into a couple of kisses than she should. How could she have been so stupid?

A sob escaped her, and she clapped her hands to her mouth. It was late and she didn't want to risk waking her parents with her pathetic crying. She only had herself to blame; she never should have allowed herself to be seduced by a handsome face and a soft Scottish burr. She'd told herself right at the start that she had no time for romance, that she should be concentrating on *Budding Stars*, but she'd allowed love to sneak up on her, and now look at the state of her – a weeping, miserable mess.

Her eyes widened. Oh God, she'd just admitted to herself that she loved him.

Fresh tears fell, and she collapsed into her pillow and cried until she had nothing left.

It was much later when she finally sat up, wiped her eyes and lifted her chin. She couldn't turn back the clock or change Rex's mind – she was too proud to go chasing after him anyway – so the only thing to do was to put this behind her and look to the future.

She had a competition to win and a job offer to accept. She had a glittering future ahead of her; Jarred had said so.

So why did she feel so awful about it?

She hadn't given Jarred an answer yet, but maybe she should start thinking seriously about it. If Rex was no longer interested in her, then perhaps it would be best if she moved away from Tanglewood altogether.

It was actually quite shocking to her to realise she'd been delaying her decision because of Rex and her feelings for him. What had happened to the ambitious go-getter who had blithely sent off the application to *Budding Stars*, wanting nothing more than to win it?

Rex had happened, that was what.

–

The phone slipped out of Rex's nerveless fingers and dropped to the carpet. He couldn't believe what had just happened – Leanne had broken up with him, and just when he'd been about to explain everything, too.

Thank God he hadn't opened his heart to her.

At least it had made the decision about moving back to Glenshona that much easier. He wouldn't have to worry about Leanne's feelings, or fret over how hard it was to leave her.

All he would have to worry about was himself.

And he was hurting like the very devil right now.

Chapter 34

'Mabel,' Leanne wheedled, knowing she sounded like a small child begging for sweets but carrying on regardless, 'I'm going to need more help in the shop. Or should I say, *you* are going to need more help.'

'Aren't I good enough?' Mabel asked. 'I thought I was doing OK.' She looked ready to cry.

'You are, you're doing brilliantly,' Leanne hastened to reassure her, 'but I've been offered an opportunity I'd be silly to pass up.'

'Oh?'

'Jarred Townsend has asked me to go and work for him.'

'That's wonderful!' Mabel cried, then she frowned, and Leanne was aware of her scrutiny. 'Isn't it?'

'Yes, it is,' Leanne replied, injecting as much enthusiasm into her words as she could muster. 'It's just there's an awful lot to think about. It's a big responsibility, and I don't know if I can—'

'Stop right there. You can do this... whatever it is. You know you can. You're young, talented and ambitious. I wish I'd been like you when I was your age. You've got to take the bull by the horns and ride it like you stole it.'

Leanne laughed, despite her apprehension. And she agreed with the other woman. Sort of.

'Would you be happy managing the shop if I employed someone else to help you?' she asked.

'Hmm, I'm not so sure about that. Don't get me wrong, I love helping out, and the money certainly comes in handy, but I'm not getting any younger, you know.'

It was as Leanne suspected: Mabel was content with things the way they were and didn't want the extra responsibility or the additional work. Running the shop single-handedly was hard work, and it wouldn't be easy for a woman of her age.

'OK. I'll start advertising. I'm sure the job centre in Abergavenny would be willing to put an advert out, and I'll stick a notice in the window, too. Stevie found Cassandra that way.'

Thinking about Cassandra gave Leanne a flashback to the conversation she'd had with Betty. The old lady had been right about one thing: Cassandra *had* given birth to a little girl, though Leanne had yet to see her. She could hardly wait to get her hands on her for a cuddle, but she'd been so busy lately, what with the flower shop, the competition and Rex, that she'd hardly found the time to brush her own hair. However, Betty had been totally, utterly and completely wrong about something else – Rex wasn't in the slightest bit interested in her.

Rex. There he was again, lurking around in her mind like a fart in a lift. She simply couldn't escape him; whatever she thought about, or talked about, he was involved somehow.

What on earth had she found to think about before she'd met him? she wondered. Her mind must have been as empty as a desert, or so full of innocuous things as to be positively vacant.

Well, she'd have to go back to not thinking about much at all, wouldn't she? Although not thinking about Rex might be easier said than done, and would need a bit of working on.

Chapter 35

Rex didn't want to bump into Leanne. He was too raw, too emotional. He could have sworn there'd been a spark between them, a growing awareness that the kisses could lead to something much more, maybe something permanent, but after what she'd said last night…

How could he have been so stupid to fall so heavily for her?

He should have listened to his instinct when it had told him it was too soon to be dating again, that he should give himself some time and space to get used to being a single man and to free himself of Jules's influence. A grunt of derision escaped him at that last thought – if he really was Lyall's father, there was no way he would ever be free from Jules. As the mother of his child, she would always be in his life.

He waited until Wednesday afternoon – a day when he knew Leanne would be on her way to London – before he ventured out into the village to take a stroll past the flower shop. He knew he was being silly and irrational, but although she mightn't be there in body, he wanted to feel closer to her, and walking past her shop was about as close as he was ever going to get now.

It was almost closing time and he'd just done a long stint in the office, so he needed to stretch his legs a little;

both he and Nell got restless if they sat still for too long. He intended to amble along the high street, then walk down to the river to try to clear his mind a little.

As he passed the flower shop, he noticed that the window looked spectacular, as usual. Leanne had created a wonderful display for wedding season, and he stopped to admire it, lingering for far longer than a bachelor with no bride on the horizon probably should.

A sheet of A4 paper secured to the inside of the window caught his attention.

Vacancy: shop manager
To start asap. Salary negotiable.
Must be an experienced florist.
To apply or for more details,
please contact Leanne Green.

Leanne's familiar mobile number was printed underneath, and he stared at the advert for a long time, reading it over and over again.

What did it mean? Did Leanne know something he didn't; did she know she was going to win *Budding Stars*? Or was she simply hedging her bets, getting the ball rolling just in case?

On impulse, he opened the shop door and stepped inside. Mabel, Leanne's elderly assistant, was busy hauling buckets of flowers into a room at the back of the shop.

'Here, let me give you a hand,' Rex offered, seeing her struggling to lift them.

Mabel looked up. 'Thank you. Some of these are quite heavy.'

He told Nell to sit, and when he was satisfied the dog was going to behave herself, he hoisted one of the buckets with ease and carried it out to the chiller, before returning for another.

'I see Leanne is advertising for a shop manager,' he said casually, as if he was simply making conversation and had no real interest in the answer.

'Yes, well, she could hardly pass up an offer like that, and I can't manage this place on my own. She did ask me, bless her, but I'm a bit past it now.'

'No, she couldn't,' he agreed, having no idea what Mabel was talking about but playing along anyway in the hope of getting some more information out of her. 'And you're not past it at all,' he added. 'I bet you've got more get-up-and-go in your little finger than I've got in my whole body.'

'Aw, you,' she said, simpering at the compliment. 'I'm staying on to help the new person, but I won't be in charge.'

Rex lifted another couple of buckets, one in each arm, as Mabel held the chiller room door open for him.

'Yes,' she continued, 'it'll do wonders for her career. She was a bit iffy about it at first, because it'll mean a permanent move to London, but she's had a good think and her mind is made up. From what she told me, Jarred Townsend sounds like a decent enough chap to work for.'

She was going to work for Jarred Townsend? Rex was astounded at the news. Leanne hadn't said a word to him about an 'opportunity', and he wondered how long she'd known about it.

'You didn't know?' Mabel asked, catching sight of his expression. 'I thought you'd be the first one she'd have told, what with you and her dating.'

'She did mention something about it,' he said vaguely, still reeling from the news. 'But I hadn't realised she'd made her mind up.'

'It was a bit of a shock to me too, to be honest. But at least it doesn't matter if she wins the competition or not, so the pressure is off her a bit. I'm glad, too, because she hasn't been herself these past couple of days. She looks far too peaky for my liking, and I think she's trying to do too much.'

'Remind me, what exactly will she be doing for Jarred Townsend?' Rex asked.

'He's opening an eco-branch of his business, and Leanne is spearheading it,' Mabel explained, giving him a strange look. 'Didn't she tell you?'

'That's right, I remember now,' he said, bending down to pick up two more buckets of flowers so Mabel couldn't see his face.

So Leanne was going to go work for Jarred Townsend, was she? She'd never mentioned a thing to him, not even a hint. Had she already received the offer when he was kissing her, or had Jarred only asked her last week?

No wonder she'd ended things between them.

'When did she speak to you about managing the shop?' he asked Mabel.

'Yesterday morning, as soon as I came in. She looked a bit upset, actually, and I thought she might have been crying. Still, I expect she must be a bit worried – it's a big decision and a huge change for her. I don't blame her for being nervous. She's lived in Tanglewood all her life, but I told her she should jump at the chance because she'll only regret it if she doesn't.'

Rex actually agreed with Mabel. Leanne *would* regret it, and with the possibility of him moving back to Scotland as soon as the baby was born, it was probably for the best that she was carrying on with her life.

It was just a pity his heart didn't agree with his head.

Chapter 36

'I hope you don't think I've influenced the result in any way,' Jarred said as Leanne slipped into the passenger seat of his car – a Porsche, naturally – and sank into the soft leather. 'Because I would never do that.'

Strangely enough, she believed him.

'You barely scraped through by the skin of your teeth,' he added. 'Actually, I gave you the lowest mark out of the five of you.'

She hadn't expected to make it through at all, if she was honest. Her performance today had been desultory at best It was only because Emma hadn't completed her unseen task in the allotted time that the other woman had been the latest contestant to leave the show. If she had actually finished it, Leanne would be the one going home. She wouldn't have blamed the judges. She would have blamed herself. It had not been her best round to date. She guessed the bookies would probably lengthen her odds of winning when this latest episode was aired.

It was weird to think that she and everyone else involved in the show knew what was happening but the programme had yet to be shown. It would be as though she was living the event twice when she watched it. *If* she watched it. She wasn't sure she wanted to see herself on screen – catching a glimpse of her face in the mirror was bad enough these days. She looked washed out and used up, as if she had all the cares of the world on her shoulders.

Even now, with a visit to Jarred's flagship shop in Kensington looming, she had trouble drumming up the necessary enthusiasm. She was just going through the motions.

She felt like slapping herself in the face to wake herself up. She was through to the semi-final of one of the newest competitions on TV, and she had the most amazing job offer on the table; she should be jumping up and down with excitement.

'I expected nothing less,' she said to Jarred, finally responding to his comment. 'I would have given me the lowest score, too.'

He pulled over to the kerb and switched off the engine. His shop was on the opposite side of the road, and she gazed at its minimalist splendour with interest. It was understated black-and-white chic, one single bloom in the window in an elegant white vase. The eye had no choice but to be drawn to the startlingly blue hydrangea. At first glance, Leanne thought the flower looked out of place – too countrified, too cottage garden – but then she understood its contrast with the sophistication of the window, and she realised the choice was quite inspired.

Rex would probably have laughed, told her she was reading too much into the whole thing, and that someone had probably forgotten to do a proper display so had stuck this in the window as a last resort.

She reached for the handle, and was about to get out – although she thought she might need a bit of help in that department because the car was so low to the ground – when Jarred spoke again.

'When you come to work for me, I'll not tolerate substandard work,' he warned, and Leanne froze.

He was so certain, so convinced she would take him up on his offer, she almost turned him down there and then. But common sense soon kicked in. Of course he expected the best from his employees; why wouldn't he? She deserved the reprimand. Thank God the total scores for all the weeks weren't totted up, and that each contestant was judged only on that day's performance. It meant a clean slate for the penultimate week. The four of them had already been given their brief, but Leanne hadn't read it yet. She'd do that just before she got into her own car for the return journey to Tanglewood, hoping it would give her something to think about on the way home other than Rex McMillan.

'I understand,' she said after a too-long pause, realising she should have spoken sooner. For some reason she seemed to be having trouble marshalling her thoughts. 'I promise I'll give you a hundred per cent.'

Jarred subjected her to a searching look. 'Does that mean you accept?'

For the first time during this long day, Leanne's smile was genuine and not forced. 'I did say that I'd let you know the second I'm removed from the competition,' she reminded him. 'I'm still in it, albeit by the skin of my teeth.'

'Ah yes, the lady wants to win. If you do, I'll wait, but not for too long. Do the interviews, the guest appearances, write a few floristry tips in *Woman* magazine or whatever. Get it out of your system, but do it quickly. I have a business to run.'

She nodded, eased herself out of the car and let Jarred lead her towards his pride and joy.

'I have seven shops in London,' he told her, 'and they all look identical. I have others in Manchester, Birmingham, Liverpool and York, to name but a few, and I am looking into opening branches abroad. My flowers are renowned for their quality and freshness, my florists for their flair and skill.'

'Do you still do arrangements yourself?' she asked him, walking into the tiled hush of the store. Just like the window, everything was black and white, with no other colours to distract the attention from the real focus, which was the flowers. Even the sheets of tissue paper were monochrome, as was the staff uniform, the ribbons – everything that wasn't a plant or part of a plant.

When Leanne mentioned it, Jarred shrugged. 'If a woman receives a bouquet wrapped in black tissue, with a black ribbon, she knows where it's from and she knows the sender has chosen the best. It's good marketing, that's all. It's also very effective.'

It most certainly was, she thought. 'What about things like weddings – will you change your colour scheme to suit the bride?'

'Of course. It's enough for me to know that the happy couple will boast that Jarred Townsend has done their flowers. I don't insist on black and white outside of the shops.'

Leanne thought of Julia Ferris, and how happy it would make her to be able to tell everyone that Leanne Green off the telly had designed her son's wedding flowers, and how she would be even happier to be able to say that Leanne worked for Jarred Townsend. The thought almost brought another smile to her lips, and she realised just how few of those she'd given out recently.

Jarred showed her around the store, which was still open at this relatively late hour, then took her upstairs to the offices. Leanne had never seen anything so plush or extravagant in all her life, and she stood there for a moment with her mouth open, her eyes wide.

'Impressive, isn't it?' Jarred said, gesturing towards the deep, white leather sofas, the Persian rugs, the paintings on the wall. 'I had the carpets specially commissioned,' he added. 'The artwork is by Boomerang.'

Who? Leanne nearly said, but she didn't want to show her ignorance. 'It's certainly...' she fished around for a suitable word, 'opulent.'

When Jarred turned to face her, it took her a second to realise there was something different about him. The cocky, almost arrogant expression was gone; in its place was something more sombre.

'This is branding,' he explained. 'Pure and simple. If you lead people to believe that what you are offering is exclusive, and you charge them a fortune for it, they'll buy it. You've been to my apartment; you know this is not me. This is the public me, not the private one.'

'Emperor's new clothes,' Leanne murmured.

'Yes!' Jarred cried, making her jump. 'You understand. I knew you would.' He led her to one of the sofas, gestured for her to sit down and sank into the one opposite. 'I am a good florist, but not a brilliant one,' he began, shaking his head at her when Leanne was about to object. 'Everyone thinks I'm brilliant, because that's what I tell them. That's what the media tells them. Even the royal family believes it. Why wouldn't they, when everyone says it's true?'

'Very clever,' Leanne acknowledged. She was in awe of this man's drive and ambition, but she was pretty certain she wasn't the same. 'I can't do this,' she said, gazing around. 'It's not me.'

'And that is what I love about you. You will be a total contrast to this side of my business. I already have the perfect place in mind.'

'Oh?'

'It's a converted warehouse – a cliché, I know – but it's all about recycling, reusing, repurposing, yes? What better way than to start at the beginning with the premises themselves? Everything, and I mean *everything*, will have started life as something else. Wait a sec, I've got some ideas to show you.'

He struggled to free himself from the sofa and got to his feet. His desk was a highly polished black monstrosity, totally devoid of anything, not even a pencil. Leanne wondered if he did any actual work there, or if it was simply for show.

There were things in the drawers, though, she saw, as he pulled out a fat folder and came to sit next to her. He opened it and thrust it into her hands.

Leanne skimmed through image after image of the inside of a warehouse, with its bare bricks and metal hanging lights. Baths had been given second lives as sofas; chests had become plant pots, their drawers open to reveal assorted foliage spilling out of them; the tables were made out of driftwood; even old barrels had been repurposed and were taking the place of the usual plastic containers for holding cut flowers; pallets had been turned into shelving – the list went on.

'What do you think?' he asked when she turned the last page.

'It's quite...' Again she struggled to find a word that fitted, one that wouldn't offend him. 'Industrial,' was what she came up with eventually.

'You don't like it?' His voice was flat.

Leanne came to the conclusion that if they were going to work together – although she was under no illusion about who would be the boss and who would be the employee, and she had an unsettling flash of Mrs Carrington and the way she treated Edie – she needed to start as she meant to go on. There was no way she was going to be a yes-man, or rather, a yes-girl. He was hiring her for her ideas, so now was as good a time as any to start expressing them.

'I do like it, but it shouts industry rather than the environment. I can see corporate customers falling over themselves to have you supply them, but I fear you'll be sadly lacking on the bride and housewife front. But then I suppose it all depends on the market you're aiming for.'

Jarred said nothing for a while, and Leanne was convinced she had seriously annoyed him.

'Hmm,' he said eventually. 'You're right.' He checked his watch. 'I'll take you back to the studios to pick up your car. You have a long way to travel this evening and I have an appointment. We'll meet up again soon.' He paused. 'I know it's a big ask, what with the semi-final coming up, but if you could spare some time to think about what the brides and housewives might want and let me know, it'll enable me to make an informed decision.'

He hauled her out of the sofa, his grip warm and firm. As she came upright, he turned it into a handshake. 'We'll make a good team,' he insisted before releasing her.

Leanne was beginning to think he was right. Jarred Townsend was nothing like his hype, nothing like she'd expected him to be. They *would* make a good team.

The idea both excited her and made her feel very, very sad at the same time.

Chapter 37

The village hall was deemed to be a better venue for the auction of the children's artwork than either the school or the Brecon Beacons Visitor Centre, for the simple reason that it was more central and easier for everyone to get to. Rex and Miss Harding had been busy putting up flyers advertising the event, and the school had sent out a text to all parents to let them know about it, so they were hoping for a good turnout.

Rex had taken out three more groups of pupils since that first time, and there was a lovely selection of artwork on display. Some pieces were actually very good indeed, though some, he guessed, would only be bid on by the child's immediate family.

After a discussion with Miss Harding in which she had enlightened him as to the possible finances (or lack of them) of some of the local families, Rex had decided on a contingency plan: if any picture was doing really poorly, then he would step in and put a bid on it himself. But he didn't want to embarrass any parents or pupils, so he'd asked Stevie if she would bid on his behalf. He already had his eye on a couple of possibles; one poor little boy especially wasn't having a very good time of it at home at the moment, with no father on the scene and his mother suffering from cancer. Miss Harding had indicated that money was tight, so Rex had already made his mind up to purchase the child's painting if no one else did.

The hall was filling up nicely with a mixture of parents, grandparents, aunts, uncles and assorted local business owners. Rex had even managed to persuade his manager to come along to place a bid on behalf of the National Park, and a representative from the hospital in Abergavenny had also promised to attend.

'Good afternoon, ladies and gentlemen,' he began, waiting for the noise to die down. With forty to fifty children here ranging in age from seven to nine, the hall was never going to be totally silent, so when he thought he had most people's attention, he dived right in.

'Mums, dads and grandparents, I know you're going to want to put your hands in your pockets for your own child's beautiful work of art, but please give everyone else a chance. This auction is to raise money for two worthwhile causes, and I know in an ideal world we shouldn't have to rely on events like this to help protect our natural heritage, or to ensure all pupils are able to take part in the end-of-year school trip, but unfortunately this is reality. So dig deep, bid high and display whichever wonderful painting you manage to acquire with pride.' He caught the eye of the hospital trust's manager. 'Mr Probert, we expect to see a whole wall of paintings in your main waiting area,' he joked.

'I'll see what I can do,' Mr Probert replied with a grin. He clearly wasn't expecting to have to pay more than a few pence for any of the children's work. Rex hoped to surprise him.

'First up is this delightful depiction of a sheep grazing among the reed beds.' He felt the need to explain, because it wasn't entirely clear what the painting actually was. 'Tamara has an abstract style and a bold use of colour,' he added, wondering why the sheep's nose was purple. 'Who will start the bidding off at five pounds?'

Tamara wriggled excitedly in her seat, her pigtails swinging about her face. 'Go on, Mummy, this one is mine!' she cried, and everyone laughed at her enthusiasm.

Her mother dutifully put her hand up.

'Five I'm bid. Who'll give me six?' Rex asked.

Tamara's hand shot up.

'You haven't got six pounds,' her mother said.

'I'm bidding for you, Mummy,' the little girl announced. 'Mr McMillan wanted six pounds, and you were only going to give him five.'

More laughter, and Tamara bounced up and down on her chair, her whole face alight with excitement.

'I think we're going to have to have another lesson on how auctions work on Monday,' Miss Harding called out with a smile.

'I'll disregard Tamara's bid, shall I?' Rex said with a wide grin on his face. This was so much fun, and the kids were absolutely delightful. A thought flashed across his mind but was gone again almost before he'd had a chance to grasp it – would he be attending things like this with his own son in the future?

That was when he saw Leanne. She hadn't been there earlier – he knew, because he'd been watching out for her – but she was there now, at the back near the door. His heart did a slow roll and his stomach lurched.

She looked gorgeous, if a little pale and tired. No wonder, what with having to charge off to London every week, and that was without all the work involved in preparing for the competition. He wondered if she'd had any applications for a manager yet.

He cleared his throat. 'Do I have six pounds?' he asked, and Sid the butcher put his hand up.

'A picture of a sheep will look good in my shop,' he said. 'A sort of before and after.'

Rex blinked. He wondered if having her picture in a shop that sold bits of the animal she had so painstakingly painted would upset Tamara, and he gave the child a concerned look.

Tamara was still bouncing.

With relief, Rex called, 'Seven?' and Tamara's mum put her hand up.

After that, the bidding took off briskly, with Sid winning the picture for a respectable £23.50. Tamara looked as though she was about to burst into tears at not being able to take her painting home with her, despite all the children being told repeatedly that they might not be able to buy their own pictures, and that they would be able to paint as many more as they wanted in school next week. Miss Harding crouched on the floor beside the little girl's chair and whispered in her ear. She soon had her smiling again, although the child had lost a little of her bounce now that she was no longer the centre of attention.

Twice Rex nodded at Stevie and twice she bid on his behalf, until Rex became the proud, if anonymous, owner of a picture of a blue sky, clouds and what was supposed to be a raven but looked more like an inkblot. He thought it was wonderful. He intended to have it framed and hung on the wall of the visitors' centre.

As the auction carried on, he found it more and more difficult not to look at Leanne. He was very conscious of her standing at the back, and when she raised a hand to bid on a lovely picture of wild primroses, he had no choice but to acknowledge her.

He was surprised how much it hurt as he nodded to her and said, 'Seven pounds I'm bid, from the lady at the back.'

Her expression was unreadable, and he would have given anything to know what she was thinking right now.

'Mister, can you please say yes to my daddy's bid?' A little voice cut into his thoughts and brought him sharply back to the task in hand.

'Oh yes, sorry.' He smiled at the boy who had spoken. 'Where were we?'

'Daddy says eight pounds and he wishes you'd get on with it.'

Rex gave the audience a rueful smile. 'Your daddy is right; I should get on with it. Eight pounds it is. Any advance on eight?'

Leanne raised her hand.

'Nine pounds. Back to you, sir.' He turned his attention to the little boy's father, who nodded. 'Ten pounds, thank you.'

He was just about to steel himself to look in Leanne's direction again when his phone rang. 'Sorry,' he said to the audience, with a grimace. 'I would normally turn it off, but I'm on call for the Mountain Rescue this weekend so I've had to leave it on. Let me just check it's not them. Miss Harding, could you take over for a second?'

He stepped off the makeshift podium and dragged his phone out of his pocket.

The call wasn't from the Mountain Rescue coordinator. It was from his mother.

He was about to ignore it when he saw he'd had several texts from her, and a sudden feeling of dread washed over him.

'I've got to take this,' he mouthed to the teacher, and briskly stepped through the side door and into the little kitchen area.

Keeping his voice down and trying not to let panic gain the upper hand, he said, 'Mum? What's up? Is it Dad?'

'No, Rex, it's Jules.'

Oh, Jules. Although she and the baby should have been the first thing to come to mind, the whole situation didn't seem real to him yet.

'Is she OK?' he asked.

'That's why I'm calling. She's had the baby.'

'*What?*' he cried, then realised that everyone in the hall could probably hear him. He lowered his voice. 'She's not due for another few weeks.'

'Babies arrive when babies feel like it,' his mother stated, then paused.

'What aren't you telling me?' Rex asked into the silence.

'The thing is…'

'Oh my God, is the baby all right?' He felt sick, and his heart missed a beat then made up for it with an uncomfortable thump.

'The baby is fine, if a little early. He's in an incubator, but he's healthy. It's…' She paused again, and Rex waited, relief making his fingers tingle. He sagged against the wall and took a deep breath.

He knew what she was going to say: that the baby was his. He realised she had been hoping all along that it would turn out to be Dean's and that was why she was sounding so odd now. He wasn't sure how he felt about the news himself – excited, terrified, despondent, overwhelmed? How was he supposed to feel?

'It's Jules,' his mother was saying.

'What about her?' Rex wondered if his son had auburn hair like him, or whether he favoured his mother. What about his eyes? Were they blue like his, or hazel like Jules's? He hoped the poor kid didn't have his toes, because—

'She's in intensive care,' his mum said.

'Oh, right.' He blinked. Was that normal for a woman who had just given birth? He had no idea. Actually, it astounded him how little he knew about the process of pregnancy, labour and birth. He did have an excuse, though, kind of, because he'd come to the party quite late. He made a note to buy a book on what to expect as a new father, because he didn't have the foggiest idea.

'Something went wrong,' his mother was saying. 'I'm not sure what, I don't have the details, but she lost a lot of blood, too much blood, and she's had a couple of transfusions, but now she's in a coma and the doctors don't know if she's going to come out of it, or if she does, what state she'd be in.' She took a breath and Rex jumped in.

'Jules? You're saying there's something wrong with *Jules*?' He didn't understand.

'Yes, love. She's in intensive care, in a coma.'

'But... *how*?'

'We don't know what happened, but from what Dean told us, the placenta was in the wrong place and Jules went into labour early and they had no chance to do a Caesarean…'

Rex let his mother talk, taking very little of it in. What did he know about placentas and Caesareans? Nothing, that was what, but he had a terrible feeling he was going to have to learn quickly if he was to have any chance of understanding what was going on.

'How serious is it?' he asked, hoping he hadn't heard his mother correctly.

'Very.' Her voice caught, and she choked back a sob. 'She might not pull through.'

'I'll leave now,' he promised, his heart pounding and a dull ache settling in behind his eyes. He felt numb and surreal, as if this was happening to someone else.

Poor, poor Jules. How could it have come to this? He'd only seen her a couple of weeks ago and she'd looked so healthy and well. His heart went out to her, to Dean, and to her poor parents.

But most of all, his heart went out to the little newborn baby who might have to face life without his mother.

Chapter 38

Leanne hadn't wanted to go to the auction, but it was for a couple of good causes and it wasn't fair to boycott the event just because the man who had organised it had broken her heart. She sidled in late, hoping he wouldn't notice her if the bidding was in full swing, but no such luck. He'd spotted her the second she walked in through the door.

His gaze hadn't lingered, however, and he didn't acknowledge her. Leanne actually thought that his mouth had tightened and his shoulders had stiffened, but it might have been her imagination, because after that he'd not glanced her way once. Except for when she'd bid on Dylan Plaister's lovely little primrose painting. Leanne had been in school with Dylan's dad, and they'd exchanged a smile. She was just about to raise her bid when a phone rang. Rex told the audience that he had to take the call, said something to the teacher, Miss Harding – who had been shooting him besotted looks, she noticed with a jealous pang – and stepped off the podium, taking his phone out of his pocket.

She wasn't sure if anyone else noticed, but when he looked at the screen, his face blanched slightly, and she hoped it wasn't bad news. She watched him walk briskly through the door leading to the little kitchen.

'Excuse me? Did you want to carry on bidding, or are you done?'

'Eh?' Leanne dragged her attention back to the podium, where the teacher was waiting for an answer. 'Um... yes.'

'Which is it?' the young woman asked politely.

'The first one. I want to carry on bidding.' She kept one ear on the open kitchen door while Miss Harding was speaking, and she could have sworn she heard Rex cry, 'What!' But no matter how hard she tried to listen, she didn't hear another peep.

When he reappeared in the hall, he looked upset and distracted. Leanne studied him as he walked up to Miss Harding, leaned in close and whispered in her ear. The teacher nodded and placed a hand briefly on his arm, and Leanne wondered if she had been wrong about Rex's reason for dumping her. Maybe it had nothing to do with his ex in Scotland and everything to do with a new love interest much nearer home, because she couldn't help noticing the way the young woman's eyes followed his retreating back.

She didn't stay to pay for or collect her picture – she'd sort it out later – telling herself it was because she had a shop to run, even though Mabel was quite capable of holding the fort for an hour. As she headed off down the street, tears pricking and chin wobbling, she saw Rex behind the wheel of his Land Rover, his expression grim. He looked both ways as he pulled out of his road, and she could have sworn he had seen her, but if he had, he didn't bother to acknowledge her.

She wouldn't cry. She'd done enough of that recently, thank you very much. Anyway, she had nothing to cry about. She had a fantastic future ahead of her and a competition to win.

So why was it that she felt like she was desperately trying to convince herself?

Chapter 39

'I'm sorry, it's close family only. Who did you say you were?'

'Rex McMillan. The baby's father.' Rex swallowed, and added, 'Possibly.'

The nurse gave him a sharp look. 'Are you related to the patient?' The patient was Jules, and he couldn't in all honesty say he was, so he shook his head.

'Can you at least tell me how she is?' he pleaded when he saw she was about to refuse to allow him in.

'Sorry, I really can't. I can let her partner know you're here. If he chooses to share her condition with you, that's up to him.'

Dean was here? Rex sighed. Of course he would be. Jules was his now, and the man had every right to be at her bedside. 'Her parents?'

The nurse gave him a sympathetic smile. 'They've stepped out to get a coffee and a sandwich. Do you want me to tell them you're here when they come back? They won't be long.'

She said this with certainty, and Rex wondered how many times she had seen this scene played out – frantic, terrified relatives sneaking off for a desperately needed break but feeling guilty about every second spent away from their loved one's side, just in case something happened.

'No, there's no need. It'll only be one more thing for them to worry about. You can ask Dean if he'll speak to me, though. Please,' he added.

He must look a sight. He'd only made one quick stop, and that was because poor Nell needed a pee. Seven hours door to door, more or less, with a swift detour to his parents' house to drop Nell off. It was late, nearly ten p.m., and he was creased and travel-weary, and more than a little strung out. Still, he reasoned, the staff in intensive care were used to seeing people when they weren't at their best. But that was no excuse for bad manners, and he'd remembered his just in time.

'Come into the relatives' room,' she said. 'It's more comfortable there and you can grab yourself a coffee from the machine. It's foul, but at least it's hot.'

Rex took her advice. Anxiety combined with his headlong drive was taking its toll, and he could use the caffeine to perk him up. He even added sugar for good measure, reckoning that the calories would give him a bit of extra stamina to see him through the next few hours. He had no idea what he was going to do beyond finding out how Jules was, and persuading the staff to let him see the baby. After that, the future was a bit of a blur. Should he remain at the hospital until something happened (he shied away from what that something might be), or should he go back to his mum and dad's house and wait for news?

Jules's parents and Dean were clearly here for the duration, and he felt he should be too, but he wasn't sure they would want him here, or if he had any right to stay.

He looked up as the door opened and Dean, his former best mate, walked through it. Rex hardly recognised him. The football-loving, pint-swilling life and soul of every party looked beaten and defeated, as if the spirit had been sucked out of him, leaving only an empty shell.

Without conscious thought, Rex strode across the room and enveloped him in a hug. Dean clutched at him like a drowning man gripping a lifebuoy, and Rex felt him shake and shudder. He patted him gently, letting his mate cry, tears welling up in his own eyes and trickling down his cheeks.

'She's not…?' he asked, when Dean's sobs subsided a little.

'What? No! I mean, not yet.' Dean pulled away and rubbed his sleeve across his face.

Rex swiped a hand at his own wet cheeks. 'Not yet,' he repeated woodenly. 'Does that mean there isn't any hope?'

Dean shrugged. He was a shrunken, older, frailer version of the man Rex had once known, his face drawn, his eyes sunken. He looked as though he hadn't slept for a week, and Rex felt nothing but a deep sadness and pity for him. He'd briefly hated him when he'd imagined Dean bringing up his son and treating him like his own, and a wave of guilt struck him. It didn't matter who played Lyall's dad, just as long as the child's mother was there. If Rex was indeed the baby's father, then the child would have two loving, caring dads. He'd have double the love, double the attention… Just please let Jules pull through, he pleaded. Lyall needed his mother.

'There's always hope,' Dean said, in a slow, dead voice, 'but mate, she lost so much blood. They gave her five units and they still couldn't stop the bleeding. They operated on her for nearly three hours. She's in the ICU; they've got her on a ventilator and there are all these tubes and wires...' He trailed off, and Rex bit his lip.

Dean sank into one of the threadbare sofas and put his head in his hands. Rex, feeling useless, got him a tea from the machine. If nothing else, it would keep his friend hydrated.

'Ta,' Dean said, without looking up, as Rex placed the plastic cup on the table next to the sofa. The surface was covered in leaflets for counselling and funeral advice.

'What happens now?' Rex asked.

'We wait.'

'Can I see him? Do you think they'll let me?' Rex plucked up the courage to ask. He didn't really want to remind Dean right now that he could be the child's father, but he was desperate to see the baby and make sure that the infant, at least, was well and healthy.

'Oh man, he's perfect,' Dean said, and Rex felt a stab of envy, swiftly quelled, that Dean had set eyes on Lyall before he'd had a chance to. 'He's got dark hair like Jules, and blue eyes, and a little squashed nose.'

Blue eyes, Rex thought. Jules's eyes were hazel. Dean's were dark brown. Blue eyes, like mine? *Oh God.*

'Hang on a sec,' Dean was saying. 'Let me check on Jules and I'll be right back to take you down to see him. He's in the skiboo.'

'The what?'

'Special care baby unit, the SCBU. He's in an incubator because he's a bit early, but he's doing OK.'

SCBU, ICU? It amazed Rex how quickly Dean had become fluent in hospital-speak. He supposed he might soon be using the acronyms with ease too, and wished with all his heart that he didn't need to, that Jules was well and healthy and that Lyall didn't need to be in the special care unit.

Dean came back and nodded his head at Rex's questioning glance. 'Jules' parents are busy with her now so it's a good time to take you to see m— the baby.'

Rex guessed that Dean had been about to say 'my son', and his heart twisted. It was so weird that the other man also thought Lyall might be his child, but maybe that was a good thing, since Dean and Jules would be living together and—

The thought hit him like a sledgehammer to the brain. What if Jules didn't pull through? What then? Who would bring the baby up? The child's father, that was who, whichever one of them that turned out to be.

He staggered and put his hand out to the wall to steady himself. In the space of little more than a couple of weeks, he'd gone from being carefree and responsibility-free to the very real prospect of being a single parent.

Then another thought came to him – they really, really needed to perform the paternity test, because if Jules… (he didn't want to face *that* word, not yet, as if by saying it in his head it might make the awful thing happen), then he didn't want to be in the middle of a fight to claim the baby. The matter of Lyall's paternity needed to be sorted out before… Again he hesitated, not wanting to face the possibility that the little boy might soon be motherless.

They arrived at the entrance to the baby unit and Rex paused. The enormity of what he was about to do punched him in the chest. He was going to meet what might be his son for the first time, and it scared him to death. What if he didn't feel that instantaneous love everyone spoke about? What if he felt nothing? He was excited and terrified, and felt sick with nerves.

'It's all right, mate, take your time,' Dean said, and Rex felt a sudden resentment that this man who had stolen Jules had seen the child first.

Oh Lord, his emotions were all over the place. He didn't know what to think, how he was supposed to feel, what he should say…

'I'm fine,' he said, although anyone could see that he wasn't.

A nurse greeted them at the door, insisting they put on hospital gowns and wash their hands. 'Your… er… baby is well and healthy,' she explained to them both, although Rex guessed that Dean had heard this before. 'He's a little small, so we'll keep him in SCBU for a while yet. This way.'

She led them into a side room, where two small bundles lay in individual cots. Along the way, Rex caught a brief glimpse of a larger area with clear-domed incubators with tiny, tiny figures inside them. The lighting was dimmed, and he only had a quick look, but seeing those little babies with wires and tubes humbled him. At least Lyall was healthy.

Dean came to a halt next to one of the plastic cots, and the expression on his face made Rex's heart constrict and miss a beat. The man looked besotted. Poor Dean, it was going to be so hard on him if Jules… and if Rex was the father. Rex would take the baby home with him – although at the moment he didn't have the foggiest idea where home was going to be – and Dean would be left with nothing. He put a hand on his former friend's arm and gave it a squeeze.

'Aye, he's bonny all right,' Dean said as Rex walked around the cot for a better look. The baby was on his side, facing away from the door, and all Rex had been able to see up until now was a mop of unruly dark hair poking out of the top of the sausage-shaped blanket.

He stood for long, long minutes staring at the face of the newborn child who might or might not be his son, and love rose up to swamp him in a tidal wave of emotion.

The little boy's eyes were tightly shut, his mouth working, lips pursing. Rex could only see his face, but it was enough, although he did long to unwrap him like the best Christmas present in the world and count those tiny toes and kiss those minute fingers.

Instead, he stared and stared, consigning the baby's face to memory. This first sight of him was so precious, and—

'Could I have a quick word?' The nurse who had spoken wasn't the same one who had shown them in. This one wore a different uniform and an air of authority. 'Not here,' she added, and gestured for the two men to follow her.

She showed them into another side room, this one with comfy chairs and bright colours on the walls. They all sat down, and Rex waited for her to begin.

'First, please let me say that I understand how difficult this is for you both. Lyall's grandparents have asked...' She paused. 'There's no easy way to say this, so... They want to determine which of you is the baby's father sooner rather than later, and to this effect a mouth swab was taken from Lyall this morning. Once we have swabs from the two of you, they will all be sent away for DNA analysis. Paternity testing isn't something the hospital would normally do, but under the circumstances...'

Rex looked at Dean and Dean stared back at him. Rex cleared his throat.

'What do we need to do?' he asked.

'I can take a swab now, if you like. Or you can wait to see a doctor, if you need it explained or if you have any questions.'

'Let's get it over with,' Rex said, and Dean nodded. 'Just one thing, though, how long will the results take to come back?'

'About a week,' the nurse said.

Rex's heart hammered. The idea that he might already be a parent was terrifying and exhilarating at the same time. The idea that he might not was just as overwhelming and he wasn't sure how he felt about that, either.

Chapter 40

Nope, nah, definitely not, maybe. Leanne was sifting through a pile of applications, not very enthusiastically. None of them had really made her sit up and take notice. Most were nothing but hopeful, a few were meh and only a couple were worth the bother of inviting them in for an interview, but even then she wasn't all that impressed.

Maybe her standards were too high, but she really did feel she needed someone who had worked in a flower shop before. Trimming your dad's hedge and weeding his raised beds didn't actually count, she decided, tossing that particular letter on the definitely not pile.

She sighed dramatically, wondering what she should do now. Should she keep advertising, or should she have another look at a couple of the maybes? Time was getting short and she really did need to have someone in place soon.

'What's up?' Saul said.

Leanne let out a squeak. 'What are you doing here?' It was late, and she'd assumed that with her parents in bed, she had the downstairs to herself.

'I live here,' he replied.

'No, technically you don't. You have your own place, so use it.'

Saul's lips twisted into a wry smile. 'I can't.'

'Why not? Had a tiff with Murray?'

'Not exactly.'

'Go away, Saul, I'm not in the mood for games,' Leanne grumbled.

'Sorry. It isn't a game. Murray has got himself a girl-friend and I'm keeping out of his way, that's all.'

'Really? Since when?'

'A couple of months now.'

'Who is she? I might know her.'

Saul filled her in on the details and Leanne enjoyed having her mind taken off her immediate problems. She was really pleased for Murray – it was about time he had a steady relationship. The same went for Saul, too, but she despaired of him ever settling down.

'I reckon he'll be asking her to marry him before too long,' Saul confided.

'Crikey, he doesn't hang about, does he?'

'You know Murray, he's the quiet one in the family. I hope he brings her to meet Mum before he pops the question, though, otherwise he won't hear the end of it,' Saul said.

'What will happen with your house?' Leanne wanted to know.

Saul shrugged. 'It makes sense for him to stay in it if he does get married, rather than trying to find somewhere else to live. I can always move back in here.'

'Great. I'm looking forward to it,' Leanne said, deadpan.

Saul smiled and shook his head, and there was silence for a while until he picked up some of the applications and rifled through them. 'No joy?'

'Not really.'

He scanned a letter. 'This one seems all right.'

Leanne took it from him and glanced at it. 'She's too old.'

'Mabel is old; this one is only in her fifties,' Saul pointed out. He picked another application off the maybe pile. 'What about this one?'

'Too young.'

'This one?'

'Too...' She hesitated.

'You haven't really got a reason, have you?' he asked. 'I get the feeling you're going to find fault with all of them. Is that because you can't let go of the reins?'

She shrugged. 'Maybe.'

'Talk to me, Lea. I might be able to help.'

Oh God, she was going to cry. 'I'm scared,' she admitted in a tiny voice, her eyes beginning to fill up.

Her brother scooted his chair closer and put an arm around her. 'What of?'

'Everything!' And she burst into noisy tears.

When she'd calmed down enough to speak properly and not simply make *ugh, ugh* noises, Saul pushed her away slightly to study her.

'Tell me, sis. What can I do to help? Is it the next round? Do you need me to get the wire cutters out again?'

Leanne snivelled and sniffed, her smile as damp as her face. But at least it *was* a smile; her brother, for all his annoying ways, never failed to cheer her up, even if it was just a tiny bit.

'No wire cutters,' she said, blowing her nose on a tissue she'd found in her pocket.

'Come on, spill the beans. A problem shared and all that,' he insisted.

'If you must know, the whole idea of leaving Tangle-wood scares me.'

'Of course it does. It's only natural. Moving to London and going to work for Jarred Townsend is a big step.'

'I don't know if I can do it. What if I'm not good enough? I might make a right pig's ear of it.'

Saul shrugged. 'If you don't try, you'll never know, will you? Do you want to get to eighty and think "I wish" or "what if"? Jarred Townsend must think you're good enough or he would never have made you an offer.'

It was odd the way everyone seemed to refer to Jarred by his full name, Leanne thought absently, then wondered when it was that she'd stopped doing the same.

'Maybe you're right,' she conceded. 'But what if I get there and he realises he's made a mistake?'

'Then you come back home and go back to working in your flower shop,' Saul pointed out. 'You won't really have lost anything.'

But she had already lost something, hadn't she? She'd lost Rex. Although to be fair, she wasn't sure whether she'd actually had him in the first place. She must have imagined the feelings and the connection between them for him to leave her high and dry so quickly and so thoroughly.

She blamed herself for the state she was in – if she'd concentrated more on the competition and less on her love life, she wouldn't be feeling as awful as she did now.

'There's more to this than you're telling me, isn't there?' Saul asked. 'If I were you, I'd be grabbing this opportunity with both hands. The Leanne I know would too. She's never been afraid of anything in her life. She's a real go-getter, knows what she wants, then goes and gets it.'

'I know what a go-getter is.' Leanne bumped his shoulder with her own. 'Idiot.'

'So why aren't you being one? I know you, Lea, and this isn't you. What's happened? Has Jarred Townsend said something, or done something? Because if he has, I'll go get those wire cutters now and pay him a visit.'

She nudged him again. 'Don't be silly.'

'Tell me what's wrong, then,' her brother demanded, 'because this isn't like you at all. Yes, I get that it's a big move and you're bound to be worried and nervous, but I've never seen you cry like this. Not even when Dad's prize ram broke your arm.'

'He was a nasty sod,' Leanne said, smiling wryly at the memory. 'It bloody hurt.'

'Stop trying to change the subject.'

'You started it!'

'Why have you cried yourself to sleep every night for the past week?'

Leanne froze. 'I haven't.'

'You have. I've heard you.'

'How long have you been sleeping here?'

'About a week.'

'Oh.'

'Yes, oh. Now, are you going to tell me?'

Leanne thought for a moment. 'It's women's problems,' she said, knowing Saul would run away faster than a rabbit being chased by a fox at the possibility that he might have to discuss such a thing with his sister. Ha, that'll shut him up, she thought.

It didn't.

'I don't believe you,' he said. 'If you've got medical issues that are serious enough to make you cry every night, then I'm telling Mum and she'll take you to the doctor.'

'I'm too old for my mother to take me to the doctor!' she protested.

'Do you want to chance it? You know what she's like when she gets going.'

Leanne fell silent. Patient confidentiality wouldn't count for a lot with their mother if she suspected something was wrong with any of her children. Leanne had no doubt Iris would make the appointment on her behalf and drag her to the surgery kicking and screaming if necessary.

'Rex McMillan,' she said eventually.

'What about him?'

Leanne worried at her lip with her teeth. It was one thing admitting it to herself; it was another thing entirely to admit it to someone else. It made everything more real somehow. 'I think I love him.'

'*What?*' Saul sat up straighter. 'You *do?*'

'I do.'

Her brother thought for a moment. 'Does he love you?'

She shook her head, not trusting herself to speak.

'Bummer.' Saul let out a breath. 'Does he know how you feel about him?'

'No.'

'Right. Maybe if you told him…?'

'Yeah, like that's a really good idea,' Leanne retorted. 'What am I supposed to say? "Hey, Rex, I know we've had a couple of dates, and we've kissed an' all, but I think I love you. Whaddya say?"'

'I wasn't suggesting you should come right out with it like that,' Saul began, then stopped. 'A couple of dates? Really? When? And *kissing*?'

'You're not being much help, you know.'

'Sorry. I don't have much experience of this kind of thing.'

Leanne raised her eyebrows.

'I've got plenty of experience in the kissing department,' he amended. 'I was talking about love.'

'Count yourself lucky. It's horrid.'

Saul put his arm around her again and she leaned in for a cuddle, feeling the dampness of his T-shirt where she'd cried on it earlier. He was all right, for a brother, she thought. Not that she'd ever tell him that.

'Is it just this Rex thing that's making you unhappy?' he asked.

'You can't even say the word "love", can you?' she teased. 'No wonder girls don't stick around. You're a commitment-phobe.'

'I haven't met the right one yet, that's all,' he replied stiffly.

'You will, one day,' she said.

'So will you,' he replied.

'I thought I already had,' was Leanne's soft, sad response.

Chapter 41

It might be twenty-five-plus degrees Celsius down in the valley, but the temperature on the mountain above Glenshona barely reached double figures, what with the elevation, and the wind blowing inexorably from the west. It was positively howling a gale up here, Rex thought, watching Nell dance through the clumps of heather and blueberry bushes.

He bent down. Fruit was just starting to form on the bushes, little hard nodules, and it would be a few weeks yet before they'd be ripe enough to pick. He used to love nothing better than clambering up the steep slopes above Glenshona, a pack of jam sandwiches in one pocket and a bottle of blackcurrant squash in the other, clutching a Tupperware box in his hand with every intention of filling it to the brim with wild blueberries.

What usually happened was that he'd eat more than he put in the container, his lips and tongue stained purple, and then he'd get distracted by a skylark's nest or a burbling spring, or something equally riveting, so the promised apple and blueberry tart his mother vowed to bake when he returned home would never materialise.

He straightened up. The jagged humped spines of mountain after mountain faded into the distance, their colours soft and muted, shrinking patches of snow still clinging to some of them. The air was fresh and clean, carrying the scents of the land he knew so well: gorse, grass, heather and the occasional hint of deer. But it was the almost-silence he loved the most; the wind susurrating through the low vegetation and the calls of nesting birds were the only noises except for his own breathing and Nell's tongue-lolling panting.

For a long time he gazed into the distance, thinking. Guilt tugged at him with sneaking, relentless fingers. Jules was down there, far to the south, in her hospital bed in Glasgow where she'd been transferred yesterday. Her parents had followed the ambulance in their Skoda, a grim foreshadowing of a funeral car behind a hearse.

He shuddered at the image. Dean had informed him that the doctors hadn't given up on her yet, but they were duty-bound to prepare the family for the worst. Dean had also gone to Glasgow, the baby too, now that he was ready to leave the SCBU, in the hope that the infant would help bring her out of her coma. Rex's heart broke for all of them.

He found a lump of rock to perch on and drew a flask out of his backpack, ignoring his sandwiches.

Nell didn't ignore them. He usually shared them with her, so she stuck her nose into his hand to let him know that though he mightn't be hungry, she certainly was.

Stroking her ears absent-mindedly, he drank his coffee and tried to keep his emotions under control.

When tears gathered in the corners of his eyes, spilling over and trickling down his chilled cheeks, he realised he'd failed. If he was going to cry, what better place to do it than on the top of a mountain where no one except his dog and a few birds would witness it? He'd tried so hard to be strong, and not to break down – because that wasn't going to benefit anyone, was it? – but he couldn't prevent the outpouring of grief and sorrow that was threatening to overwhelm him now.

Giving in, recognising that he had to let it out, he put his head in his hands and sobbed.

He seemed to be crying for everyone – for Jules, for Lyall, who might be left motherless, for Jules's parents, for Dean, for his own parents, who had the possibility of a new grandchild to consider and were trying to be supportive and strong for him and the baby. He was also crying for himself, and even though he thought he was being selfish for mourning what could be the imminent loss of his own dreams, he couldn't help himself.

Leanne, with her creamy skin and her smiling brown eyes, filled his mind. He could almost smell her flowery scent, almost feel her in his arms. He'd been on the brink of telling her he loved her, consequences be damned.

Thank God he hadn't.

Feeling drained and empty, though somewhat calmer and more focused, he continued with his walk, but not before remembering to feed his sandwiches to a grateful Nell. If he was hungry later, he'd grab something before he left for the hospital. He planned on visiting this evening; he needed to see the baby. He had yet to cuddle the little boy, and the urge to hold him was impossible to ignore.

Was this what fatherhood was all about – this over-whelming longing to be near your child? He smiled ruefully. He might be desperate to hold him, but he was terrified at the same time. What if he dropped him, or hurt him in some way? Crikey, he hadn't appreciated how simple life had been only a couple of weeks ago. The prospect of being a parent – and the dread of being a single one, at that – had turned him into one giant mess of uncertainty.

One such uncertainty was to do with his job. He was supposed to be back at work tomorrow. Luckily, he hadn't been scheduled to work this weekend, but he had to return at some point. As much as he didn't want to leave Glenshona, he had to go back to Tanglewood until the results of the paternity test were in and he knew one way or the other what his future would be.

He checked his watch. It was time he made his way back down. He wanted a shower before he set off for the hospital and maybe a bite to eat. He still didn't feel hungry, but he knew he needed to keep his strength up for what was to come.

Just one more minute, though, because it was so peaceful up here. The lack of people, the wide-open spaces, the heather-scented air, the huge sky – it all gave him room to breathe and think, although he'd not managed to arrive at any clear decision or course of action yet.

The view from the top was breathtaking, and he took a moment to savour it.

Bloody hell! His phone ringing made him jump; he hadn't anticipated being able to get a signal up here.

It was Dean.

Oh God…

He froze, a part of him not wanting to answer, not wanting to hear what he knew Dean was about to tell him.

'Hello?' His voice broke and he coughed to try to cover it.

'Rex, mate? I've got some news.'

'Go on.' He was holding himself rigidly, his shoulders tense, his head aching.

'She's come out of it.'

'*What?*'

'Jules. She's woken up.'

Rex's legs gave way and he slumped down onto the grass. Nell, thinking this was a new kind of game, jumped on top of him.

'Nell! Get off!' Rex pushed her away. 'Sorry, did you say Jules is awake?' He could hardly believe it.

'Yeah, she is.' Dean sounded relieved and exhausted.

'That's fantastic news. Tell her I said hi. Oh...' A horrible thought occurred to him. 'Is she OK?'

Dean immediately knew what he meant. 'A bit confused and really tired, but yeah, she's good. They're going to keep her here for today, then transfer her back tomorrow. They reckon she could be home next week. She's even breastfed Lyall.'

'Brilliant. I'm so happy for her, and for Lyall. I hated to think of the poor little chap without his mother.'

Dean let out a sigh. 'Me too.'

An awkward silence followed, then both of them spoke at once.

'You first,' Rex said.

'I was going to say, I think it might be best if you waited until Jules and Lyall are out of hospital before you visit. Is that OK?'

'No problem,' he said, although he really would have loved to visit the baby and hold him for the first time.

After asking Dean to give Jules his regards and the baby a kiss for him, he ended the call. For the second time that day, he had tears in his eyes, but this time they were due to relief.

With a slightly lighter heart, he hiked back down the mountain. Now if only he could get Leanne Green out of his head… But a part of him really, really didn't want to forget her.

Chapter 42

Leanne swallowed hard. If she'd thought the contestants had been under pressure before, it was nothing compared to the pressure that the four of them still left in the competition felt now. There was only one more round to go after this one, and then the winner would be revealed.

She didn't know whether to giggle hysterically or to burst into tears. The whole thing seemed rather unreal. She couldn't claim to have grown close to her fellow florists, but there was a degree of camaraderie mixed in with the intense competitiveness she was sure they all felt. She wondered if the contestants of *Bake Off* felt the same; on that show the bakers seemed to be the best of friends and highly supportive of each other. Her fellow *Stars* weren't, she felt. They were in it to win it, come hell or high water or a fight over a bunch of asters.

Not that anyone would be using asters this morning, because the theme for the unseen task was 'Green'. Not a bloom or a bud in sight.

For a change, each contestant had been allocated a set number of leafy stems, plus the usual assortment of oasis in various shapes, string, wire, tape, vases, twine, a wreath, glue, raffia and moss.

Rory was his usual sleek, polished self. He shot his cuffs and cleared his throat. 'Ladies and gentlemen, you may have noticed that the chiller and the stockroom are locked, and that you each have identical items on your benches. You can use all of the items or some of the items. What you make is entirely up to you. Today we are giving you free rein in your designs.' He lowered his voice and leaned forward, as if he didn't want the judges to hear, which was difficult considering they were standing right next to him. 'They want to be wowed. Think outside the box.' He straightened up again, then boomed out, 'You have one hour, and your time starts... now!'

Green. Great. Wonderful. Even though 'green' was supposed to be Leanne's forte, she didn't have a clue what she was going to do. She might as well grab her handbag and go home right now, because everyone else was twisting and snipping with enthusiasm. Or was it manic determination to produce *something*?

She stood there for far too long, idly rolling a leaf between her fingers, her mind a terrifying blank. She rolled another one. The first had uncurled slightly. Could she do anything with that, or had she simply destroyed a part of her allocation?

An itch at the back of her mind was irritating her. Bag, handbag...

She had it!

Selecting the largest leaves, she began rolling them into tubes, fastening them in place with a dab of adhesive. When she had about forty or so, she laid ten side by side and stuck them together. She did the same with nine more leaves, placing them on top of the first, then added another layer, then another, fewer leaves on each successive one, until she had a shape with a flat front and back and curved sides. After that, she built the edges up with yet more rolled leaves, and inserted two twine handles. Then she tied leaves into a kind of a bow around them and stepped back.

She had made a handbag. It wasn't perfect, but with the time constraint it wasn't too bad. At least the shape was right – it looked like a hobo bag, only firmer and smaller, and with more definition.

She thought it was quite cute. She only hoped the judges did too.

By now, she was exhausted and beginning to think that if she never saw another flower for as long as she lived, it would be too soon. She suspected she was starting to quite dislike flower arranging, floral displays, floral competitions, people who judged floral competitions... In fact, she came to the conclusion that she didn't even like flowers themselves any more, or anything green for that matter. She was fed up to the eyeballs with it. The only thing she wanted to do was fall into bed and sleep for a week and forget she'd ever agreed to come on this stupid show. What on earth had possessed her to enter it in the first place?

But when the four remaining contestants lined up for the judges' verdict, she remembered the reason – because she knew she could do this, that she was good enough, ambitious enough – and her drive and enthusiasm returned in a rush of desperate longing to get through to the final.

After all, with Rex out of her life, what else did she have?

Chapter 43

The envelope was on the hall table when Rex arrived back from the supermarket. He'd offered to do the shopping for his parents. It was the least he could do, considering he was still staying with them. Besides, it kept him busy. Jules had been released from hospital yesterday, a day later than expected, and he was due to visit her and the baby this afternoon. Tomorrow, Sunday, he had to make the long journey back to Tanglewood. The National Park Trust had agreed to the time off, but they were expecting him back in work on Monday.

He couldn't wait to see Lyall. That brief glimpse of him in the too-sterile environment of the SCBU had been nowhere near enough, and Dean had made it clear that he wasn't needed – or wanted? – at the hospital. But now that Jules and the baby were home, he was dying to pay the little boy a proper visit.

Putting the carrier bags down in the hall, he drew in a deep breath as he eyed the envelope. The bungalow was still and silent. Both his parents were out, and he was grateful for the solitude. This was something he preferred to face on his own.

He knew what the letter contained. All his post went to his Tanglewood address, but he had given his parents' address for this particular matter. After all, he hadn't known how long he was going to be here, so it seemed sensible.

He stood there for a long time looking at it. Seeing the result in black and white would make it so final. If he *was* Lyall's dad, there was no coming back from this. The irrefutability of the results in that letter was a solid weight in his heart.

Slowly he reached out a hand, noticing it shaking a little, and with his thumb and forefinger grasped the envelope and picked it up.

It was light and insubstantial, hardly heavy enough for the enormity it contained.

'Just do it,' he muttered, and tore the envelope open and drew out the letter in one swift motion, before he gave himself a chance to change his mind.

The words *DNA Profiling Test Results* jumped off the page. Underneath were the words *Alleged father* followed by his own name, and *Child* followed by Lyall's. He noticed that Jules had used her own surname for the baby.

And underneath that was the result.

He stared at it for a long time.

Probability of paternity 0%

He nodded to himself once, then carefully folded the letter and put it back in the envelope, which he replaced on the hall table. He debated whether to call Dean, but there didn't seem any point. Dean would have had the results today too. By now, he would know who Lyall's father was, and that it wasn't Rex. He didn't know how he felt about that, but he did know there was a splinter of sorrow in his heart; he hadn't realised until now how much he'd accepted the prospect of being a father.

This was for the best, he said to himself as he threw his things into his holdall and gathered up Nell's bed and bowls. Jules and Dean would be proper parents; together with Lyall, they'd be a complete family, without the complication of stepfathers and birth fathers and visiting rights, arguments over who the boy should spend Christmas with and the minefield of feelings and emotions that went with it.

When his phone rang, he realised he'd almost been expecting it.

'Hi, Jules.' He heard how flat his voice sounded.

'I just wondered if you were still coming over this afternoon?' She was cautious, her tone careful.

'There's not much point, is there?'

'You've got the results?'

'Yep.'

A pause. 'I would have thought you'd be over the moon that Dean is the father.'

'Ah well,' was all he said, but he heard the catch in his voice and guessed Jules had probably heard it too.

'I didn't realise you wanted kids so badly,' she said.

'Neither did I,' he admitted.

'Dean told me you didn't get to hold him.'

'Who, Dean? Nah, if he wants a cuddle, he can ask you for one.'

Her chuckle floated over the airwaves, and he was pleased he'd lightened the mood a little.

'Silly, I meant Lyall,' she said.

'I know you did,' he replied softly.

'You can still come over if you want.'

'Can I pop in and see him another day? It's just that...'

Jules seemed to understand. 'Of course you can. Any time.'

'Bye, Jules, and I'm glad you're better. Give my best to Dean.' He found he meant it too.

But a part of him still grieved for what he'd so nearly had. An even bigger part of him grieved for what he'd actually had and lost.

Leanne.

Chapter 44

'Saul,' Rex said in greeting.

'Rex,' Saul replied.

Both men fell silent, reaching for their respective pints and taking a long swallow.

Rex was drowning his sorrows for the second evening in a row. Once he'd arrived back in Tanglewood in the early afternoon, he'd spent his Sunday sorting out the house after a week away – laundry, food shopping (what little there was in the cupboards and fridge had gone stale or past its use-by date) and catching up on emails. He'd also napped a lot; he hadn't realised how weary he'd been. He'd kept himself busy yesterday and today, because he was back at work, but the evenings had stretched out before him, long and lonely. Everywhere he'd looked he'd seen memories of Leanne: sitting on the sofa, lying on the floor with her nose buried in the soft fur on the top of Nell's head, or taking the plates out to the kitchen. He'd come to The Hen and Duck for yet another pint (or three) and the hope that a change of scenery would take his mind off things; if that didn't work, the alcohol might help numb the ache.

Not for the first time since he'd got back, he wondered if he was doing the right thing by staying in Tanglewood.

He couldn't keep running away, he'd told himself sharply. He didn't want to move back to Glenshona now that there was no reason for him to do so. Yet he didn't want to stay in Tanglewood either, because of Leanne. Well, the memories of her at least, because he wasn't entirely sure whether she was still in the village or if she had left for good to move to London and accept Jarred Townsend's fabulous job offer.

'Any news?' Saul asked, breaking the silence.

'Nah. You?'

'Not really.'

Silence again. More pint sipping.

Rex finished his beer. 'Fancy another?'

'Why not?' Saul tipped his almost-empty glass at Mads, who was serving behind the bar. 'Same again, mate.'

Rex didn't mean to, but the words just slipped out of his mouth. 'How's Leanne getting on? You know, with the competition an' all?'

'She's through to the final,' Saul said, but he didn't sound too thrilled about it.

'That's good, isn't it? It's what she wants.'

'I suppose.'

'How does she feel about it? I know she was worried,' Rex said.

'She still is. It's a big step and I'm not sure her heart is in it.'

'In what? Winning the competition, or taking Jarred Townsend up on his job offer?'

'You know about that?'

'Yeah.' Rex didn't mention that it wasn't Leanne who had told him but Mabel. Though it didn't matter who'd told him; the outcome would be the same – Leanne was still going to live and work in London.

'She's lived here all her life. Moving to London will be a huge change,' Saul said.

'Did she find a manager for the shop?' Rex asked.

'Not yet.' Saul's face closed up and Rex wondered what he'd said to offend the other man. Then he took a sip of his ale, screwed his mouth up and said in a rush, 'Between you and me, I don't think she's trying too hard.'

'Why ever not?'

Another grimace from Saul; Rex thought he looked as though he had a bad case of heartburn.

'I can hear her, at night,' he said.

'Hear what?' Was she working in the middle of the night? Rex expected she must be, what with the competition ratcheting up. He was so proud of her, getting through to the final, but the pressure on her must be incredible.

'Crying,' Saul said.

'Oh.' Rex sipped at his pint, using the action to give him a second or two to think. 'Why?' he asked eventually.

'I don't think she's happy. She seems...' Saul paused, and Rex wondered what he was about to say. 'Fragile, brittle. Driven. But not in a good way.'

'It's the pressure,' he said. 'It's bound to be getting to her.'

Saul shook his head slowly. 'I don't think that's it.'

'What do you think it is?'

He picked up his glass and looked at Rex over the rim. 'I dunno, mate, but she's been like it for at least a week. She seems to have lost her spark. You don't know anything about that, do you? I mean,' he added quickly, 'she's not said anything to you?'

'I haven't seen her for a while,' Rex admitted.

Saul raised his eyebrows. 'I thought you two were getting close.'

'It… ah… didn't work out.'

'That's a pity. I thought you'd be good together.'

So did I, Rex nearly said. And they had been, hadn't they? Until he'd found out Jules was expecting, and Leanne had broken up with him. A part of him wanted to confront her, to hear her say to his face that she hadn't felt anything for him. He wanted to barge back into her life and try to convince her that they'd been good together, that their relationship had been the start of something wonderful.

But she'd made her intentions more than clear when she'd posted the advert for a shop manager – she was going to London to work for Jarred Townsend, and Rex wasn't going to try to stand in her way, no matter how much he wanted to drive over to the farm and beg.

Chapter 45

Leanne had been awake since before the sun came up, the flat silver light of pre-dawn creeping into the sky with imperceptible slowness. Unable to sleep (this was getting to be a regular thing), she got dressed and slipped out of the house, her hiking boots on her feet and a down jacket on her back, although she knew she'd probably end up taking the jacket off after a mile or so.

Birds filled the woodland with song, calming her shredded nerves a little; not completely, but being outdoors did help. Her problems and worries faded a little when faced with nature in the raw. With the dramatic peaks and valleys all around, she became very aware of how this land had been here long before she'd been born, and would still be here long after she had turned to dust. The image wasn't depressing but reassuring – life would go on and she was only a tiny, tiny part of that. It was humbling.

Right now, she felt extremely grateful to be able to witness a brief window in the lives of the creatures all around her: animals getting on with the business of mating and bringing up young, the eaters and the eaten. She understood how lucky she was compared to the robins (not so visible now with other birds all around and the leaves hiding them from prying eyes) and the wagtails, the voles and the rabbits. Her problems were nothing next to theirs. She didn't have to struggle for survival every day, and if she made the wrong choice, her life wasn't on the line. No sparrowhawk, falcon or fox would be waiting to pounce; only the fear of failure and a return to Tanglewood with her tail between her legs.

She had the flower shop (she wasn't going to give that up), she had a place to live, even if it was on her parents' farm — she actually had nothing to lose by taking Jarred up on his offer. Although she'd already made her decision, she was waiting until tomorrow to tell him officially.

Tomorrow was the final.

The thought made her tummy churn and her heart flutter. She so desperately wanted to win. The competition had consumed her life for the past three months. She'd put so much effort into it, had immersed herself in it totally (more or less), and she deserved to come first, damn it! But there was hardly a hair's breadth to choose between the three finalists, and she was well aware that the win could go to any one of them. It all depended on performance on the day, so the producers said, although Leanne did have her suspicion that the judges had a favourite.

Slowly and with great care not to make any noise, she tiptoed along the narrow, barely there path. A blackbird called a warning overhead, protesting at her presence, and she mentally shushed it as she opened the door to the hide and slipped inside, closing it behind her softly.

She had a couple of hours before she needed to leave. There was nothing else to be done; the last flower-arranging task she had been set was ready and her overnight bag was packed. The only thing left for her to do was to say goodbye to her old life. The new one was calling, its demands increasing until it would overwhelm her tomorrow. Whether she won or not, her life would never be the same again. Unless she made a spectacular arse of herself.

There I go again, she thought, letting my doubts and insecurity have the upper hand. Jarred would not have made her the offer if he didn't believe in her, so it was time she believed in herself, because that was the only thing holding her back.

Once, she might have turned her back on this future for a different one entirely, but it was not to be. The man who had stolen her heart hadn't wanted it, had given it back to her in jagged pieces, leaving her bruised and sore.

For a moment, she wondered what she was doing here, at the beavers' dam, the place where she suspected she had begun to fall in love with Rex. She could have walked the steep paths above the farm just as easily, although with considerably more puffing and panting. It would have achieved the same result, which was to soothe her, steady her and centre her. So why had she come *here*?

Then she realised that it was to say goodbye. Not just to her easy, familiar flower shop life; she was saying goodbye to the farm she had grown up on, to this landscape that had helped her to flourish and thrive, to the family who had allowed her the space and the boundaries to become who she was now, and to the friends she had shared her sandwiches at school with and in whose ears she had whispered the name of her first crush.

But more than that, she was here to say goodbye to the man she still loved, despite the way he had disappeared out of her life, and the way he had let their budding relationship wither and die until it was nothing but memories and a pain in her heart that might never fade.

'Rex.' His name felt strange on her tongue, like some exotic food she had never eaten before.

She closed her eyes, almost feeling his arms around her, his warm lips on hers, the taste of him, his scent.

When she opened them again, it was with a whispered 'Goodbye' and the image of his face seared on her heart.

Chapter 46

Crying, he'd said. Rex mulled it over, again and again. Why would she be crying, and every night, too? He imagined her getting ready to leave for London later today. Should he call by the flower shop and—

No. He shouldn't. He'd only be torturing himself, like a kid picking at a scabby knee, hurting but unable to stop.

But Saul had said she'd been crying. Why?

Rex had got the feeling that Leanne's brother had been trying to tell him something. The question was, *what*? He'd spent half the night thinking about it, worrying at it and annoying the hell out of Nell, who had been trying to sleep. He'd even got dressed and taken the dog for a walk, padding past the flower shop just to feel closer to Leanne.

Nothing had worked.

Lonely and sad, he'd taken Nell down to the river, remembering the last time he'd done exactly the same thing, and wishing he could turn the clock back.

Too late now, of course.

But why had she been crying?

He was still asking himself the very same question, over and over again, and still not arriving at an answer that made any sense, when he popped into Peggy's Tea Shoppe for breakfast. He had bread and cereal at home, but the thought of eating alone at his kitchen table filled him with dread, so he'd snapped Nell's lead on and was now sitting on his own in the cafe. At least there was Betty and Stevie, and although they didn't have much time to talk with him, they did provide some company.

He sat at his usual table and stared at the noticeboard. There was no advert for Border collie pups for sale today. In some ways, he almost wished he'd never spotted it in the first place, although if he hadn't, Nell wouldn't now be lying quietly at his feet hoping he'd drop a bit of croissant.

He would also never have met Leanne, and that didn't bear thinking about. Better to have loved and lost, and all that. Who'd said that? He tried to remember, anything to keep his mind off memories of Leanne sitting opposite him in this very tea shop.

'Stevie?' he called. 'Who was it who said "better to have loved and lost than never to have loved at all"?'

Stevie wandered over to his table, wiping her hands on a cloth. 'Dunno. Shakespeare probably. He said most things.'

Betty followed her. 'Alfred, Lord Tennyson,' she said.

'Was it? I always thought it was Shakespeare,' Stevie said.

'Everyone does. It was definitely Tennyson, from his poem "In Memoriam".' Betty pulled out a chair and recited, 'I hold it true, whate'er befall; I feel it, when I sorrow most; 'tis better to have loved and lost than never to have loved at all.'

'You are a dark horse,' Stevie called over her shoulder as she approached another customer to take an order.

'They used to teach proper stuff when I was in school,' Betty commented, 'like your times tables and poetry. I never thought this one would come in handy, though. It goes to show how wrong a person can be.' She placed both hands on the table, leaned forward and looked Rex straight in the eye. 'What have *you* been wrong about?'

Rex blinked. 'Um… lots of things?'

'You've got that right.'

'Excuse me?'

'I'm talking about Leanne Green.'

'What about her?'

Betty shot him a disapproving look. 'You know what I mean.'

'I don't.'

'I don't know exactly what's gone on between the two of you, but I know something has, and I also know it's nothing good. She's got a face like a wet weekend in June, and you're quoting Tennyson at me. Now, are you going to tell me what's up, or do I have to force it out of you?'

Despite himself, Rex burst out laughing, then halted, surprised. That was the first time he'd felt like laughing since he'd learnt about Jules's pregnancy. 'How do you suppose you're going to do that? Beat me? Torture me? Refuse to serve me croissants?'

'No. I'll go ask Leanne.'

'I doubt if she'll tell you either.'

'One of you will,' Betty vowed grimly, determination written all over her face.

'Bloody hell, you're worse than the Spanish Inquisition,' Rex muttered.

'I've been around a bit, and seen a bit too, in my time. Go on, you can tell me, I'm not easily shocked.' She gave him a wrinkle-faced smile. It was meant to be expectant and hopeful, but it reminded Rex of the expression on the Wicked Queen's face in 'Snow White' when she was disguised as an old woman and was trying to persuade Snow White to eat the apple.

'Not on your life,' he said. He really didn't fancy airing his problems in the middle of a tea shop to an octogenarian with an attitude problem.

Betty clapped a hand to her mouth. 'It's not that bad, is it? Who have you slept with and feel so guilty about that you can't face that poor young girl? You should be ashamed of yourself. Oh, wait, you are, and that's why you've split up with her.'

Rex sighed. 'She split up with me, not the other way around.'

'She never did!'

He shrugged.

'Why, what did you do?' the old lady demanded. 'You've bound to have done something for Leanne to have ended it.'

'Nothing. Please stop it with the random guessing.'

'I can keep this up for hours, so you might as well tell me.'

She probably could, Rex thought, but he wasn't going to give her the chance. He pushed his chair away from the table and got to his feet.

'You haven't finished your croissant,' Betty pointed out.

'I've lost my appetite. Stevie, can you tell me how much I owe you?' he called.

Stevie glanced around from arguing with the coffee machine (she seemed to do that a lot), took one look at his face, another look at Betty's, and asked, 'Has she been annoying you?'

Rex shrugged.

'She tends to do that. I've always found it best to let her get on with it, whatever it is,' Stevie said. 'Give me a sec, Bert is being a pain.'

Bert. She called the coffee machine *Bert*? Was everyone in this tea shop barmy?

Betty said, 'Him and Leanne have fallen out and he won't tell me why. If you make him sit back down and eat his croissant, I'll winkle it out of him.'

'Betty, I can't make him do anything.' Stevie turned her attention to Rex, as did everyone else in the cafe. Rex's cheeks grew warm. 'Why have you fallen out? I thought the pair of you were in luuurrrve.'

Rex's cheeks grew hotter and he mumbled under his breath, 'I thought we were too.'

Betty cupped a hand to her ear. 'What was that? I didn't quite catch it.'

Stevie stopped fiddling with Bert, wiped her hands and came out from behind her counter. 'Seriously,' she said to him, 'you may as well tell her. For a start, she'll find out one way or another, and you never know, she might be able to help. If it wasn't for her, I wouldn't be with Nick, and Tia and William wouldn't be engaged. Our Betty is a right little matchmaker.'

'I don't want to know what it is you've done, or think you've done, or should have done and haven't…' Betty turned to Stevie. 'Have I covered all the bases?' Stevie nodded. 'As I was saying, I don't want to know – oh bugger, yes I do, but you're not going to tell me – but the way I see it, you're as miserable as the devil at an angels' tea party right now, so it can't get any worse. You think you've lost her anyway, and you really will have if you don't pull your finger out of your whatsit, get off your behind and go and tell her how you feel. If it don't work, so be it, but at least you've tried.'

Stevie nodded. 'She's right.'

'She broke up with me, remember?' Rex said.

'Pish. You must have given her a good reason.' Betty scowled at him.

'I didn't,' he protested, ignoring the fact that if he'd managed to actually tell her his news, she would have had a very good reason indeed. 'She said she didn't think we were any good together.'

'Believe me, my lad, she doesn't mean it.'

'She sounded pretty convincing to me,' he replied. This conversation was pointless.

'And you just let her walk away? You didn't bother to fight for her, to tell her you love her? Shame on you.'

'She's moving to London, taking a job there,' he protested. 'What's there to fight for?'

'Her heart? Your happiness? Look, sunshine, if you don't let her know how you feel, you'll regret it for the rest of your life. What have you got to lose, eh? A bit of pride? Pah! Go for it, I say. Get over yourself and go get her!'

Rex froze, thinking frantically. Betty *was* right. He needed to gather his courage and tell Leanne what had happened and how he felt. But...

'I can't, not right now. Later, when she comes back from London,' he said.

Betty put her hands on her hips. 'You're making excuses.'

'What if I spoil her chances in the competition by getting her all upset?'

'What if you don't? What if you put a smile on her face again and give her the opportunity to decide what she wants for herself? She's a grown woman. All she needs you to do is to let her know she has another option.'

Chapter 47

With one last look around her bedroom, Leanne picked up her overnight bag and trotted downstairs.

'Got everything?' her mother asked, as she always did.

Leanne nodded. Her car was packed with the things she intended to take with her for the prepared task.

Iris stepped towards her and pulled her into a fierce hug. 'Are you sure you don't want us to come with you today?'

'I'm sure.'

The moral support would be nice, but there was nothing her parents could do, and they'd just be hanging around until tomorrow. Besides, she was meeting Jarred tonight, so she wouldn't see much of them anyway.

There was a party planned for tomorrow evening, when the winner would be announced in front of the finalists' families. Leanne had packed a dress, the one she'd worn to The Manor's summer ball last year. She wasn't planning on staying long, only until about ten o'clock, then she'd make her way back home.

So why was she acting as if she was going away for good? Why did everything feel so final?

Because it was; because very soon she'd return to London and this time it *would* be for good. She had no idea how any of it was going to pan out, where she was to live, whether she would have an office. These were the details she would have to thrash out with Jarred. She didn't even know whether he'd expect her to start working for him on Monday, or whether she'd be driving back and forth to London for the next few weeks or months until things were finalised.

No wonder she was terrified.

'Good luck,' her mother whispered into her hair. 'Not that you'll need it. You're going to win, I just know it.'

Was she? Leanne wasn't so sure. But it was reassuring to know that her mother had so much faith in her.

As she got into the car, she finally understood why she was feeling so glum.

Ever since their very first kiss, she'd planned to ask Rex to accompany her, to be by her side when she celebrated winning, or commiserate with her for being a runner-up.

The other two finalists were either married or had a partner, and suddenly Leanne felt very much alone.

She really would have loved to share this moment with Rex, but she'd have to face it without him, just like she'd have to face the rest of her life.

Chapter 48

Rex almost fell in through the door, Nell tumbling after him, and he leaned against the counter to catch his breath. He couldn't remember the last time he'd moved so fast, but it was imperative he told Leanne how he felt about her before she left for London.

He hadn't intended to beat the Olympic time for the hundred metres, and neither had he intended to dive into the flower shop, panting and dishevelled, looking as though the hounds of hell were after him. But he was here now, and he was determined to say what he had to say, no matter what.

There was one slight problem with his plan – Leanne wasn't behind the counter. Mabel was.

'Is she out the back?' he asked, peering around the older lady and hoping to catch a glimpse of the girl he loved.

'No, she's setting off early this week, so she decided not to come in today. Is there anything I can help you with?'

He looked around helplessly, as if he expected to see her hiding behind a bunch of chrysanthemums, and caught sight of the painting she'd won at the auction, now framed and hanging on the wall. That was the last time he'd set eyes on her. Such a lot had happened since then and he wanted to tell her all about it, to tell her he loved her. If it wasn't too late.

Speaking of too late… 'What time was she planning on leaving, do you know?' he asked.

Mabel checked her watch. 'In a couple of hours, maybe. She didn't exactly say.'

'I might catch her at home, then?' he asked, hope flaring.

He heard Mabel say 'You might' as he shot out of the door, an excitable dog hot on his heels.

Another mad dash, this time to his Land Rover, then a slightly careless drive out to the farm, a little too fast for the narrow lanes. He slewed into the farmyard, scattering gravel and small stones.

Iris was out of the front door in a trice. 'What's wrong?' Her expression was worried, and Rex hastened to reassure her.

'Nothing, sorry, I shouldn't have…' He gestured to the vehicle. 'I'm in a bit of a hurry, that's all.'

'So I see,' came the sardonic response. 'I thought there'd been an accident.'

'Sorry,' he said again. 'Can I speak to Leanne?'

'She's not here.'

'Oh.' He paused, letting the information sink in with dismay. 'She's left already, then?'

'Yes. You've got her phone number, haven't you? Why don't you call her?'

He shook his head. What he had to say would be better said face to face and certainly not while Leanne was driving.

Then he had an idea. There was nothing stopping him following her. 'Which hotel is she staying in?'

Iris gave him a sharp look, but went inside to fetch the details. 'Here,' she said when she came back out. 'I'm not sure I'm entirely pleased about this,' she continued, handing him a sheet of paper. 'If you upset her, I'll never forgive you.'

Rex grimaced. He couldn't promise that he wouldn't do precisely that, and he felt a bit of a heel. But as Betty had so rightly said, if he didn't try, he'd always be wondering, and he didn't know if he could live with the 'what if'.

'I'll try not to,' was the best he could manage under the circumstances. 'Thank you.'

He'd turned the key in the ignition when he realised Nell was still in the car. He could hardly take her to London, could he?

He switched the engine off again and climbed out, calling for Nell to follow. The dog jumped down and Rex gestured at her, giving Iris a helpless look.

She sighed. 'I'm sure Saul won't mind looking after her for a couple of days. When will you be back?'

'It depends,' he said.

Iris nodded. 'Good luck. You're going to need it. I don't know what's gone on between the two of you, but she's not happy. Don't make me regret giving you the name of the hotel.'

'I hope I won't,' he said, clambering back into the driver's seat.

He was about to pull away when his phone rang. He thought about ignoring it, but he was supposed to be working today, and he'd had so much time off already, he thought he'd better answer it and at least try to explain. At this rate, he was going to get the sack.

It wasn't work, though; it was an automated call from the Mountain Rescue team.

He listened to the message and his heart sank when he realised he had no choice.

He'd have to ring back and advise of his availability. His conscience wouldn't let him do anything else.

The coordinator picked up on the second ring.

'I'm on my way,' Rex said.

'I'll text you the details,' she told him. 'And Rex, you need to be aware that the missing person is a child. The police are involved, and a search-and-rescue dog and handler will be there as soon as they can.'

A child? Dear Lord, no. Despite his intense disappointment at not being able to hightail it to London, he was very glad indeed that he'd decided to answer the call, because they'd need all the help they could get.

He gave Iris a wave and drove away without telling her of this new development, thinking that once the child was found, he could follow Leanne to London. He had no doubt they *would* be found safe and well, because to think anything else was simply too awful to contemplate.

With his focus firmly on the task ahead, he pulled into the second farmyard of the day, this one vastly different to the first. For one, it was smaller, and for another, it was crammed full of vehicles.

He got out of his car and made for the makeshift command post, which was being conducted out of the back of a Range Rover. He recognised most of the faces as being people he'd trained with previously. Once they were all assembled, they were briefed by the police.

The child, Billy Morrow, aged eight, had been missing since before breakfast. His mother had gone to wake him, but his bed was empty. The police didn't suspect foul play at this time, but were assuming Billy had gone for an early walk. His coat and wellies were nowhere to be found, and neither was his drawing pad and pencils, which was why the authorities were treating this as a missing person and not anything more sinister. The little boy had been drawing a great deal recently. Apparently he had developed a keen interest in it ever since he had sold a painting at the auction, and had taken to disappearing into the field at the rear of the farmhouse. Until today, he'd always come back.

Rex took a deep breath, perched on the open back of the nearest vehicle and dropped his head into his hands.

This was all his fault. If he hadn't held that stupid auction, none of this would have happened.

Chapter 49

'Billy! Billeeeee!' The shouts echoed around the mountains, bouncing off the hills and filtering into the folds between them where steep-sided valleys hid.

Four hours later, and the search was widening and growing ever grimmer. Rex couldn't stop thinking about the boy's poor parents and what they must be going through, and he kept wondering where the search-and-rescue dog was. It should have been here hours ago with its handler.

The decision had been made not to wait for the dog, but to begin the search immediately, and Rex was glad they had, because, as was typical in these wild Welsh uplands, the weather was closing in. A mist had settled on the mountaintops and was steadily creeping down the hillsides.

Rex shivered inside his waterproof jacket. He wasn't cold or wet, thanks to the thick waxed-cotton fabric, but he would bet everything he owned that Billy probably was. The sooner they found the little laddie the better.

The searchers had started off strung out in a loose line, but the uneven, rugged terrain filled with dips and hollows had soon scuppered that, and now Rex was further away from the guy on his left than he wanted to be. The whole idea was that every square foot was covered, because it was surprising just how small a little boy could be if he was lying down. Even a clump of heather could conceal him.

'Billeeeee...'

Rex shivered again. The call was drawn out and eerie, the encroaching mist adding to the atmosphere.

Please let him be safe, please let him be safe, he chanted silently, using a long stick to push aside a low-growing bush and peering hopefully underneath it.

Nothing.

He moved on, clambering down one of the steep-sided little valleys that had been carved out of the bulk of the mountain by fast-flowing water. The stream splashed and gurgled noisily; if Billy was calling for help, his voice would be unlikely to be heard above the sound of it.

Taking care on the slippery grass and rocks, Rex cut across towards the stream itself, aware of the fascination that water could hold for small children. All the time, he was praying he wouldn't find the boy, because if the lad was down here in this narrow, shadowed crease in the hill, it might not be good news.

What was that?

Convinced he'd seen movement out of the corner of his eye, he stepped towards a dark hollow between some rocks, and let out a startled yell when a rook took flight in front of him.

'Bloody bird,' he muttered under his breath, following its soaring flight as it skimmed the contours of the hill. Rooks ate carrion, so just to be on the safe side, and with his heart in his mouth, he inspected the hollow.

It was empty, and he sagged in relief, leaning against the side of the outcrop, feeling the cold, hard stone under his hand.

Another noise made him jump as his two-way radio crackled into life.

'The child has been found safe and well. I repeat, the child has been found. All units return to base. Copy.'

'Copy.' Rex hardly managed to get the word out, so great was his relief, and he hurried back to the small-holding for a very welcome mug of scalding coffee.

'Where was he?' he asked as the hot drink was thrust into his hand.

'You know that deserted sheep pen about a mile or so that way?' The man he was speaking to pointed towards one of the ridges above the house. 'He was huddled in there. The cloud had come down and caught him unawares, so the sensible lad found some shelter and stayed put. He's a bit scared and very cold, but he's OK.'

'Thank God,' Rex said, finishing his coffee with such haste he burned the roof of his mouth. Now that the boy was home safe, he had somewhere else he desperately needed to be.

Stripping off his waterproof overtrousers and throwing his jacket in the back of the Land Rover, he dived into the driver's seat, switched on the engine and headed for London and the woman he loved.

Chapter 50

The restaurant was subtle, understated and elegant – everything Leanne had come to associate with Jarred. He liked the finer things in life, and who could blame him? He'd built his business up from scratch, she'd discovered, starting life selling flowers from a makeshift market stall, bunking off school on Thursdays because that was the best day. To think that he now owned a multimillion-pound enterprise was startling and quite admirable.

Her new boss was a confusing mixture of ruthless, determined businessman with one eye on the bottom line and the other on his profits, and courteous gentleman who opened the door for her and gallantly took her wrap before handing it to a hovering waiter. In a way, these contradictions only served to make her nervous and throw her off-kilter. She almost felt like this was a date, although Jarred had never given her any indication that he was interested in her except for her green fingers.

She would have preferred to meet in his office rather than being taken out to dinner.

They talked shop for a while, both of them careful to avoid any mention of the competition tomorrow. He had some fresh ideas, based on the comments she'd made last time, and he was eager to run them past her while they ate their meal.

When he'd finished, she gave him her honest opinion. 'That's more like it! I love the way you want to take this new venture in a totally different direction to the shops you currently have.' She giggled. 'Hobbits? It's perfect!'

She slid the computer drawings back across the table, and Jarred folded them carefully and put them in his briefcase. The man was a genius – his vision for his new business was now split into two, one branch for the corporate end, the other one aimed more at the man (or woman) in the street. The mock-ups of the shop he had just shown her had reminded her of a hobbit's house, or rather, what a flower shop might look like in Middle Earth, and she loved everything she'd seen so far.

'I particularly like the cuteness of it, but isn't it going to cost a fortune?' she asked.

'I've had someone do a quick costing, and it's coming in at roughly the same financial outlay per opening as the mainstream stores,' he told her.

'Will it attract the higher-paying customer?' she wanted to know, eager to learn as much as she could.

'Yes.' Jarred sounded certain. 'I will make sure of it.'

He picked up his glass of mineral water and tilted it towards her. 'To our new venture.'

Leanne clinked her glass against his. She *was* excited about this – she *had* to be, because there was nothing else in her life to be excited about.

Chapter 51

Finally, he'd arrived! Many hours later than he'd intended, but at least he was here. Negotiating the crammed streets, Rex remembered why he hated the city. There were too many cars, people, roads, buildings, traffic lights. It was too noisy, too frantic, too… everything.

What he needed was space, and growing things, and a chance to see the sky clearly and not with a foreground of roofs and concrete. When he pulled into the underground car park of the hotel Leanne was booked into, it was with a sigh of relief. Until he saw how much the parking charges were. *And* he was expected to pay using his mobile phone. When did that become a thing?

'Have you a booking, sir?'

'Not as such, no.' He didn't even have a toothbrush.

The girl behind the reception desk checked a screen, frowning. 'We've got a premier suite available. Is that all right for you?'

Rex had no idea whether it was or wasn't, but he nodded anyway. Then he paled and felt faint when she told him the price. He wanted a bed for the night, not to buy the whole darned place. He presented her with his credit card anyway, and winced as he keyed in his PIN.

After she'd run through her spiel of how to use the key card, the checkout time, payments for any extras (like breathing!) and when breakfast was served, she pointed him in the direction of the lifts.

'Can you tell me which room Leanne Green is in, please?' he asked when he could get a word in edgeways. Just saying her name made his heart miss a beat. Involuntarily, he glanced at the ceiling; she was here somewhere above his head, and he felt a bit sick as he thought about what he was going to say to her. His mouth was dry and he swallowed nervously.

'Sorry, I can't disclose any information about our guests,' the receptionist said.

'But I'm a guest too,' he replied.

She shook her head. 'Sorry, sir, data protection. I'm not allowed.'

Rex grunted. 'Can you call her, then? Are you allowed to do that?'

'Yes, sir, I can do that for you.'

She played with her screen again, then picked up a phone. To his annoyance, it was angled so he couldn't see the number she dialled. He wasn't going to find out that way.

The receptionist gave him a professional smile as they waited, and Rex tried not to tap his fingers on the desk in impatience.

'Pick up,' he muttered under his breath.

A few seconds later, the girl put the phone down. 'Sorry, sir, there's no answer. If you ring down to reception later, we can try again. Just dial zero from your room.'

Rex thought about trying Leanne's mobile, but he was scared she mightn't take his call. He'd also been scared that she might have refused to speak to him once the receptionist had told her who it was, so in one way he was almost relieved she hadn't answered.

He decided to pop to his room, freshen up a bit, then check out the restaurant. He knew from what Leanne had told him about some of the other evenings before the filming days that all the contestants and some of the TV company staff ate together. It was nearly seven thirty, so if she wasn't already at dinner, she probably would be soon.

After a quick shower – luckily the hotel provided the basics: a cheap toothbrush, toothpaste and shower gel, as well as a shower cap, which he wondered if anyone actually ever used – he pulled on the clothes he had been wearing since he'd got dressed that morning and made his way to the dining room, wishing he'd taken the time to pack a clean shirt. He was aware he must look a right sight in his hiking boots, walking trousers and T-shirt. He'd left his fleece in his room. It smelled faintly of dog.

Standing in the doorway, he scanned the room.

'Table for one, sir?'

'Er…' He craned his neck. There was a group of diners over on the far side of the restaurant who he guessed might well be who he was looking for. 'Is that the *Budding Stars* lot?' he asked, pointing.

'Yes, sir, are you wanting to join them?'

'No, but can I have a table nearby but out of the way a bit?'

The maître d' gave him a wary look and raised an eyebrow artfully.

'My girlfriend is one of the contestants,' Rex lied. 'She's not expecting me. I want to surprise her.' He gave the other man a wink and a smile.

The expression on the face of the maître d' didn't alter. 'Certainly, sir.' He clicked his fingers and a waiter came over with a menu and a price list, and Rex was led to a table close to the *Budding Stars* group.

He sat so he could see the door, and opened the menu, holding it up so it almost covered his face, with just his eyes showing. He felt like a stalker, and not a very good one at that, so he lowered it again and glanced at it at while letting the sounds of the restaurant wash over him.

How much? For a single rump steak? And that was without any sauce. If he wanted a splash of peppercorn sauce to go with it, it would cost an additional £3.50. He checked out the rest of the items on the list and was glad he had no intention of ordering anything.

He was too nervous to eat, and although he'd had nothing since his coffee and croissant earlier that day, he didn't feel in the least bit hungry. Actually, he still felt a little sick, his stomach doing a strange flip every so often. He did order a drink, though, a soft one. He really could have done with a pint, but he suspected it mightn't be a good idea.

A man's voice coming from the *Budding Stars* table filtered into his thoughts.

'Shall we order? It doesn't look like Leanne's joining us. Seven thirty, the itinerary said, and it's quarter to eight now. I'm absolutely starving.'

Rex's ears pricked up.

'Yeah, well, I bet she's seeing Jarred. It wouldn't be the first time,' a female voice said. 'If she wins, it'll be a fix. Talk about sleeping your way to the top.'

'Now, Desiree, we've got no proof that's what she's doing.'

The woman snorted. 'What else are they going to be doing? Playing Scrabble?'

'Well...' The first speaker sounded doubtful.

Rex slowly put his menu down, then stood up and walked out of the restaurant. 'Charge the drink to my room,' he called to the maître d' on the way out.

So, Leanne was with Jarred Townsend, was she? From what he could remember, he was sure she had told him that neither the judges nor the presenter, Rory, stayed in the same hotel as the contestants. Which meant she would have to walk back through the hotel's front entrance at some point tonight (*or tomorrow morning*, a sly little voice said).

Rex picked a comfy-looking chair that gave him a good view of the revolving doors and settled down to wait.

He wanted to be here when she returned, because there was no way he was letting her go without a fight.

Chapter 52

Leanne was exhausted. Although it wasn't late, she'd been up since goodness knows what time. Actually, she'd not slept much at all last night, and her walk to the beavers' dam this morning seemed like days ago. Time seemed to have become distorted and stretched, and she had the impression she was living two days for every one that passed. She guessed her strange thoughts were the result of tiredness, nerves and unhappiness. It was going to take her a long time to recover from Rex.

Jarred had insisted on escorting her into the hotel foyer, leaving his car parked illegally directly outside the building and not caring one hoot. He was totally driven and focused when it came to his work, but anything else was treated with a distinct lack of care. It made for an interesting mix, and Leanne had a feeling she would enjoy working for him (alongside him?) even if he was demanding, exacting and had impossibly high standards.

She wondered if he was going to kiss her on the cheek, and she paused just inside the revolving doors, bracing herself. She was relieved when he held out a hand instead. Taking it in her own slightly damp palm, she returned his firm handshake.

'Good luck for tomorrow,' he said. 'You'll need it.'

She would?

'You all will,' he continued. 'There's hardly anything to choose between the three of you. It will all come down to how you perform on the day.'

They'd been told the very same thing numerous times. No matter how brilliant a person was last week, if they bombed this week then they were out of the competition.

Jarred patted her on the shoulder and gave her a smile and a nod. 'See you on set in the morning. I'll let the winner have his or her glory at the party tomorrow, and announce my new business venture the day after.'

Leanne blew out her cheeks as she watched him walk away. This was all moving so fast that she wondered if she'd be able to keep up. A little voice in the depths of her mind wished she didn't have to.

—

Despite his best intentions, Rex was only half awake. The foyer was overly warm, and the chair was deep and squishy. He'd been up since the crack of dawn and hadn't slept too well the night before, then he'd been on the go all day looking for missing Billy Morrow, and that was without the mental toll that such a search exacted. Add to that the emotional roller coaster he was riding when it came to Leanne, his mad dash to London and the news that she was probably with Jarred Townsend, and it was no wonder he was shattered. On the one hand, he felt he could sleep for a week, but on the other, his brain refused to switch off, and every time his heavy lids drooped, images of soft brown eyes and a gorgeous smile popped into his head.

As if thinking about Leanne had made her magically appear, there she was, walking into the hotel, Jarred Townsend at her side, his hand on her elbow, almost like a policeman escorting a prisoner. Did the man think she was about to run away?

When they stopped and turned to each other, Rex could no longer watch, convinced he was about to see the pair of them kissing. He closed his eyes, wishing he'd never come to London, wishing he'd stayed in Tanglewood with his memories, because these new ones were definitely not to his liking.

Unable to stop himself, and thinking he must like pain because why else would he do something so silly, he opened his eyes.

Leanne and Jarred weren't kissing.

He rubbed his face and squinted. They were shaking hands. He blinked, trying to get his head around this new development. Actually, it wasn't a new development at all, he realised, because he already knew Leanne was going to work for Jarred. Shaking hands was perfectly reasonable. Believing a bit of idle gossip was his own fault.

He could understand why the other two contestants thought the way they did, though. It would never have occurred to them that Jarred Townsend had offered Leanne Green a job. He would have jumped to the same conclusion as them if he had been in their shoes.

He watched Jarred pat Leanne on the arm and walk away, then studied Leanne's expression. She was giving nothing away – her face was inscrutable.

He got to his feet and walked slowly over to where she stood waiting for the lift, debating whether to announce his presence now, or to follow her to her room and speak to her in private.

Deciding on the latter, he waited for her to step into the lift, then made a mad dash for the stairs, bounding up them three at a time. He felt like a cop or a secret agent, chasing the bad guy through a hotel, but he was already panting when he reached the next floor, falling through the fire door and into the corridor.

The lift was still going up.

He repeated the performance three more times, feeling less and less like an action hero with each floor he reached.

When the lift finally stopped ascending, he heard the ping as the doors opened before he'd put his foot on the top step, and used the handrail to drag his weary body onto the landing. He wasn't cut out for all this cloak-and-dagger stuff, he thought, as he cautiously opened the door to the hallway and peered around it.

There she was, walking away from him, her key card in her hand. He made a note of which door she stopped at, then waited for her to unlock it and go inside.

Room 406.

His heart thumping, his breathing loud in his ears, he wondered if maybe it would be better to wait for a minute, to compose himself and get his breath back. He didn't want to try to tell her he loved her while sounding like a steam engine with a cold. Besides, he was scared of what might happen next. He had an awful feeling she might take one look at him and slam the door in his face, and he'd have to resort to shouting into the crack between the door and the floor.

When he realised his breathing wasn't so much to do with having pelted up several flights of stairs, and that his heartbeat wasn't about to return to a more sedate rhythm any time soon, he knew he had to do it now.

Taking a deep breath, he lifted his hand and knocked.

Leanne changed into her PJs. She was tired, irritable and overwhelmed, and felt out of her depth and excited all at the same time. The only thing she wanted to do was to fall into bed and sleep for a week, even though she strongly suspected she wouldn't be able to sleep much at all.

She should be concentrating on the competition tomorrow, but all she could think about was her conversation with Jarred. He had been pleased when she'd accepted the job, as she'd hoped he would be, and had wanted to start planning her role right away, filling her already overloaded brain with talk of advertising, bottom lines, executive markets and other stuff that sounded like a foreign language to her befuddled mind.

She knew it had been a mistake to tell him tonight; she should have waited until the winner had been announced, because she had trouble finding room for both the competition and the job in her mind right now, especially when there were still so many thoughts of Rex in it.

She washed her face, revelling in the feel of the fluffy towel as she patted her skin dry, then turned back the covers and sat on the edge of the bed.

Please, please let me get some sleep tonight, she prayed as she kicked off the complimentary hotel slippers, swung her legs onto the bed and slid them under the sheet.

Someone knocked on her door, and she paused in the act of pulling the covers up to her chin. She wasn't expecting anyone, and she wondered if it was actually the room next door and the sound had travelled.

The knock came again.

Surely it couldn't be for her?

When the knock came for a third time, she swore, and threw back the bedclothes. Whoever it was wasn't going to go away, and they'd better have a good reason for disturbing her at this time of night. She had a competition to win tomorrow.

Hesitating with her hand on the handle, she wondered if it might be Jarred, and if so, what he could possibly want. Uneasy now, but deciding to get on with it and see who it was, she opened the door, and gasped.

—

Rex's first thought when the door opened was that Leanne looked delectable. She was standing there in pink PJs with little white dogs all over them, her hair ruffled and her eyes sleepy. The sleepiness evaporated like steam from a kettle when she saw him, and her mouth became a round O of shock.

'Rex?' she gasped, clutching one hand to her chest, the other firmly on the door handle.

'That's me,' he said.

'I can see that.' She sounded cross and put out. 'What I meant was, what are you doing here?'

'I came to see you.'

'Why?'

It didn't look as though she was going to invite him in any time soon, so he asked if she wanted to go somewhere more public to talk. She looked slowly down at her PJs, then back up at him.

'Maybe not,' he amended. 'OK, I'll say what I've got to say out here and then I'll leave you in peace.'

Wordlessly she stood to one side, holding the door open, and he sidled past her. As soon as he was inside, he halted and turned to face her.

'I wanted to tell you how I feel about you. I know you probably don't feel the same way...' He grimaced. 'You told me as much the other night. I know you've got a fantastic job opportunity and a whole new life ahead of you, but I had to come here and explain things to you.'

He took a deep breath. 'The weekend I visited my parents, I know I was a bit offhand, and you might have thought I was ignoring you, or that I didn't care, but I had a lot going on. I'm sorry.'

'I did think that,' she said levelly, neither her tone nor her expression giving anything away.

'Will you let me explain? Will it do any good?'

He studied her as she worried at her lip with her teeth, and he wanted nothing more than to gather her in his arms and kiss the haunted expression off her face.

She nodded. 'It might.'

Gathering his resolve, he carried on. 'It all started when I found out that my ex-girlfriend, Jules, was pregnant,' he began, speaking quickly, trying to get his story out before Leanne lost patience and told him to leave. From the expression on her face, she didn't appear to be all that happy with what she'd heard so far.

Without meeting her gaze, he soldiered on, leaving nothing out.

And when he'd finished his story, he ended with the only words that mattered.

-

Leanne couldn't believe what she was hearing. Poor Rex, he must have been so hurt when he discovered the girl he'd once loved had cheated on him, and so confused about the baby and everything. She let him speak, saying nothing, unable to find the words to express the indignation and sadness she felt on his behalf. She wanted to reach out and gather him into her arms, but she sensed he needed to finish his tale, that unburdening himself to her was the best thing for him.

She could hardly bear to think about that poor little baby, facing the first few days of his life with the possibility of never knowing his mother. There was something very endearing about the way Rex had half fallen in love with the child, without even knowing if Lyall was his or not. He'd make a fantastic dad, she knew, and a shiver went down her spine at the image that popped into her head – a little auburn-haired boy with eyes like hers. It almost made her cry.

When he finally ground to a halt, his story done, she swallowed convulsively, trying to hold back the threatened tears.

Then he said the only thing she wanted to hear from him.

'I love you.'

He looked so earnest and so loving, yet utterly terrified.

She took her time replying. Not because she wanted to make him suffer, but because she had to be certain that she was doing what she was about to do for the right reasons. What she was thinking of was momentous, and would change her life forever. She never wanted to look back and regret the decision she was about to make, so she nodded once, slowly, while she searched her heart and scoured her soul, and made certain she was choosing the path that was truly right for her. For both of them.

Finally she met his gaze. He'd been watching her, and she noticed that the hope had slowly faded from his eyes. He seemed cast adrift, lost, empty, as if he had pinned everything on coming here tonight and putting his heart in her keeping.

'I love you too,' she said.

'But?'

'No buts,' she replied firmly. Definitely, absolutely, positively no buts. She'd never been more certain about anything in her life as she was about that. No strings, no provisos, no conditions – nothing except love.

Rex continued to stare at her, but his expression was no longer the hurt, guarded, defeated one of a few moments ago; now it was full of wild hope and brimming with love.

'I don't think I realised exactly what I'd almost lost until I thought I'd lost it,' he said.

'You should have told me earlier. I thought you were about to end our relationship, so I got in there first.'

'I think I was scared of what you might say,' he admitted. 'When I did pluck up the courage, you told me it wasn't working out between us.'

'We're a right pair of idiots,' she said.

'Yes,' he said softly. 'We certainly are.' He crossed the room in three strides and Leanne sank into his embrace, his arms tight around her, promising to never let go.

For the first time in ages, she felt at peace. This was where she belonged, and this was where she intended to stay.

When Rex's mouth claimed hers, his kiss swept her away, and she went with joy in her heart and gladness in her soul.

Chapter 53

The competition was over. Done.

Leanne hadn't seen Rex all day, not until the three contestants had been ushered off set and sent back to their hotel, where Rex was waiting nervously for her in the lounge.

'Well?' he demanded, after sweeping her into his arms and kissing her soundly.

Leanne chuckled when Desiree tutted at the sight of them embracing.

'She thinks you're sleeping with Jarred Townsend,' Rex told her, kissing her nose.

She shrugged. 'I guessed as much. She must think I'm awful. First Jarred, now you.'

'She'll think even worse of you when you win. And just you wait until Jarred announces that you're going to be working for him!'

'Oh, don't.' Leanne shuddered. 'It doesn't bear thinking about. Besides, I might not win.'

'Of course you will. You're the best by far.'

She giggled. 'How do you know?' she protested. 'You haven't seen what the other two can do.'

He let go of her and led her to a couple of free seats. She sank down into hers gratefully. Last night had been yet another night with very little sleep, but for a far more wonderful reason.

They had talked into the wee small hours, neither of them quite yet able to believe that the other truly loved them, then kissed a lot and talked some more, until Rex told her he was off to bed to let her get some rest before the final in a few hours' time.

Leanne hadn't realised how exhausted she was until she closed the door behind him, with promises to meet him for breakfast, and leaned against it, almost too tired to move. She didn't care – she was happier than she could ever remember being. Now all she needed to do was to win this darned competition.

But it hadn't been the competition that had been on her mind when she slipped into sleep; it had been Rex, and her heart sang with happiness.

'Never mind,' he said, as if reading her thoughts. 'Only a few more hours and it will all be over. Why don't you have a nap, followed by a long soak in the bath before you get your glad rags on? I'll do the same, and come for you at about seven?'

'You don't have any glad rags,' she joked. He'd told her he'd arrived without even a toothbrush to his name.

'Ah,' he said with a glint in his eye. 'I went shopping while you were playing with flowers.'

'You make it sound as though you had a harder time of it than I did. I was trying to win a competition, I'll have you know!'

'Have you been out there?' he asked, a look of horror on his face. 'I have, and it's full of people. Thousands of them, and they all want to get in your way and stop you from doing what needs to be done.'

'Like shopping?'

'Exactly.'

'You don't like cities much, do you?' she teased.

'Not really. But I'll learn to like London if I have to – honest.'

Leanne knew he wouldn't. He'd hate every second of every minute that he'd spend here. But the fact that he was willing to move to the city to allow her to carry on her career made her feel all warm and fuzzy.

'How's Nell?' she asked abruptly.

'She's good, thanks. I left her with your mother.'

Leanne gasped. Her mother! Oh dear...

'Mum and Dad should have arrived by now,' she began worriedly. What kind of daughter was she to have forgotten her parents?

'Relax, they've already checked in. I rang your dad and asked him what time they were planning on arriving, and I was here to meet them when they did.'

Leanne narrowed her eyes. 'You were?'

'Yes.'

'What did you tell them? About us, I mean?'

'Nothing. I didn't have to. They guessed. Your mum's delighted. Your dad not so much. I'm just grateful that he left his shotgun on the farm.'

'I'm sure he's pleased deep down, but I'm his only daughter so he's bound to be protective.'

'I don't blame him,' he said. 'Now off you go – I can't wait to see you in your dress.'

She did as he suggested, but instead of hopping straight into bed, she gave her mum a call.

'Well?' Iris demanded.

'I can't tell,' Leanne said. 'It's so close, and the other two are brilliant. If I win, it will be a miracle.'

Iris huffed. 'I wasn't talking about *Budding Stars*.'

'Oh, I see. You mean Rex?'

'Of course I mean Rex. Did he tell you he came looking for you yesterday morning, but you'd already left? I can't believe he was delayed by joining the search party for Billy, but at least the little lad was found safe and well, the rascal.'

'Rex blames himself for the boy going missing in the first place, because of the auction,' Leanne said.

'The daft idiot,' Iris said with a smile in her voice. 'He's a good one. You want to hang on to him.'

'What does Dad think?'

'He thinks Rex is sound, but he's not going to tell him that because he wants to keep him on his toes.'

Leanne laughed; that sounded like her dad. She sobered. 'I intend to keep him, Mum,' she vowed.

'Good. You've been as miserable as sin these past couple of weeks. Maybe you'll have a smile on your face now.'

'I have,' she said.

'Right. Gotta go. Some of us take longer than others to get ready, you know. Oh, and Lea?'

'Yeah?'

'I'm so very proud of you.'

Leanne blinked away the sudden sting of tears. 'Thanks, Mum.'

She was still feeling quite emotional as she soaked in the bath later. Her mood only started to change when she took her dress out of the wardrobe and slipped it on, turning this way and that in front of the mirror, admiring the way it nipped in at her waist and flowed over her hips. The deep fuchsia made her skin glow and her eyes sparkle, and she felt good in it.

Calmer and more centred now, she came to the conclusion that with Rex by her side, it didn't matter if she didn't win. It would be the cherry on the top of her little cake of happiness, but that was all.

Squaring her shoulders, she stood in front of the mirror, intrigued to see a different Leanne staring back at her. This Leanne looked serene, confident, sophisticated, and there wasn't even a hint of green-smudged fingers or foliage in her hair.

A year ago, faced with the same situation, she would have been squealing with excitement and wondering if the drinks were free and whether gin was included, and she recognised she had grown up a lot since then. The competition had helped with that, but Jarred and his job offer had played a more important part. Rex too had had a hand in it, although his world of mountains and moody skies, buzzards and beavers was a far cry from the streets of London and Jarred's slick, shiny lifestyle.

She felt ready to move on to the next stage in her life, and with Rex's love and support, she knew she was capable of anything.

With one last look at the woman she had become, Leanne stepped out of her hotel room and went to meet her future.

–

Leanne's right hand was being held tightly by Rex. Iris, sitting on her other side, reached for her left. Her dad looked as nervous as Nell when the dog knew she'd done something wrong.

As for Leanne herself, she was strangely unperturbed by the whole thing. It was as if all the stress, the frantic activity and the intense focus of the last three months or so had drained away, leaving her an empty vessel ready to be filled with something new and exciting.

She still wanted to win, but it didn't seem as important as it once had, and she was a little sad about that. But the joy of seeing such love shining from Rex's eyes eclipsed everything and everyone, including *Budding Stars*.

Rory was about to announce the winner. The cameras were moving into position, aiming their lenses at all three contestants, waiting to film their reactions.

The presenter made a little speech, but all Leanne could think was, just get on with it, and suddenly she was as nervous as hell and her hunger to win came back with a vengeance, hitting her in the sternum and making her feel sick. She found she did want this after all – badly.

She caught Jarred's eye and grimaced. His face was expressionless, giving no hint of the verdict, and she looked away, back to Rory, who was flourishing an envelope. Idly, almost abstractedly, she wondered who had done the flowers, because there were floral arrangements everywhere, and she guessed Jarred's company was probably responsible. If the show was a success and ran again next year, who would design them? This year's winner, perhaps?

Rory was opening the envelope with infuriating slowness. He read it carefully, then raised his head. Anyone would think he didn't already know, Leanne thought to herself. She disliked the drama and the drawing out of the tension, the milking of every drop of theatre for the benefit of the viewing public, even as she understood why it was being done.

She gripped Rex's hand tighter and gritted her teeth, before remembering the camera pointed at her face. Being constantly on show was one thing she certainly wouldn't miss.

'…and the winner of *Budding Stars* is…'

Silence. Not even a cough or the clink of a glass.

The seconds stretched out, and time slowed. Leanne's fixed smile made her cheeks start to ache.

'Desiree Chalmers!'

The crowd erupted, and Leanne found herself clapping and smiling along with everyone else, disappointment sweeping through her.

'Come up here, Desiree,' Rory said.

Leanne watched as the other woman was presented with a crystal flower plaque, along with a bunch of understated creamy roses. She recognised the signature black ribbon and tissue paper instantly.

'It doesn't matter, I'm still so very proud of you,' her mother said in her ear.

Rex's arm was around her. He didn't say anything. He didn't need to.

But Leanne did, and she picked her time with care, waiting until Desiree had made her speech (Leanne herself hadn't even considered preparing a speech in case she won – it simply hadn't occurred to her) before congratulating the other woman and commiserating with Peter. She was asked to make a comment to camera, which she did, and circulated as instructed, accepting the good wishes of total strangers and the supportive comments of two of the judges.

When she found herself standing in front of the third, she drew him to one side.

'Jarred,' she began, not sure how to go on.

'It's OK,' he said.

'I'm not talking about not winning.'

'Neither am I.'

This threw her for a moment, and she didn't know what to say.

Jarred said it for her. 'I have eyes. I can see you haven't been happy. You're not the same girl I interviewed. Somewhere along the way, you lost your sparkle. Tonight, of all nights, I see you have found it again.' He jerked his head towards the table where Rex and her parents were sitting.

Leanne met Rex's gaze, and a rush of love filled her heart. He was determined to make things work between them, even if he had to leave his beloved mountains behind. A small smile spread across her lips – there weren't many calls for park rangers in the big city.

'I can't work for you, Jarred. I'm so sorry.' She felt like crying. She hated letting him down, especially when he had such faith in her, but she had to follow her heart, and her heart belonged to Rex.

Jarred made a face. 'I know.'

'You do?'

'I just said so, didn't I? Your sparkle is back, and I know the reason why.'

'I can't ask Rex to leave everything behind and follow me to London,' Leanne said. 'He'd shrivel and wilt here.'

'Like a rose bush planted in the wrong place?'

'Exactly.'

'Yet he's asking you to give up your dream?'

'He's not. He doesn't know I've changed my mind. I'm so sorry I messed you about.'

'I'm glad this is purely your decision, but you must do what is best for you.'

'No, I need to do what is best for *us*. For me and for Rex.'

'Oh, all right. You win.' Jarred threw his hands in the air with a theatrical sigh.

Leanne smiled. 'Actually,' she said, 'I didn't.'

'I think you'll find you did.' He looked meaningfully at Rex. 'I have a proposition,' he added.

'What?' Leanne asked cautiously.

'Stay at home, I don't care. I don't need you here. You can work just as easily from there, in your little backwater village. I'll employ you as a consultant, although it will be a pain having to find someone else to front Eco-Branch.'

'Is that what you decided to call it, Eco-Branch?'

'Yes, why? I think it's perfect.'

Leanne pulled a face.

'Let's see you come up with a better one,' he challenged her. 'That can be your first job. Your second is to visit some new premises with me.'

'I told you, I don't want to live and work in London.'

'You don't have to. Do you think you can manage to come to the city once a week? Or would that be too arduous for you?'

'You're serious, aren't you?'

Jarred nodded. 'Of course, it won't be the same as heading up Eco-Branch, but your talent won't be completely wasted.'

She laughed. 'If you're going to employ anyone, it should be Rex – he's the brains behind my designs.'

Jarred rolled his eyes. 'Perhaps it's fortunate you're going back to the sticks then. You might be more useful to me there.' This was said with a smile, so she knew he was teasing. 'I have to go, networking to do. I'll be in touch.'

She watched him walk away and shook her head. That man was full of surprises.

Then she looked back at Rex, waiting patiently for her. He was full of surprises, too, but right now she had one for him. She couldn't wait to see his reaction when she told him she wasn't moving to London after all, and that she intended to live in Tanglewood with him and Nell, and that she would love him forever and always, the way he'd told her he loved her.

She might not have come first tonight, but she'd won much more than a competition – she'd won Rex's heart.

And that was the only thing that would ever matter.

Acknowledgements

A heartfelt thanks to Jackie Godfrey at Field Day Flowers in Abergavenny, who most kindly allowed me to use her shop's name. I fell in love with this gorgeous florist's shop the very first time I saw it, and it's the inspiration behind the flower shop in this book.